PRAISE FOR JOHN D. NESBITT

". . .a remarkable work . . . Nesbitt is a true artist. . . . *One-Eyed Cowboy Wild* has as its most stylish feature dialogue which is simply superb."

— *WESTERN AMERICAN LITERATURE*

"John Nesbitt knows working cowboys and ranch life well enough for you to chew the dirt with his characters as this tale unfolds."

— *TRUE WEST*

"Spur-winner Nesbitt doesn't write traditional novels or routine shoot-em-ups. *Gather My Horses* is an emotional story, full of believable people with rich detail and a sense of purpose. Nesbitt breathes life, rich in characterization, to this beautifully written novel."

— *ROUNDUP MAGAZINE*

"Nesbitt demonstrates himself a skilled wrangler of detail and character."

— *PUBLISHERS WEEKLY*

FORGOTTEN ROSE

ALSO BY JOHN D. NESBITT

FORGOTTEN ROSE

JESS DELAINE
BOOK 3

JOHN D. NESBITT

WOLFPACK
PUBLISHING
— EST 2013 —

Paperback ISBN 979-8-89567-073-6
Ebook ISBN 979-8-89567-072-9
LCCN 2025932241

for Betty Hayano

FORGOTTEN ROSE

1

DELAINE SWAYED IN THE SADDLE WITH THE MOVEMENT of the horse, keeping an eye on the country around him and from time to time watching where the animal placed its feet. The dry grass was pale, and little bits of it rose with the movement of the dark hooves. The horse's brown shoulders rippled, and its dark mane bobbed. Delaine raised his head, felt the warm air on his face, and tensed. A faint crying sound caused him to look overhead. High above, a thin stitch against the dull blue sky brought back to his memory the source of the sound. Sandhill cranes. They flew higher than the wild geese, and their sound was more distant. He had not heard them for all the years he had been away, and he did not recall hearing them the year before, when he came back to Wyoming. But here they were, going about their yearly migration. He had seen them up close only once, years before, three of them in wheat stubble, with their curious-looking red caps and light-colored plumage. He had thought of them many times, rising and flapping away at dusk.

Full sunlight was pouring down at present, bringing a faint perspiration to his face and shining on his horse's mane and neck. Time alone on the rangeland was often the best time.

———

THE TOWN of Overton came into view, and the horse clip-clopped along. It did not need much guidance to turn in to the Sweet Auburn Café. Delaine swung down, wrapped his reins around the hitching rail, and went in.

As the doorbell stopped tingling behind him, a dark-haired figure emerged from the kitchen. Delaine's pulse jumped. Rachel was wearing a white apron and a dark-blue dress, as she often did. Her bronze complexion was pleasing to see. She paused as she smoothed her apron.

"You came back in good time," she said. "Coffee?"

"I could go for some."

The café was empty at mid-afternoon. He took the table nearest the kitchen and set his hat on the chair next to his.

Rachel returned with a crockery mug and a coffeepot. As she poured the coffee, she said, "How did it go?"

"I found a job."

"Oh, that's good. Where?"

"North of Sayers."

She set the coffeepot on a hot pad. "How far is that?"

"A little more than ten miles west to Sayers, then about five miles north."

"That's a ways."

"I can come back if I get a day off. And like most ranch work, it's just for the season."

"Ranch work again. That's good."

"Better than working in the stable." He sipped his coffee. "This fellow has hunters coming in. Guests, they call 'em in the bigger ranches. This one isn't a regular guest ranch, just a cattle ranch, and not a very big one, with antelope and deer hunting nearby. He's got a group coming in to hunt antelope, then another bunch to hunt deer. After that, we'll do fall roundup, which he says won't be that big of an operation."

"But it's work."

"Oh, yeah, and not that far away."

"When do you go?"

"Tomorrow. I'll vacate my room in the morning."

Rachel gave a faint smile. "Will you have time this evening?"

"I hope to." He smiled. "Any ideas?"

"One of the families I know has a visitor. A man from Trinidad, Colorado. He is some kind of a relative of theirs, so he has stopped here. He is looking for a daughter who ran away."

Delaine's smile left him. "How old is she?"

"Seventeen, I think. And he is one of those old-fashioned men, who expect the young man to ask permission to come and visit, and then ask permission for her hand, and all that."

Delaine grimaced. The families that Rachel socialized with were Mexican, and he assumed the man from Trinidad was, as well. The mention of a jealous father brought up images from Delaine's time in New Mexico. "That's rough for some of them."

"Yes, it is. And here is what I was thinking. Since you know the people, and you speak the language, and

3

you know something of the country around here, the main roads and more, I thought you might be willing to meet him and offer any advice you might think of."

Delaine tipped his head. "I guess I could. I like to be of help when I can."

"Good. I thought you would. How would you like to come by for me at about eight, after everyone has had supper, and we can walk from there?"

"That sounds fine."

———

THE FAMILY'S name was Mendoza, Rachel said as they walked to the Mexican neighborhood. She stopped at a house with a low roof and grey stuccoed walls. She rapped on the doorframe with the head of her house key.

A middle-aged woman with a full face and tied-back hair opened the door. "*Ay, Señora Valera, pasen ustedes,*" she said, stepping aside.

Delaine recognized the woman from gatherings he had attended with Rachel, but he had not met her. He gave brief responses in Spanish as she introduced Rachel and him to people sitting around the living room.

The last one introduced was the man from Trinidad, Tiburcio Martínez. He was a slender, dark man, weathered and tough-looking, shorter than average, with a greying mustache that reminded Delaine of a maguey rope. He sat apart from the others on a deep-stained wooden chair and did not stand up or offer his hand. He cast his dark eyes over Delaine and nodded.

La señora Mendoza spoke for him, in Spanish.

Don Tiburcio had come from Trinidad, in Colorado, in search of his dear daughter, who was taken away, or stolen.

Delaine allowed himself another glance at the man, who had a sullen air about him. He wore a close-fitting denim jacket with a blanket lining, unbuttoned, so that a pistol in cross-draw fashion was visible.

La señora Mendoza continued. It was thought that el señor Delén, the gentleman friend of la señora Valera, who knew many things about this area and the people, might have some ideas to help Don Tiburcio in his search.

The guest of honor folded his hands in his lap and spoke to the hostess. *"Él no tiene vela en este entierro."* He does not have a candle in this burial. He added, *"No tiene caso,"* which could mean anything from "It does not have significance" to "He does not matter."

Delaine nodded, as in respect. The family had taken the trouble to recommend him and introduce him to the visitor, and he had been rebuffed. He told himself that was fine. It was easier for him anyway.

La señora Mendoza put her hands together and dipped her head forward. *"¿Un ponche?"* she said. *"Vamos a tomar un ponche."* A punch? Let us drink a punch. Still smiling, she stood in the center of the room while her husband wheeled a cart from the kitchen, bringing into view a crystal bowl of pink punch and a matching set of glasses.

The husband poured four glasses for the ladies present, and the wife handed them around. He poured three glasses for the men and improved each with a dollop of brandy from a brown bottle.

La señora Mendoza handed Delaine his glass, and after he had sampled it, she said, still in Spanish, "And you, Señor Delén, you do not work at the corrals this year?"

"No," he said. "I have work at a ranch."

"Oh, how good."

———

THE EVENING AIR had a chill as Delaine walked Rachel to the home where she rented a room.

She said, "It is too bad that Don Tiburcio was so… closed with you."

He noted that she used the form *Don* also, a mode of reference for an older man who deserved respect. He did not feel that the man from Trinidad had shown much courtesy in return. "I don't mind it," he said. "It's his business, and I could see he was not happy about any of it."

"Well, you know how fathers are. I understand that she was his *consentida*—the pet or the favorite one." She paused. "As you know, I lost my daughter when she was very young. Don Tiburcio's case is different, and his jealousy may seem excessive or out of place, but he is a man who feels he has lost a daughter. Or to put it in another way, any girl who runs off or is taken away is someone's daughter."

Delaine said, "I can appreciate that. And I still think I should be able to do something, knowing as I do, a little of the language and the people who speak it, and knowing a little about the country around here, as you said earlier. But he says he doesn't need any help, and he doesn't even say it to me. I just try not to take it as anything personal."

"That's the best way. And maybe he will need help later. Do what you want to do."

Delaine shrugged. "I want to be useful in a way that I think I should. I just have to wait to see if it happens."

———

DELAINE RODE into the town of Sayers at about noon, when the sun, now moving south each day, had him and his horse even with their shadow on the right. He had seen the town in passing when he came through before, and now he looked for a place to eat.

The main street ran east and west, as it did in Overton, with the railroad running parallel a few blocks to the south, and beyond that, the river.

He came to the main cross street, which was called Pearl Street and led north to the ranch country where he would go later. Past Pearl Street a few buildings on his left, he found the Millbrook Café.

He tied his horse and went in. The interior of the café was like many of its kind, with a center aisle and a row of tables on each side. On the left wall, a lithograph illustration showed a wooden mill building, a millwheel, a pond, and a stream. Near the print, a man sat at a table. Delaine took a seat on the other side of the aisle.

He waited while the man at the other table spoke to the waiter in a stern tone and sent his plate back to the kitchen. Delaine minded his own business.

The waiter did not appear for several minutes, and when he did, he carried a steaming plate on a small tray above his shoulder. At the other man's table, he lowered the tray and set the plate down. "I hope this is better," he said.

The patron raised his head and sniffed. "I should

hope so." He had his left side to Delaine, and on the right side of his plate, he had a newspaper. He gave it his attention as he applied himself to his meal, and the paper allowed him to look away from anyone else in the café.

The waiter stood at Delaine's table. "Something to eat?" he asked.

"What do you have?"

"Our plate special today is roast beef, potatoes, and gravy."

"Is that what the gentleman is having?"

"He ordered a steak. Quite different."

"I'll have the plate special."

"Right away."

Delaine found the meat, potatoes, and gravy agreeable to the taste and in a good amount. He drank from a cup of coffee.

The man at the other table cleared his throat and called for the bill. Delaine could see that he had not eaten everything on his plate and had tossed his napkin on top of the remnants.

When the waiter returned with the change and withdrew, the man stood up. Delaine observed him with a sideways glance.

He was a tall, slender man, in his fifties, Delaine guessed, with dark hair grey at the temples and a full mustache going grey. He wore a pinstripe suit with a gold watch chain showing on his waistcoat. From the chair next to him, he took a tweed overcoat and a dark hat and put them on. The newspaper remained on the table as he strolled out.

Delaine thought it would not have been a surprise to see him take up a gentleman's walking stick as well.

The waiter asked Delaine if he would like to read

the newspaper that the other man had left. Delaine thanked him and said, no, he needed to be on his way to a job that was waiting for him.

———

DELAINE RODE north out of town, following the trail his new employer had told him to take. Five miles out, he found a foot-high pile of rocks with a bleached-white cow skull on top of it. He turned right and rode two miles east. As he traveled, he observed a ridge running north and south that made it impractical to cut across country on a diagonal. The ridge started out bare in the south, with tan bluffs and vertical shadows, and became spotted with pine and cedar trees that grew thicker as the ridge progressed north. Across the ridge and a little to the north would be the Silver Pine Ranch, where Delaine had worked the year before. The ridge itself was still four or five miles away.

Delaine was prepared for a small ranch layout, so he was not surprised when he found it. As with many ranches in this country, the headquarters were built in the lee of a rise in the land that would offer some shelter from the winds coming from the north and west. Such a location meant early shadows on cold winter days. Even in the early afternoon of a warm autumn day, the spare setting spoke of exposure to the elements. The ranch house, the bunkhouse, and the barn were all weathered structures, facing one another on three sides of a bare ranch yard. No trees grew anywhere near, and no flower beds or rosebushes grew around the house. A bare clothesline was the most domestic item in view. No children's toys or benches or chairs or wash-tubs or buckets were left out to be buffeted by the wind or pelted by hail. No chickens clucked or crowed, and no dog rose up to bark. Only a horse from the corral nickered as Delaine rode into the yard.

The barn door was open, and a man appeared in its shadow. Delaine recognized him as Percy Calvin, the ranch owner. The man raised a hand in greeting and walked into the sunlight as Delaine brought his horse to a stop and swung down.

"Found it all right," said the boss. He was dressed the same as the day before, in a dusty dark-brown hat, a white work shirt with a collar and a full row of buttons, a brown wool vest, and grey wool pants tucked into brown boots.

"Just as you said, sir."

"Call me Percy."

"Yes, sir."

"And yours is Jess."

"That's right. Jess Delaine."

The boss smiled. He was a little below average height, with a sturdy build and a thick chest. He had pale blue eyes and the stubble of a man who shaved once a week. "Mize well put your things in the bunkhouse." He led the way.

Delaine tied his horse at the hitching rail and took down his folded coat, his bag, and his bedroll. He followed the boss into the shadowy interior.

"Find a bunk," said the boss. "We got six in all, and two of 'em are in use. We'll have the three of you for huntin', then two more before we go out with the wagon for roundup." He stepped out of the way. "Ed 'n' Art should be along in a little while. That's one thing. Never gets lonesome out here."

"That's good," said Delaine. He set his belongings

on an empty bunk. "I suppose I can leave my rifle and scabbard on my saddle if we're going out to hunt before long."

"Should be all right in the barn."

The boss led the way outside, where he paused to cast a glance around the ranch yard. He took off his hat and dragged his left shirt cuff across his forehead. The sun shined on his bald head. He had light-brown hair around the fringe, and his pate was white down to a line above his eyebrows. His face was tanned and weathered.

"'Bout time for a change in the weather," he said. "But the good days keep on comin'." He put his hat on. "You can take your horse to the barn. You'll find a place for your saddle. Leave your horse in that little pasture in back with the other saddle stock."

Delaine was about to move away when Percy spoke again.

"How long have you been in Overton?"

"About a year. I've worked out of a couple of places in that time, but I also worked in town at the shipping pens and the delivery stable."

"Didn't you say yesterday that you're from Wyoming?"

"That's right. I grew up here. Then I was down in New Mexico for several years, and I decided to come back."

The boss smiled. "Man always wants to come back home."

"I suppose so." Delaine waited to see if the boss had more to say.

"Go ahead. Ed 'n' Art should be along pretty soon."

"Is there something you'd like me to do after I put my horse away?"

The boss gave his easy smile. "Oh, there's always work."

———

DELAINE WAS STANDING in the ranch yard, wondering where the boss was, when a wagon came rolling in from the north, piled with hay. Two horses were pulling the wagon, and two men sat on the seat.

The driver pulled the horses to a stop in a thin cloud of dust. "Are you the new man?" he asked.

"That's right. Percy's around here somewhere."

"He's right there." The driver pointed behind Delaine.

Percy's voice carried as Delaine turned around. "Got 'er made, uh? Well, just back it up to the barn." He spoke to Delaine. "You and Ed can unload it, and Art can get started on supper."

The driver shook the reins, and the wagon moved. When he stopped to back up, the other man jumped down to give directions.

Delaine stood clear until the wagon was in place in the barn. The driver did not pay him any attention as he climbed down from the seat and headed to the bunkhouse. The other man came out of the barn. He had the sturdy build of a range rider. He wore a brown hat with a dent on each side of the crown, and he had thick, wavy, brownish-blond hair and dark-blue eyes. He wore a dark-blue wool shirt, a bright blue neckerchief, a grey vest, denim trousers, and scuffed brown boots. As a decorative touch, he wore buckskin-colored wrist cuffs with red and blue beads.

He offered his hand and said, "I'm Ed Hiller."

"Jess Delaine."

"If you want to get started on the load, I can unhitch the horses. You can see where we've been stacking it."

Delaine found a pitchfork and went to work moving hay. The first part of the load was easy, as he was standing on top and pitching down. Hiller seemed to be taking his time with the horses. After a while, he appeared with a pitchfork in his hands.

"I'll work on this end if you don't mind," he said. "I don't shovel or pitch the other way very good. I can if I have to."

"I don't mind." Delaine was glad for the help, and the two of them went at it. Delaine kept a lookout for the shiny tines of the other man's pitchfork.

When they had the wagon empty, Hiller set Delaine to work pumping water for the horses while he put away the pitchforks and poured grain for the wagon horses, which he had left in a small corral next to the barn.

To Delaine's surprise, Hiller relieved him at the pump handle.

"What do you think of the Lazy T?" Ed asked.

"Is that the name of this place?"

"It's the brand. It came with the place when Percy bought it."

Delaine shrugged. "It all looks good enough to me."

"It's all right." Hiller paused in the pumping and spoke in a lower voice. "It's just that if you know one thing from the start, it's a little easier to work here. Percy's what you might call thrifty."

Cheap, Delaine thought. "Lots of men are. It's how they get by."

"In some ways, he's like anyone else. He keeps just one man for the winter, and that's Art. That's all right but on roundup, he gets by with one man less. You'll see."

Delaine nodded and let him go on.

"Just so you know. He'll tell these hunters not to tip anyone on their own but to give him the tips, and he'll divvy it up even. But I wouldn't expect to see any of it."

"I wouldn't have thought about it. I never worked in a place where someone tipped the help."

"Neither have I, but they do it at the dude ranches and some of these higher-level outfitters. So it's something the guests know to do."

"Well, I won't think about it."

"Better that way. Other than that, it's not a bad place to work. He doesn't try to work you without grub, and he doesn't try to beat you out of your pay, or not much. I wouldn't be surprised if your pay started tomorrow."

"Yes, but I'll eat today. I never worry about that. When I was in New Mexico, I heard a saying that came from Spanish. You know, the Mexican people have their skinflints, too."

"I'm sure."

"It went, 'If there are days when the duck swims, there are days when he doesn't even drink water.' So I take things as they come. If someone tries to beat me out of my wages, I don't have to work there. But there's always going to be some days harder than others."

"You can bet on that." Hiller resumed pumping

and said, in a louder voice, "We'll finish here and go see what Art has for supper."

———

LAMPLIGHT WAS SHINING in the bunkhouse, and warmth spread out from the cookstove. Delaine craned his neck. Two black cast-iron skillets sputtered with beef frying in bacon grease, and the mixed aroma hung in the air. The cook had his back to the eating area, where a stack of tan crockery plates sat on the table next to a platter of boiled peeled potatoes.

Delaine and Hiller, having washed up at the pump, hung their hats on pegs. Hiller waved at the benches that ran along each side of the table.

"Sit where you like. Art sits at the end, I tend to sit on that side, and Percy on this side."

"Then I'll sit on that side as well."

Before they sat down, the cook turned around from the stove. He had a mitten on his left hand and a large two-pronged fork in his right. Without his hat, his features were more visible than they had been earlier. He had brown eyes, dull brown hair, and a matching mustache. The left corner of his mouth tucked back as he said, "I'm Art. Meredith."

"Jess Delaine."

"Has Ed got you indoctrinated?"

"Only insofar as telling me that this is where the food was."

Meredith raised his eyebrows in what seemed to be a gesture of tolerance. "It won't be long."

Before he turned away, Delaine caught a full view of him. He was about thirty-five, of average height and build, not muscular and not soft. He wore a collarless three-button wool work shirt, suspenders under his cloth vest, and striped wool pants tucked into stovepipe boots with mule-ear pulls. He wore a sheath knife and a gun and holster even in the kitchen.

The bunkhouse door opened, and the boss came in.

"Smells like food," he said as he took off his hat. "That's the good stuff. No one ever goes hungry at this outfit. Isn't that right, Ed?"

"That's right."

"When I first came to this country, I worked for an old fella named Donovan. Poor as a crow, as they say. No flesh on him." Percy touched his cheekbones with his open hand. "He'd work you so late in the day there was no time to have anything more than a crust of bread before you turned in. He'd say, 'We'll eat good tomorrow.' But we just about never did." Percy hung his hat near the others.

Meredith had turned away to the kitchen area and now returned with a cast-iron skillet that was still sizzling.

"Here's grub," he said. "And to hell with anyone who doesn't like it." He set the skillet on a folded cloth on the table and turned away.

"That won't be anyone here," said the boss. "Did they feed you that good down on the ranch grandy, Jess?"

"Sometimes."

The boss looked around and smiled. "Jess worked down in New Mexico for a spell. What was the main thing you ate there, Jess?"

"It was ranch food, so it wasn't all that different from here."

"Biscuits and beans one day, and beans and biscuits the next. Ha-ha. And someone else's beef."

Meredith returned with the second skillet. "Mexican beef is always tougher'n hell. Poorer kind of cattle."

"But Jess was in *New* Mexico, not old Mexico. Isn't that what you said, Jess?"

"That's right. And it's not all the same. I worked on some of the mountain ranches in the north, and they were nothing like the *llano*, the dry plains."

Meredith whacked the heavy fork on the lip of the skillet. "Dig in," he said. "There should be plenty for everyone."

2

DELAINE AND HILLER FITTED OUT FOUR SADDLE HORSES
and two packhorses for the boss to take to town. Percy
saddled his own horse and left with the string of six,
saying he would fetch the four hunters and meet the
crew in camp.

Delaine and Hiller loaded a wagon with camp
gear, including two packsaddles and pads, a bag of salt
for the heads and hides, grain for the horses, two
canvas tents, poles, bedrolls, a field box, a chuck box
with cooking utensils, and all the food supplies that
Meredith set out for them. By midday they were ready
to go, with Delaine and Hiller on horseback, Meredith
driving, and a horse with Meredith's saddle tied to the
rear of the wagon.

They traveled about four miles north and west into
a broad, treeless grassland, tawny with greyish-tan
bluffs in the distance. They went up a long, low grade,
and for a few minutes toward the top, Delaine could
not see any country ahead. When they came to the
crest, the grassland came into view again, this time a

wide basin with a thin row of trees in the bottom showing a watercourse.

Meredith drove the wagon to a place that had been the site of camps in the past. Stumps and logs were arranged around a fire pit of blackened stones, and cottonwood and box elder trees offered shelter as well as a place to hang meat. Meredith stopped the wagon and said, "Here we are."

He began to give orders, as he had done through the morning. Delaine could see from Hiller's responses that Meredith was the lead man in this setting, so he fell in as well and followed directions.

Delaine and Hiller laid out the first tent, pegged it down, raised the ridge with the poles, and stretched the guy ropes. They went on to do the same with the second tent. Delaine understood that one tent was for the kitchen, and Meredith and Percy would sleep there as well. The other tent was for the four hunters. Hiller and Delaine would sleep out. Meredith set up his kitchen while the other two men unloaded the gear into the respective places.

They set the field box on the ground, and Hiller raised the lid. He lifted a couple of articles and poked at others, showing Delaine an assortment of ropes, pulleys, meat saws, meat hooks, and triangular iron gambrels, which he called singletrees. In the bottom of the box lay several folded canvas game bags that had the stains of old blood that had not washed out.

Hiller said, "Percy keeps the field glasses and skinning knives in the bag we set in the tent."

"Seems pretty well equipped."

"One other thing," said Hiller. He reached into the wagon and took out a long, narrow canvas bag that rattled. He opened the drawstring and pulled out a bipod made of long dowels. "Shooting sticks."

"I'm familiar with them," said Delaine. "I even made one for a fellow last year."

"Then you should be all right."

With a set of longer ropes from the wagon, they put up a rope corral about thirty yards from camp, using a layout that showed signs of earlier use. The ground was worn, and some of the trees had notches cut into them, just as a couple of trees at the campsite had spikes driven into them.

With the saddle horses and the wagon horses stripped and in the corral, Delaine and Hiller made their way to the campsite. Meredith had a fire going and was sitting on a stump, smoking a cigarette.

"Percy should be here with the hunters before long," he said. "This firewood doesn't make very good coals. Takes a lot, and the coals don't last long."

Delaine wondered why he started the fire so soon, but he said nothing. He thought Meredith's eyes were glassy, as if he had had a couple of nips, but he considered that the effect might come from a reflection of the fire.

Hoofbeats caused the three of them to look around. Two men on horseback rode in from the northwest side of camp. They did not stop several yards out but rode up to the center of camp and dismounted.

"The things you see," said Meredith.

The closer of the two men stepped forward in something of a swagger, with his hand on the buckle of his gunbelt. He wore a brown hat with a high, dented crown. He set it back on his head and said, "Where's the whiskey?"

"Ain't got none," said Meredith.

"Don't give me that. I know what a hunting camp is."

"Percy's bringin' it from town."

The newcomer said, "That's some shit."

His companion's spurs clinked as he stepped closer. "What do you know, Art?"

"Nothin'."

The first rider said, "Got a new helper?" He nodded toward Delaine.

"Aide dee camp," said Meredith. "Goes by Jess Delaine." He raised his cigarette, and before taking a drag, he said to Delaine, "This is my brother, Ben."

Delaine nodded across the campsite and said, "Pleased to meet you."

"Same to you." Brother Ben moved so that he stood with his feet apart, and with his reins in his left hand, he took out a sack of Bull Durham. Looking down but keeping his shoulders squared, he began to roll a cigarette with an air of authority.

Delaine saw that the man was larger and more muscular than his brother but had similar dull brown hair and brown eyes, with a mustache grown out more than the stubbled beard. He wore a dark-blue wool shirt with a single breast pocket, a leather vest, denim pants, and rough leather boots.

Art Meredith said, "And this is his pal, Lou Crawford."

Delaine observed the second rider. Beneath his grey hat, he had hair the color of last year's straw, brownish stubble, and light-brown eyes with a heavy brow. He wore a tan flannel shirt, a dust-colored cloth vest, dull brown canvas trousers, and broken-down brown boots. "Pleased to meet you as well," Delaine said.

"All the same to you." Crawford's eyes roved around the camp.

Brother Ben Meredith popped a match and lit his cigarette. "What kind of hunters have you got comin' in?"

His brother answered. "Antelope hunters."

"I know that, or you wouldn't be way out here."

"Then I guess I would just say good ones, which is to say that they pay."

"I know that, too."

"I don't know what you mean."

"Doesn't matter. Just makin' conversation."

Motion caught Delaine's eye. Crawford had taken out a plug of tobacco and was cutting off a chew with his jackknife. He had his head tipped to the side and was gazing straight ahead. He clicked his knife shut, lowered the plug, straightened his head, and shifted the lump to his cheek. He took a bite down, shifted his jaw, and spit out a small stream. "Seems to me that a good huntin' camp ought to have camp whores."

Art Meredith raised his cigarette, held it near the corner of his mouth, and said, "Then I guess this ain't a good one."

"We weren't goin' to stay long, anyway," said his brother. "Just stopped in to say hello."

"No harm."

Brother Ben spread his shoulders, raised his head, lifted his cigarette, and took a drag. Delaine expected him to say something and realized that might be the effect the man was trying for. After a long moment, Ben took a last drag and tossed the rest of his cigarette into the fire. "I guess we'll go," he said. "Good luck with your hunters."

"Thanks," said Art.

Crawford said, "We'll come back when you've got some women."

Art said, "Stay out of trouble."

Crawford's lower lip was wet as he smiled and said, "That's my middle name."

Delaine was waiting for one more exchange, but Ben gave a hitch to his belt buckle and turned to mount up.

When he was aboard, he pulled his hat forward and said, "So long."

"So long," said his brother.

Crawford had swung up, and he raised a hand in farewell.

When they were gone, Hiller said, "Where is it that they work, Art?"

Meredith sniffed and rubbed the bottom of his nose. "The Big Eight," he said.

"That's what I thought, but I wasn't sure."

Delaine waited to see if Meredith was going to say any more, but the man was looking at the last bit of cigarette he held between his thumb and forefinger. He pinched it and threw it into the fire.

———

PERCY ARRIVED in early evening with four men on horseback and two pack horses carrying duffel bags and padded rifle cases. Delaine and Hiller unpacked the gear, stripped the horses, and turned them into the rope corral.

Back at the fire, with darkness gathering at the

edges, everyone including Meredith was holding a tin cup. In another minute, Delaine and Hiller each had a cup as well, with an inch of whiskey in it.

Delaine listened to the conversation. He learned that the four hunters were from Cleveland, Ohio, and knew each other from a hunting club there. They all wore sporting clothes and had an air of affluence about them. As Percy poured them another round, Delaine saw them as being accustomed to paying others to do things for them and to wait on them. He thought they must be paying quite a bit to have someone do what they could learn to do themselves if they cared to, from finding the animals to taking care of them after they were killed. As it was, they came for the privilege of pulling the trigger.

Delaine noticed that none of them talked about their work or businesses or how they made their money. He assumed it was because they all knew each other and had had plenty of time to talk about their enterprises when they were on the train.

In spite of their differences in appearances, they had an air of sameness about them. Delaine imagined he would get to know at least some of them as individuals when they went out to hunt.

Meredith had boiled a pot of potatoes and now brought out two cast-iron skillets to fry the steaks. He said he would cook one round for the hunters and then one round for the help.

Delaine and Hiller brought more firewood and water and stood back to make themselves inconspicuous.

Footfalls and the snapping of twigs in the grove of trees caused everyone to look at the southern edge of the campsite, where a man on horseback came out of the darkness and stopped.

The detail that Delaine recognized first was the rope-like mustache, then the denim coat. He had not seen the man wearing a hat earlier, but the style he now saw, which people called a straw hat but was made of palm fiber, was a natural fit for Tiburcio Martínez.

Perry called out, "Who's there?"

"A traveler. Can I come in?"

"Come on ahead. Get down from your horse and take it slow."

The man came forward on foot, leading the horse. A coat of coarse wool was tied on top of the duffel bag in back of his saddle. His features were not very visible, but Delaine was sure that everyone could see his dark complexion.

"What do you need?" said Percy. "Are you lost?"

"Not really," said Martínez. "I saw the fire and didn't know what kind of a camp it was." His deliberate enunciation had an identifiable accent, but his English was clear.

"It's a hunting camp."

"Ah-hah. Well, I don't want to bother you."

"No bother so far. Are you looking for something?"

"Yes, I am looking for my daughter."

"Well, she's not here."

"I can see that. And I would not expect her to be here with your group. She was stolen away by a single man, a person of low class whose name I will not repeat."

"I"m sorry to hear that," said Percy, in a matter-of-fact tone. "Like I said, this is a hunting camp. And this is cow country. Anyone who comes to camp is welcome

25

to eat. The second round of grub should be ready in a little while."

"No, thank you," said Martínez. "I did not expect to stop and eat. For that matter, I had something earlier. I was just curious about who had a camp here."

"There's no problem with that. This is public land, as far as that's concerned. So anyone has a right to be here. You, too, if you're a citizen."

"Which I am. From the state of Colorado." The man had had his coat buttoned when he first came in, but Delaine saw now that the coat was open and the pistol in cross-draw position was in view.

Percy moved his head as he looked the man over. "Just for the record, my name is Percy Calvin. I've got a ranch called the Lazy T. You're likely to meet other outfits out on the range here."

Martínez nodded as his gaze moved from one man to another. He seemed to recognize Delaine but gave no show of it. "Very well," he said. "I will be on my way. My name is Tiburcio Martínez. I am from Trinidad, Colorado." He pronounced the four Spanish words with a Spanish inflection.

"I hope you find what you're looking for."

"So do I. Thank you."

Martínez led his horse away and mounted up at the edge of the firelight. The steps of the horse with the rider faded in the night.

Percy said, "You never know who you'll meet. I wonder why he isn't on the main trail."

"He said he wasn't lost, but you never know," said Meredith.

"Well, it's not our worry," said the boss. "Let's have a good evening in camp."

———

DELAINE AWOKE in the dark as the toe of a boot poked him.

A voice said, "Time to get up."

When the person moved on and did the same with Ed Hiller, Delaine placed the voice as Art Meredith's.

Delaine sat up. The kitchen tent glowed from lamplight from within, and a flame was beginning to build in the fire pit.

Hiller said, "We need to grain the horses and start gettin' 'em ready."

Percy had laid out the plan the night before. Each hunter would have a guide with a packhorse, and they would set off in four different directions.

Delaine and Hiller fitted out four packhorses, four riding horses for the hunters, and their own two. The sky was beginning to show grey in the east as they walked to the fire.

The hunters were sitting in the same places as the night before, on a large cottonwood log and two stumps. Percy was standing up and drinking coffee.

"Git it down fast, boys," he said.

Meredith gave them each a tin plate with three flapjacks and pointed at a jar of molasses on the tailgate of the wagon. Delaine smelled bacon and saw one hunter eating a strip by hand.

The boss said, "Pour your coffee now so it can be coolin'."

Delaine and Hiller sat cross-legged on the ground and made short work of their breakfast. The sky in the east was beginning to turn pink.

Percy handed Delaine a pair of binoculars, old and heavy, that looked as if they might have been left over from the Civil War. "You're responsible for these field glasses, but if your hunter wants to look through 'em, let him. He'll carry his own shooting stick, but you keep an eye on it, too."

Delaine was assigned to a hunter named Charles Hale. He was about forty-five, with a flushed face that was filling out. He had brown hair and blue eyes and did not wear a mustache or a beard. He wore a jacket and pants of deep green wool, of a texture that Delaine was sure was expensive, with leather trim and buttons. He had a cap of the same color, with a short beak and a band that would fold down over the ears. The night before, he had smoked tailor-made cigarettes from a leather case, and he had one going now.

"I think it would be a good idea to finish that before we leave camp," said Delaine. "We don't smoke on horseback. Too much danger of a grassfire."

Hale gave a brief look of resentment, took a puff, and tossed the rest of the cigarette in the fire.

"I guess we're ready," said Delaine.

"Will you let me get my gun?"

"Sure. Do you want to carry it, or shall I tie a scabbard onto the saddle?"

"I'll carry it on a sling."

Delaine held the horse and stirrup as the hunter grabbed the pommel with one hand and the cantle with another, heaved himself up, shifted his right hand, and swung his leg over. At one point, the rifle slung on his shoulder pointed at Delaine. Each hunter had the same horse and saddle as the day before, so Delaine did not have to adjust the stirrups when the rider was seated. When he was sure that the man had the reins secure, he went for his own horse and the packhorse.

The eastern sky was a deep pink beyond the ridge,

and as Delaine and his hunter rode northeast out of camp, the sky faded. Before long, it was yellow, and the sun rose all in a minute.

"What we need to do," said Delaine, "is try to get within a couple of hundred yards of any antelope. You can get closer on horseback than you can on foot, but it doesn't do to shoot from horseback, unless you want a hell of a wreck, so what we try is to see some at a distance and try to sneak up closer with some kind of higher ground between us."

"Who goes first?"

"We can ride or walk side by side, but however we go, I prefer not to have that gun barrel pointed at me."

"I don't have a live round in the chamber."

"That's even better."

Hale lagged behind and had to make his horse trot to catch up. "I don't like the way this gun bounces on my shoulder," he said. He unslung it and set it crossways in front of him. After it bumped on the swells of the saddle a few times, he carried it in the crook of his arm. Five minutes later, he said, "I'm tired of this." He stopped the horse, lengthened the sling strap on the rifle, and lifted the strap over his head so that the rifle rode on his back with the strap on a diagonal across his chest. He nodded to Delaine, and they went on.

"You want to make your fist shot a good one," Delaine said. "Any antelope that have been shot at are goin' to be much harder to get up on, so the first chance of the season is the best one. You want to run it through your mind several times, how you're going to get into position, get set, and shoot when everything comes together."

"Where's the best place to hit 'em?"

"In the front quarters. The head is too easy to miss,

and you don't want to destroy the head or horns if you want to have them mounted. Antelope have a ruff of hair on the back of their neck, so the neck isn't as thick as it looks. If you can get 'em through the heart and lungs, that's the best."

"How are they to lead? They run fast, don't they?"

"I wouldn't shoot at one that's running. It's too easy to gut-shoot 'em or just hit a leg. They can run all day on three legs. And if you shoot at one that's running, you'll shoot at another, and you're ruined for the day. It's better not to get into a bad shot to begin with."

"Have you guided many hunters?"

"Not all that many. I made all those mistakes myself, long ago. The best thing to do is to be sure that's the shot you want to take and bear down to make it a good one."

"One shot, and it's all over?"

"That's the best way. There's too many things that can go wrong."

Delaine did not know how much he had convinced the man. He knew that many men who considered themselves sportsmen, as this group seemed to do, were used to hunting birds and small game and might shoot any number of times in a day. For some, restraint was hard to learn. It had been so even for himself, growing up on the plains.

The sun rose higher, and daylight spread over the landscape. Delaine and his charge rode on, going up and down the swells of the grassland.

Delaine stopped. More than half a mile away, a group of white dots materialized into a band of about eight antelope.

"Let's drop back," he said. The specks went out of view.

He studied the contours of the land. All was quiet, with the packhorse breathing behind him. He swung down from the saddle.

"Let's go around to the east," he said. "Keep the sun out of our eyes. We can edge our way up and peek over every once in a while." He untied the shooting stick from the packsaddle and handed it to Hale. "You might want to practice with this a couple of times. Lay the forearm of your rifle in the little crossbuck at the top, and hold the two of them together with the butt of your rifle snug against your shoulder. Open the legs to lower it, close 'em to raise it. You can get a pretty steady aim if you hold tight, and like I said, there should be a moment when everything comes together. It the animal moves, you regroup until it stops."

"What if they take off?"

"No need to throw lead at 'em. There's always a good shot later, better than a bad one now."

Delaine led the horses about four hundred yards, and Hale followed. "Let's go up and take a look." He leaned forward and walked uphill. As he reached the crest, he took off his hat and rose until his eyesight cleared the rim. He saw the tan and white of separate animals, and he sank back.

Hale had come up alongside.

Delaine whispered, "We're closer than we were, but I think we can do better. Let's go around a ways further."

Delaine led the way for another three hundred yards, with Hale following. Again, they made a slow approach to the ridge, and the shallow basin came into view. The antelope were still grazing, and they looked close enough.

"I think this is your chance," Delaine said. "Give

me your horse, and get yourself steady." He took the other man's reins. He was going to have to hold the three horses, but he also wanted to stay focused on the antelope and keep track of what happened after the shot.

Hale breathed hard as he settled into place, shifted, and shifted again.

Delaine, with his hat off, raised his head. He counted seven antelope. One of them was a buck with dark horns well above its ears, grazing in the rear of the little group.

The rifle blasted, and the buck lurched. He lowered his head and took off at a dead run, veering to his left after about sixty yards and tumbling in a small cloud of dust. Delaine held onto the horses and had them settled in a moment.

Hale levered in another shell.

"I think you hit him good enough," said Delaine. "That's the way they run when you hit 'em good. Let's walk over. If he tries to get up, you can shoot again, but I don't think you'll have to."

The buck was lying with its white underside facing the men as they walked down the slope and up the other side.

"How far do you think it was?" Hale asked.

"A little under two hundred yards. Maybe a hundred and fifty. You could step it off."

"It's not important enough."

As they walked up to the fallen animal, Delaine pointed at a spot of red where the tan color of the coat gave way to white, behind the front shoulder. "That's where the bullet went in. Good shot. Didn't make a mess of it, I hope."

"How could it?"

"Sometimes a bullet hits a bone and goes off course, tears up the stomach. Seems easier to gut-shoot an antelope than a deer. They're a little smaller. But we'll see soon enough. We'll roll the guts out of him right away."

Hale stared at his guide.

"I'll do it," said Delaine. "You can hold the horses, and if I need you to hold a leg aside, I'll let you know."

Delaine took out his folding knife and went to work. He opened the abdomen, and the warm, gamy smell rushed out, but the intestines were not shot up. The animal had fallen with its back uphill, so the innards spilled out without Delaine having to drag the carcass around. He trimmed the colon and the bladder from the outside and from within, and he felt a relief when he had those parts cut away and tossed aside.

He pulled at the intestines again to get the stomach and liver outside the cavity. He cut the diaphragm, and then came a wave of blood. With his sleeves rolled up, he reached in with both hands, his left index finger guiding the back of the knife blade as he held the knife in his right hand.

Farther in, his hands found the way. He grasped the windpipe and gullet and slashed until it all came free. He drew the knife out, set it on the dry grass, and reached in again to get a purchase with both hands. When he pulled, the front of the animal contracted, so he pushed against the sternum with his forearm as he pulled on the heart and lungs. A minute later, he had the pulpy mess lying on top of the gutpile. He stood up to straighten his back, and he held his hands out in front of him. he was drenched in blood halfway to his elbows.

"If you can pour water, I can try to keep from

getting blood on his horns when I tip him up to empty out the blood."

"That's a pretty strong smell."

Delaine nodded. "That's antelope for you. Even the blood has a stronger smell than a deer's. We'll be glad we got this one cleaned out right away. Then the sooner we get him to camp and skin him, the better."

Hale poured water from Delaine's canteen and stood back with the horses. With his hands cleaner, Delaine took the animal by its horns and lifted it, twisting the carcass so that the pool of blood flowed out onto the ground.

Delaine lowered the head and smelled his hands. Sure enough, the pungent smell had transferred from the horns. Not wishing to waste more water, he rubbed his hands with dirt.

"I don't know anyone who likes antelope liver," he said, "much less the kidneys. If you want to take the heart, I can cut it loose."

"Leave all the guts here," said Hale.

"Fine with me. Now if you can hold that packhorse steady, I'll see if I can host this carcass up on top."

Delaine knew that the head was the most cumbersome part, as it was heavy and tended to flop around, but if he grabbed the animal by the hocks and horns, it would sag in the middle. He took the hind legs in his left hand and the front legs in his right, and as he lifted it, he put his knee under the animal's shoulders and gave a forceful pull and heave all at once. The carcass cleared the crossbuck of the packsaddle and sank into place. The horse shuffled but did not move far.

"Whew!" said Delaine. "Let me get him tied down, and we'll be ready to go."

Ten minutes later, he was rubbing his hands with

dirt again and feeling a relief at having this part of the work done. He took his reins and the lead rope for the packhorse from Hale and led the two horses away a few steps. As he looked back to make sure he had not left anything lying on the ground, a rifle shot blasted from the other side of Hale's horse.

Delaine hung onto the reins and lead rope of his two horses as the third horse bolted away. Hale stood by himself with his rifle in his hands.

"I don't know what happened," he said.

"You put in a new shell after you fired."

"I know. But I didn't have my finger anywhere near the trigger."

Delaine thought, *Maybe you didn't*, but he said, "Just leave it as it is. You know you don't have a live one in there now. If you hold these horses, I'll go get the other one."

The loose horse stood about fifty yards away with its reins on the ground. Delaine walked around and approached the animal from the front. He admitted to himself it was his fault. He should have told Hale to take out the live shell when they were sure that the antelope was dead.

———

DELAINE AND HALE were the first ones back to camp. They had heard other shots, but they had not seen anyone from their party. The sun had not yet reached its high spot, and the shady area around camp was cool. Delaine hung the antelope from a cottonwood limb and put the horses away.

Hale stood by, watching, as Delaine skinned the

antelope. Hale had gone to the tent and brought out a flask wrapped in leather.

"Brandy," he said. "A little for the nerves." He had taken off his jacket and was standing in the sunlight. He lit a cigarette. Delaine saw that he had narrow shoulders, thin arms, and a full abdomen.

Delaine had hung the antelope on a gambrel, so the skinning was not awkward. His main concern was not to let too much hair fall on the meat, and when he got down to the shoulders and neck, he took care to keep the cape and head in one good piece with no cuts in the hide. When he had the piece free, he salted the wet side of the hide, closed it, and rolled it.

"The good thing is that you made a good, clean shot," he said.

Hale had lit another cigarette. He blew away smoke and said, "Those horns aren't very big, are they?"

"Oh, about average for a full-grown buck, I think. And he was the only one with horns in that bunch."

"I wish I had held out for something better."

Delaine felt his spirits sink. He could still smell the blood and antelope stench on his hands, and he had worked hard. He reminded himself that this was a paying customer, or client, and Percy was the boss.

The sound of horse hooves saved him from having to grit his teeth and not say anything.

Three riders came in from the north side. The one in the middle was tallest. He rode a bay horse and had a gun and holster in view. He drew his horse to a stop and looked over the camp. He wore a wide-brimmed hat and a red bandanna, a sand-colored shirt, a brown leather vest, and a pair of pale, yellowish gloves. He raised his head, and the sunlight showed on brown hair, blue eyes, a flushed complexion, and a stubbled face.

"Who are you?" he asked.

Delaine said, "I work for Percy Calvin. This is his hunting camp, and this is one of his hunters."

The man had large facial features, and his throat moved as he swallowed. "We don't care for hunters. We don't like people trespassin' or shootin' in the direction of our cattle."

"I just do my work."

"Sure, you do."

"Do you mind if I ask who you are?"

"We ride for the Big Eight." The man pointed over his shoulder with the thumb of his large right hand. "Our headquarters are back that way."

Delaine took in the man to the left, who rode a sorrel with a blaze and white socks.

The man had dark hair, a full beard but not very long, and darting eyes. He wore a brown hat with a flat brim and a rounded crown, along with a grey shirt, a brown cloth vest, and brown wool pants. He rested his hand on a six-gun that rode high on his hip. "We don't like hunters," he said, "or tenderfeet, or men of leisure, or people from cities who eat prissy things."

Delaine turned to the third man, who rode a plain brown horse. He had mouse-colored hair and a matching mustache, a narrow face with a protruding nose, and washed-out blue eyes. He wore a blue denim shirt with no vest, but like the others, he wore a gun. He seemed to feel as if he was called upon to speak, for he tipped his head toward his fellow riders and said, "Like they say."

The man in the middle spoke again. "We heard shots, so we came over to see what was going on."

Delaine nodded in the direction of the red-orange carcass hanging in the shade. "Just an antelope. I was about ready to put a bag over it, but you can see for yourself."

"I can see," said the man in the middle. "But we don't like it."

The three men turned their horses and rode away.

Hale took a long breath and spoke to Delaine. "Who did they say they were?"

"An outfit called the Big Eight."

"And you don't know them?"

"I can't say that I do even now, since they didn't say their names, but I've heard of the outfit before."

3

ART MEREDITH CAME IN WITH THE SECOND ANTELOPE. His hunter was the oldest-looking of the four, in his early fifties or so. Delaine had caught his name as Alex Broom. He had dark-brown hair going grey, a trimmed mustache, a heavy face, tired brown eyes, and a slumping build. He lowered himself from his horse and gave a long sigh, then gave the reins to Hiller, who had come in with his hunter empty-handed.

Meredith and Broom gave a short account of the hunt. Broom had gotten his animal with three shots, the first one being in the hindquarters, the second across the spine, and the third high in the shoulders.

Meredith said he would rustle up some grub if someone else would skin the antelope. By the time Delaine untied the lash ropes and slid the carcass to the ground, Hiller returned. Meredith told him to skin the animal, so Delaine took care of the other two horses.

Hiller had the animal hanging and halfway skinned when Delaine returned. Broom was smoking a cigar and watching. He was dressed in brown tweeds with leather trim, in the style common with sportsmen, and he wore lace-up leather boots that were narrow enough for riding. He was telling Hiller about hunting ducks and geese. He would rather hunt in a blind than a boat. Hiller continued skinning, pulling the hide downward and trimming when he needed to.

Percy came in with his hunter. They, also, had had no luck. Delaine took their horses and put them away.

The hunters went about cleaning up as Meredith worked on the meal. A couple of the men shaved. Delaine brought water from the creek, using one pailful to help Hiller wash his hands and knife.

When the group was gathered around the fire, Percy spoke. "These antelope tend to lay up around the middle of the day and then come out again around three or four. We're gettin' close to that time now, and I don't want to rush anyone's meal. So unless someone wants to go back out this afternoon, we can rest up, and those who have yet to get an animal can start out fresh in the morning."

Everyone assented, including those who had already killed their game. Percy brought out a bottle of whiskey, and everyone drank to the success so far and to the future prospects.

The hunters fell into conversation among themselves. Hiller and Delaine went to feed the horses. When they were finished with that chore, Delaine saw Percy standing by himself near the two covered carcasses.

"Pretty good so far," Delaine said as he walked near.

"Oh, yeah," said the boss. "Anything can happen. I've shot as many as nine in one day myself, and I've gone days when no one in the party has killed a single one. You and your man did good."

"Yes, we did." Delaine lowered his voice. "We did have a small incident, at about the time I was finishing with the work here in camp."

Percy gave his attention. "What was that?"

"Three men came in on horseback. Said they rode for the Big Eight. They said they didn't like hunters."

"They don't have to. We've got a right to be out here."

"They said they didn't like trespassers or people shooting in the direction of their cattle. One of them even went on about how they didn't like people from the cities. I didn't talk back."

"It's just as well. They can be pushy and overbearing, and there's no need to make things worse. But there's not much they can do, as long as we stay on public land. Their range is off to the west and north of here."

"That's what I gathered."

"Don't worry about it. But thanks for lettin' me know."

———

DELAINE AND HILLER had only four saddle horses and two packhorses to fit out the next morning. When they returned to the fire, the two hunters for the day were eating bacon and fried potatoes. Delaine and Hiller served themselves from the skillets. The night before, Percy had assigned his hunter to Delaine, and Hiller would stay with the same hunter as on the first day. No one seemed to be in a hurry, and no one spoke loud, as if was to be assumed that Percy and two hunters were still sleeping in the tents. Meredith stood by with a cup of coffee in one hand and a cigarette in the other.

The sky was grey as Delaine rode out of camp with his hunter. The man's name was Richard Wesley. Delaine guessed him to be about the same age as two of his companions, around forty-five, but he had a younger appearance, with blond hair, blue eyes, a clear complexion, and white teeth that showed when he smiled. Around the campfire the evening before, he had mentioned playing tennis and baseball. He did not smoke, and he was one of the two who had shaved during the day.

For hunting, he was decked out in a tan wool outfit with a dark-brown shooting patch on his right shoulder. He wore a wool hat of the same shade of tan, and he had dark-brown boots.

His rifle rode in a forest-green padded canvas gun case strapped to the packsaddle along with the bipod. He sat straight up in the saddle, smiling.

"It sounds as if you did well yesterday," he said.

"I thought so. I don't know how satisfied he was with the animal itself. I think he might have liked to have gotten a bigger set of horns."

"They looked about the same as the other pair."

"They were nothing to scoff at. But still, I'm sure Percy wants everyone to be satisfied."

"Oh, yes."

"So I think it's a good idea to decide ahead of time what you'll be satisfied with and what you won't. That helps you have your mind right. I know from my own experience that if you're only half-hearted about a shot, you're liable to make a bad one. Part of making a good shot is wanting to. The rest is a matter of getting into good position, holding steady, and shooting at the right time."

"I think you're right."

"Like I told your friend yesterday, you go over it a few times. Think about it."

"Visualize it."

"You can practice it as well. Go through the motions of getting set up with the shooting stick."

"I did a little of that yesterday."

"You want to hold it tight in that notch and snug against your shoulder. You don't want your rifle to jump when you fire."

"That's what I do. Hold tight."

"Good. If you want to practice anymore, just let me know."

"I think I'm ready."

They rode out into the grassland. The day seemed like a replica of the day before, with a scarlet sunrise and then golden sunlight pouring over the plains. The world was quiet, with the swishing and plodding of horse hooves and the occasional twit of a bird.

They saw cattle and at one point a coyote, yellow in the morning sun.

"He would be good for a rug," said Wesley.

"Go ahead and try if you want to."

"Nah. It was just a thought."

"Just as well. I think it's better to stay focused on what you came out to hunt and not make unnecessary noise ahead of time. There'll be chances for other things later. Coyotes, prairie dogs."

"I agree."

"I've been out hunting elk, in the high country. Everybody is quiet and serious, and then a member of the party shoots the head off a blue grouse."

"How are coyotes to clean?"

"That's another good reason not to shoot one. They're good for fleas and ticks." Delaine reflected, *Of course, you wouldn't have to do it.*

"Better not. If there's a chance after everyone's got their antelope, it might be interesting."

"This one's gone, anyway."

"Right."

They followed the rise and fall of the land, taking it slow on the crests and relaxing into an easy fast walk across the low spaces.

Shape and color registered in Delaine's mind, and he stopped. "Let's go back," he said. He turned his horse and led the packhorse down the slope. "Saw something," he said.

He swung down, and Wesley did the same.

"This would be a good time to take down your rifle and your shooting stick. I don't think we're close enough where we are. I think we'll have to work our way around, but we can sneak up here and take a look."

Delaine set off on his slow, forward-leaning walk with the reins and the lead rope in one hand. As he neared the crest line, he took off his hat. He inched up until he saw the scene again. His pulse ticked when he saw horns. He sagged back.

"Five of them," he said. "One of them is a buck. He's got horns well above his ears."

Wesley nodded, took off his hat, and edged up for a peek. He settled back and said, "How far away do you think they are?"

"Four hundred yards or more. I think we should try to get closer."

"Which way?"

"If we go to the right, we can keep the sun out of our eyes, but I think we can get closer if we go to the left."

"Let's try that." Wesley turned toward the sun and pulled the short brim of his hat forward. "Sun's a little higher," he said. "It might not be too bad."

"Do you want to look at him through the glasses?"

"No, I think he's good enough."

Delaine led the way, keeping well below the ridge. He knew it was possible to look up later and find the scene bare, but this was the way to do it, stay out of sight while making the move. Antelope had great vision, and movement caught their eye.

After more than a quarter of a mile, Delaine decided to give it a try. He leaned into his uphill walk, crested in slow motion, and pulled back. The animals were larger objects than he expected.

Wesley came up to him.

"I think it's a good distance," Delaine whispered. "You can give me your reins if you'd like."

Wesley had been carrying the bipod and his rifle. He handed the reins to Delaine, nodded, and pushed his hat down onto his head.

Delaine said, "Put in a shell before you go up, so the sound won't carry as well."

The lever clicked, and the brass cartridge went into the chamber.

Delaine took off his hat and inched his way up, hanging onto the three horses and hoping to be able to keep track of anything that was hit.

Wesley settled in, shifted, sighed, and shifted again. The rifle blasted, and the antelope flinched, but it did not bolt. The sound that came back was not the satisfactory *thwop* but more of a *plunk*. The four

45

does had jumped around and stood watching the buck.

"I think I hit him," Wesley whispered. "Should I shoot again?"

"I think you need to."

The hunter levered in another shell, tensed, and fired again. The buck did not move.

"Don't shoot at his head," Delaine said. "Aim for his shoulders."

Wesley fired again, and the animal crumpled. The four does raced away.

"Why did he just stand there?" Wesley asked.

"That's what they do sometimes when they're gutshot."

"Damn. You think I hit him too much in the middle?"

"It's done now. We'll see."

Wesley rose to his feet with the rifle and the bipod in his hands. He had an expression of dismay on his face.

"Don't worry," Delaine said. "He's down. Before we do anything else, let's be sure you don't have a live shell in the chamber. You can hand me the shooting stick."

"I'm sure I didn't mount another one."

"Open it up anyway. The fellow yesterday touched off a shot by accident, so it's better to be sure."

Wesley worked the action, flipped out the empty casing, and pushed down on the next cartridge to keep it from coming up. He closed the action.

"Thanks," said Delaine. "We might as well put that in its case now. The shooting part is over."

"I guess it is."

After putting the rifle away, they led the horses across the swale and stood over the fallen buck.

"Those horns are all right," said Wesley. "I hate to think of what kind of a mess you're going to have, though."

"Sometimes it happens. If you can hold the horses, I'll let you know if I need you to help here."

Delaine took out his knife and went to work. The animal was a mess as soon as he opened the abdomen. Bits of mash appeared, and then a shapeless, soupy quantity of it that smelled much worse than anything the day before. Delaine knew the odor would sink into his hands and forearms, but there was nothing to do other than plunge in.

He cut the intestines loose, trimmed out the colon and bladder, cut the diaphragm, and pulled out the heart and lungs. The smelly green particles, mixed with blood, stuck everywhere. Wesley poured a whole canteen of water for Delaine to clean up, and most of the blood and green matter came off, but some of the mess stuck to the hair on his arms and in the crevice of his knife.

He lifted the front end to try to wash out some of the cavity with blood, but the animal had not bled inside as much as it would have done if it had run.

"That's as good as I can get it now," he said. "I'll see what more I can do in camp."

The buck was about the same size as the one the day before, so Delaine handled it the same way to get it up onto the packhorse. He caught his breath, uncurled the rope, and began tying on the load.

———

AFTER SKINNING the antelope and salting the cape, Delaine went to work on cleaning the carcass. The green, vomit-like matter stuck to smooth surfaces and penetrated the meat wherever it had been cut by the knife or torn by a bullet. After much scraping with his knife blade, Delaine decided to cut out the loins, or backstraps.

"I don't think these shoulders are worth saving," he said. They were bloodshot and permeated with the green smelly mash.

"That's fine," said Wesley.

Delaine cut away the shoulders. "These backstraps are good," he said. "I think I should cut them out so they don't absorb any of that smell, then cut away the carcass and leave the hindquarters hanging by themselves, together."

"Go ahead." Wesley stood by the pail of water at his feet.

Delaine cut out the two long strips of loin and draped each one on a meat hook after hanging the hooks on the same branch as the gambrel. With a saw, he cut across the backbone right next to the hindquarters, and the fouled part of the carcass fell to the ground.

"None of this rib meat is any good," he said. "I can cut out the tenderloin inside the ribs by the spine there, but I don't know how good they would be at this point."

"Throw it all out," said Wesley. "What you've got there is good, and I don't expect to use any of it for table meat, anyway. Percy says most fellows have their antelope made into jerky and sausage and shipped to them."

"Good enough. I'll stick these two shoulders inside

the rib cage and drag this thing a long ways from camp. This'll attract coyotes and magpies like nothing else."

———

DELAINE WENT OUT in the afternoon with Hiller and the remaining hunter. At the very least, he could help lift a carcass onto a packhorse.

The fourth hunter was named Andrew Lowell. He was a little taller than average, and slender, with dark hair and eyes. He was the other one who had shaved during the free time the afternoon before. He wore a grey herringbone shooting jacket and dark grey wool pants, with a lighter grey wool cap of the style that had a band that folded down over the ears. The band was tied in front, above the beak, with a black lace. He had black boots as well.

In camp, he smoked a straight-stem briar pipe of a deep reddish brown, and he had an ivory-handled pocket knife, short and slender in the style called a penknife, with a disk on one end that he used for tamping his pipe. In the conversation the evening before, he talked about having hunted ducks and geese in Michigan. He said he would like to go to Canada to hunt a moose.

Hiller led the small party north and west, in the direction of the Big Eight, as Delaine understood. The afternoon sun had crossed the high point a while earlier, and a light haze hung in the sky. The plodding of horse hooves combined with the rustle of saddle leather and the snuffling of the horses.

Half an hour of riding took them to an area where the rolls in the land were closer, so they came to a stop more often as they approached each rise, Hiller going first and then motioning for the others to move on.

At one crest, he held his hand out to signal for the others to stop. He backed his horse and turned it downhill. His face had an open expression as he slid off his horse and stood close to Lowell and Delaine.

"There's a big bunch here," he said. "About fifteen or so, and more than one with horns. This could be your chance."

Delaine dismounted and held the packhorse as Hiller unstrapped the gun case and untied the leather strings that held the shooting stick. Lowell had let himself down and had straightened his clothes. He took the rifle and the bipod and nodded to Hiller.

Delaine held all four horses while Hiller ushered Lowell up the hill, whispering. The two men settled into place, and Hiller helped the hunter adjust the legs on the bipod.

Delaine looked away, to lessen the hunter's feeling of being watched. He heard the click of the rifle, and at the edge of his vision he saw Lowell repositioning himself. Time passed. Delaine wondered if the antelope were walking or milling. Maybe the hunter was waiting for a buck to step into the clear. Maybe he was indecisive.

The rifle shot crashed, breaking the stillness of the afternoon. Hiller spoke. Lowell jacked in another shell. They both stood up.

Delaine walked uphill, leading the horses.

Hiller said, "There were three bucks. I didn't know which one he was aiming at. When he shot, the bucks and does ran in every direction, and I couldn't keep track. I didn't see anything go down, and I didn't see anything limping."

"I thought I hit it," Lowell said.

The animals had regrouped more than four hundred yards away, and a couple of them were looking back.

Hiller said, "You don't want to shoot at another one until you're sure, and those are pretty far 'way. We can go look for the one you think you shot. The grass is not high at all. If there's something down, we should see it."

Lowell nodded.

Delaine handed reins to the other two men and held onto his own horse and the packhorse. They made their way on foot down the slope toward the bottom of the wide, grassy draw. The antelope in the distance were beginning to mill around. The draw ran downhill in their direction, to Delaine's right, and the animals were up the slope from the bottom.

Out of habit, Delaine looked to his left, where the draw ran uphill, and he saw a small white mound. "There's something," he said.

The three of them turned and walked in that direction. As they advanced, the intervening ground lowered, and the shape became more visible. It was a dead antelope.

Hiller said, "I didn't see anything run this far up, but you never know. This could have been out of sight from where we were. It looks kind of limp, as if it could have been shot before."

When they reached the antelope, it was laid out in the position of an animal that had run itself out and fallen. Its left side was up, and a red splotch showed.

"Which way was it facing?" Delaine asked.

Lowell said, "To the right."

"Well, this is where the bullet went out, and the blood is fresh."

"Then that's my antelope."

Hiller stepped close and nudged the animal with the toe of his boot. "It hasn't been here any time at all. This is the one you shot. I just didn't see anything up here. But they were running every which way, and he might have gone out of sight from where we were standing."

Lowell heaved out a large breath. "Well, I'm glad of that."

"We might as well go to work," said Hiller. "I'll gut this one."

Delaine spoke to Lowell. "I think it would be best to take the live shell out of the chamber."

The hunter leveled his gaze but did not speak. He seemed to resent being told what to do by someone who wasn't assigned to be his guide.

"People forget," Delaine said. "Then they go to do something with the gun later, and it goes off, like Mr. Hale's did yesterday."

"He's right," said Hiller. "You're done hunting anyway. Or done with the shooting part." Hiller smil3ed. "I know how you feel. I've heard it before. You come all the way from Ohio, and you get to shoot one time. But it could have been different. You could have shot all day and missed, or you could have made a mess out of one and let it get away. You did good."

"I know." Lowell pointed the rifle away and took out the shell.

Hiller pulled the animal around, stepped over it to keep its hind legs spread, and leaned into his work. "Do you like the horns?" he asked.

"They're all right. They all seem to be about the same."

"They are, this time around. Yours have these white tips, though, so that's a little special." Hiller cut from the inside out to open the belly. "Percy was right about these antelope comin' out around three, wasn't he?"

———

THE SKY WAS a broad splash of orange and vermillion as Delaine brushed and combed the first horses in the morning. Camp had an air of bustle. The night before, Percy had told the hunters again how they could expect the meat and the heads and capes to be handled. The men were packing their bags as Meredith banged skillets in preparation for cooking breakfast.

Four antelope in two days of hunting was not bad, as Delaine considered it. Nothing had gone wrong. With men and guns and animals, even when the whiskey stayed in camp, there was great potential for something going out of control. Things were in order now, and the hired men had a calm, clear morning to roll up the rope corral, strike the tent, and pack the wagon. As Percy had outlined the plan, they would all go back to the ranch, transfer the carcasses and heads to a lighter buckboard, and continue in a group to town.

Delaine was tying a pair of the hunters' bags onto a packhorse when his blond-haired hunter from the day before spoke to him in a friendly tone.

"What would you think about trying to shoot a coyote now?"

"You can ask Percy. If it's all right with him, you can stake out that place where I threw the remains of your antelope yesterday."

"Thanks."

————

THE SUN WAS CLIMBING in the sky when the group moved out of camp. Percy rode in front with the four hunters, all on horseback. Meredith drove the wagon, towing the horse with his saddle. Delaine and Hiller took up the rear with the packhorses carrying the hunters' bags and gun cases. Nothing came of Richard Wesley's try for a coyote, but he seemed pleased to have had the opportunity.

At the ranch, Hiller went out to the pasture to catch two fresh horses for the buckboard. Delaine put away the extra horse and saddle, then transferred the game bags and the heads and capes to the lighter wagon. Meredith backed the camp wagon into the barn, and Delaine unhitched the horse while Meredith and Hiller hitched up the new team. Meredith put out a quick lunch of cold beef and biscuits, and the party was on it way again.

With the group strung out along the trail, Delaine recalled the visit from the Big Eight riders and told Hiller about it. Hiller cast a glance in Meredith's direction and kept his voice low as he answered.

"They're a pushy bunch, all right. That fella you described as the one in the middle would be Ross Mitchell. Big rawboned bully. I think their boss lets him do it. The one with the beard is Nate Jonas. And the third one sounds like Arnold Hand. He's not much danger himself, but he rides with the other two."

"What kind of boss do they have?"

"His name is Albert Marcus. He keeps his main residence in Omaha. From what I've heard, he's got daughters and doesn't want them to be exposed to all of us ruffians out here. He comes and goes. He's got other business interests, too."

"The fellow with the beard made fun of people from the city. Said they were prissy."

"I 'magine he didn't mean to be talking about his boss. I don't know how prissy Marcus is, but they say he doesn't like dogs. Thinks they're low class, and won't let anyone have 'em around."

"That's odd."

"It's what I've heard. I don't know him myself."

———

PERCY, still in the lead, turned at the pile of stones and the cow skull and headed south into town. The sky was broad and hazy, and the afternoon was still. Delaine swayed in the saddle, and a light drowsiness came over him.

His horse stopped. He realized the company had come to a standstill up ahead and the halt had transferred back to him and Hiller. He heard voices, but he could not pick out words.

"What is it?" he asked.

Hiller stood in this stirrups and sat down. "I don't know. Seems like some kind of a commotion. Let's ride up and see."

Each of them led a packhorse as they rode past the buckboard and caught up with the party ahead, which was bunched around something on the ground.

"Looks like a man," said Hiller.

They rode around the group until they found an open spot and turned in. The body of a dark-haired man in a coarse wool overcoat and denim pants lay at full length on the trail.

"Who is it?" said Hiller.

Delaine shifted his horse to get a better look.

Percy said, "I don't know but what it might be that fella that came by camp the other night. Said he was from Coloradda."

"I think so," said Delaine. The body had looked bigger to begin with, because of the overcoat, and the hat of palm fiber was missing, but the dark face and rope-like mustache were those of Tiburcio Martínez.

Percy said, "I wonder what he's doing here. It can't be good."

"Not for him," said Alex Broom, the heavyset hunter. "Or for us, if we're going to have to stay around as witnesses."

"Let's not get excited," Percy said. "This doesn't take everybody. Let me think a minute." He took off his hat and wiped his cuff across his brow. The sunlight fell on his bald head for a few seconds until he put his hat on again. "I don't think we should move the body, in case it got here in some wrong way, and I don't care to put him in with the fresh meat and all. So I think most of us can go on into town. I'll leave one man here to watch over him until someone comes out." Percy raised his head from staring at the body and looked around. "Ed, I think I'll have you stay here."

Hiller had an uncomfortable expression on his face, but he said, "Whatever you think is best."

Meredith came up in the buckboard and pulled it around. "Who is it?" he asked.

Percy said, "It looks like that fella from Trinidad, Colorado, that stopped by our camp the first night."

Meredith raised his chin and cast a glance. "The Mexican. Yeah, that looks like him."

Delaine observed Meredith and Hiller in turn. They were both looking at the dead man; but in a way that Delaine could not pinpoint, they did not seem to be seeing the same thing. Maybe it was because Hiller saw an unpleasant task ahead for himself.

Delaine gazed at the body. A corner of the wool overcoat was turned up, and the denim jacket was visible. Delaine remembered seeing the wool coat tied onto the back of the man's saddle. From the first meeting in Overton, he remembered the lined denim jacket, the pistol in cross-draw position, the self-assured posture, and the man's dismissal of Delaine's offer to help. None of these details seemed to matter now. As Delaine saw him, Tiburcio Martínez was a man who had thought he was justified in trying to get his daughter back, but he had come to the end of his trail.

4

THE TOWN OF SAYERS CAME INTO VIEW, AND THE TRAIL from the ranch country became Pearl Street. Delaine observed the familiar buildings on the corner where Pearl Street and Main Street formed an intersection. The hotel was on the right, and the bank was on the left. On the south side of the thoroughfare, The Mercantile sat on the right, and The Emporium occupied the southeast corner.

Percy turned right, taking the group past the hotel and down the block to the butcher shop, across the street and one building east of the Millbrook Café. Delaine dismounted and carried the game bags inside, one by one, as the hunters gave their names to the butcher, who made out string tags and noted how to process the meat.

On the street again, the group turned left at the next cross street, headed south halfway to the railroad tracks, and stopped at a building where a sign in the window identified W. Olejnik as a tanner and taxidermist. Delaine carried in each head and cape, and again the hunters had name tags put on their possessions.

The entourage turned around, reached the main street again, and headed east. They stopped short of the hotel. Percy had the riders line up the horses along the hitching rail, while Meredith parked the buckboard on the south side of the street, in front of The Lookout Saloon.

The hunters discounted and gathered their personal effects from their saddlebags while Delaine unloaded the bags and gun cases from the packhorses. A man from the hotel carried the items in.

As Delaine put the last of the lash ropes into a pannier, Percy appeared at his side.

"I'll go in and settle accounts with the hunters and make sure they're all set to catch the train tomorrow. Then I'll find the deputy and tell him about the man we found. You can join Art at the saloon. It looks like he already went in. I'll find you when I'm done, and we'll all go back to the ranch together."

"All right." Delaine saw to it that all the horses were tied, and he headed across the street. It occurred to him that none of the hunters had taken the trouble to say goodbye or to thank either him or Meredith.

The sun was slipping toward the hill in the west. A few horses were tied in front of the saloon. Meredith had parked the buckboard parallel and had tied the reins to the brake handle.

Inside the saloon, the world changed. Overhead lamps lit up the place, and voices mixed with laughter and the thump of a dice cup. A man stood by the piano, but no one was playing or singing.

Delaine made his way to the bar, which ran the length of the wall on the left side. Behind the bar, a pillar of dark varnished wood rose on each side of a set of three oval mirrors. Above the mirrors hung a painting of a landscape scene in which two early frontiersmen, dressed in fringed buckskin outfits, stood on a level area on top of a cliff, looking out over a plain with buffalo grazing. On the bottom of the frame, a brass plate was etched with the words "The Lookout."

Delaine ordered a whiskey and turned to one side so as not to be staring at the mirror. His drink came, and he set a quarter on the bar. As he lifted his drink, the man on his right turned to him.

"Oh, I thought you were someone else," he said.

Delaine gave a half-smile.

"Haven't seen you before. Do you work around here?"

"I work on a ranch north of town. We came in to leave off a set of hunters. I expect we'll go back out as soon as the boss is ready." Delaine gave a thought to Hiller, alone on the rangeland, waiting with a dead man as the day grew short.

"Hunters? It is that season, I guess."

"Antelope. I believe the next group will hunt deer."

"Hah. I guess you could say I'm a hunter of sorts. I study birds. But I don't shoot them. Some ornithologists do, and collectors. I'm a biologist, a field scientist. I just study them. By observation and note-taking."

"I see. Any special kind?"

"Migratory birds. At this time, around here, I'm on the lookout for sandhill cranes and blue jays."

"I heard the first of the sandhill cranes the other day. Up high."

"That's them." The man smiled. He was an unassuming sort, wearing a battered brown hat with a flat crown, a tan-colored canvas jacket with large pockets, canvas trousers, and lace-up field boots. He was below average height, leaning forward with a stoop in his shoulders.

"It must be interesting," said Delaine.

"It is."

"Do you travel with your work?"

"Yes. I was studying plovers during the summer, out on the prairies of Kansas and Nebraska. Small birds. They call 'em the 'Prairie Ghosts,' because they blend in with the dry grass."

"And they migrate, too?"

"Oh, yes. Of course, there's different kinds of plovers, some with longer legs and brighter colors." The man took off his hat and scratched the back of his head. A few strands of light-brown hair lay across the top of his balding head, illumined by the lamplight. He raised his head, and his grey eyes caught the light as well, shining for a moment like molten lead. He put his hat on and held out his hand. "Name's Anthony Stevens."

"Jess Delaine."

"A pleasure. So do you know the range very well hereabouts?"

"Getting to know it."

"That's the way. There's always more to learn. Even about the here and now. And then you've got your paleontologists and paleobiologists."

"Who are they?"

"The ones who study dinosaurs and all the other ancient life forms."

"I've heard of them."

"Yes, they're out here, too. When you think you've gotten as far away as you can get from people, you'll come upon one or two of them, with their little picks and brushes and screens for sifting sand."

Another man's voice interrupted. "Have you got a new student?"

Delaine turned to see the man who had been standing by himself near the piano. He was an inch shorter than the field scientist, with a slack build and one shoulder lower than the other. He wore a loose-fitting, wrinkled, dull brown suit with a white shirt that needed to be laundered, no necktie, and flat shoes with the heels worn on the outsides. He had a folded newspaper in the pocket of his coat. His head was of normal size, large in proportion to his body, which seemed to have been stunted. He did not wear a hat and had thinning hair, with unwashed strands combed across the top and uneven lengths growing down over his ears. He had large brown eyes, a broad area around his mouth, and a sallow complexion; he did not wear a beard but needed a shave.

"Oh, hello, Mason," said the biologist. "I was just talking to this fellow. I just met him. He's a range rider."

The man named Mason nodded. He lifted an empty glass and set in on the bar. "Thanks for the drink."

"Think nothing of it." The biologist paused. "Here, I've forgotten your name already."

"Delaine."

"Right. Mine's Stevens. I imagine you remember better than I do. This is Mason Mardell."

Delaine met the shorter man's eyes, which had a sullen cast to them, as if he was used to people not liking him. "How do you do?"

"Well enough." Mardell held out a hand that was half-covered by the sleeve of his coat.

Delaine shook.

Stevens said, "I've got to be going. Pleasure to meet you."

"Likewise," said Delaine. He sensed that Stevens was leaving him with Mason Mardell. He thought that if he bought the man a drink, he might go back to the piano. "Buy you a drink?" he said.

"Sure."

Delaine signaled, and the barman brought a drink. Mardell took a sip but showed no sign of leaving.

"Work on the range, huh?"

"That's right. We just had a group of antelope hunters, and we brought them back to town. As soon as the boss comes, we'll go to the ranch."

"Hunters, eh?" Mardell raised his thin eyebrows. "You're lucky you don't have competition. North of here about fifty miles, where they've got the big herds of antelope, there's hunters go in there and kill 'em by the hundred. They just take the backstraps and the hams, don't even bother to gut 'em or even skin 'em the rest of the way. They pack the meat in barrels, in brine, and they ship to the markets in Omaha."

"I've heard of that kind of plunder."

Mardell shrugged. "Just another kind of business." He had a weak-looking chin, which he shifted to one side. "How many did you get?"

"Just four. One per hunter."

"Ah, that's nothin'."

"It all went well."

"That's good." Mardell raised his head and looked around. "Who do you work for?"

"A man named Percy Calvin."

"Sure. I know him. Has a place north of town."

"That's right."

"Is that it for the hunters, then? Just four?"

"I believe he's got some deer hunters coming in before long."

"More of the same, just different. Out in the same country?"

"More or less. You don't find so many deer on the open prairie."

"Sure. And that's all cattle country. Maybe some sheep. Ranches scattered out all over."

"I don't know where they all are, but that's what I understand."

Mardell's eyes moved, and he drank from his glass. "There's a thousand ways to make a livin'."

"Oh, yes."

"Not as many freighters or pack strings as there used to be, once the railroad came through. But they still need to get goods out into the back country. You look like you might have done some of that work yourself."

"I've done a little packing, is all. But I'm not a real diamond hitch man."

"There's someone to move just about anything, sooner or later."

Delaine thought the man was taking the conversation somewhere, and there seemed to be a note of insinuation. Delaine had heard about contraband like opium, that went to the gold-mining towns. He nodded.

Mardell raised his chin, rolled his head, and settled his eyes on Delaine. He had a leer on his face. "It's got a different name in every language." He raised his free hand and rubbed his thumb against his fingertips. "But it's all the same. Even the Chinese girls, though you hear jokes about how they're different."

Delaine did not answer.

Mardell waved his hand. "But that's all just business, too. Supplies for the logging camps and mining camps."

Delaine felt as if he was being invited to ask more. Talk of shipping women like produce or commodities was bound to raise curiosity, but he did not want to play in. He did not want to seem as if he was ignoring the man, however, so he nodded.

Mardell raised his thin eyebrows, and the strand of hair across his bald forehead went up and down. "There's things to know, even in a place like this, that people would never guess at."

Delaine wondered if there was any substance to the man's talk or if it was just something to make him seem knowledgeable and important. But Delaine did not want to encourage him to go on.

"I thank you for the drink," said Mardell. "I won't bother you anymore."

Delaine was familiar with that kind of self-deprecation. "No bother," he said.

"Thanks." Mardell turned and walked away with an uneven gait.

Delaine set his drink on the bar and gazed at the mirror. He thought again of Hiller, waiting on the rangeland.

Meredith appeared behind him in the mirror.

Delaine turned around. "Is Percy here?"

"Not yet." Meredith drank from a glass of whiskey. "Who was that you were talking to?"

"I think his name is Mason Mardell."

"No, I know him. I mean the one before that."

"Oh. His name is Stevens. He said he was a biologist. He studies birds that migrate."

"Bug hunter."

Delaine recognized the term as a general one that working men used in reference to field scientists of all kinds, whether they studied insects, birds, mammals, plant life, minerals, or fossils. "There are lots of birds that migrate. He said he studied sandhill cranes, among others, and I told him I heard the first ones of the season just a few days ago."

"Yeah, I heard 'em, too. They cry like a baby shut up in the house. Ugly, too, if you ever see one up close. What did Mardell have to say?"

"Not much. He talked about men who shoot antelope in large numbers and ship the meat in barrels."

"He has a lot of talk. What else did he say?"

Delaine felt no more comfortable with Meredith's inquisitive manner than he did with the other man's innuendo. "Nothing in particular," he said. "Just vague talk."

"Yeah, he's got plenty of that."

————

CIGARETTE SMOKE MIXED with the haze that drifted out from the kitchen. Meredith had fried the bacon a little longer than usual, and smoke had escaped from the firebox of the cookstove. Meredith and Hiller were smoking cigarettes as Delaine washed the dishes.

Percy said, "Ed 'n' Art, I think I'll have you work with those ten horses in the pasture that haven't seen much work since spring roundup. You know which ones. We're sittin' on our thumbs right now, waitin' for the deer hunters, but as soon as we've finished with them, we want to go into fall roundup."

Meredith cleared his throat, nodded, tucked back the corner of his mouth, and tipped his ash in a sardine can.

Hiller said, "We can expect that deputy to come out and ask a full round of questions as well."

"Oh, yeah," said Percy. "But I don't think he'll hold us up all that much." After a pause, he spoke to Delaine. "Jess, I've got a little job in mind to keep you busy."

Delaine met his gaze and nodded.

"I want to go after the cactus in the horse pasture. That's the way it is with horses. They cut up a pasture so bad that after a few years, seems like all you've got is sagebrush and cactus."

"Any special way you want me to do it?"

"Use the wheelbarrow that's in the barn. You'll find a hoe as well, in there with the shovels and diggin' bars. You can make a pile in one of those gullies on the lower end."

"Do you want me to start at this end?"

"Mize well."

———

DELAINE FOUND a heavy field hoe that looked as if it had not seen work for a while. He thought a rake would be useful, but he did not find one. The pitchforks had wide spaces between the tines, and he thought most of the prickly pear would fall through, so he took just the hoe and the wheelbarrow, as Percy had told him.

At the horse pasture, he saw a scattered population

of the low-lying, pale-green cactus, some of it turning yellow against the dull ground. A rake would be handy for pulling the plants out by the roots, but he worked with what he had. He knew he would not be doing much good if he cut the growth off at ground level and left the roots, and he did not want to dig up too much dirt with the corner of the hoe, so before long, he developed a method of bearing down on the hoe and dragging the plants. Some were small and consisted of only a lobe or two, while others grew out for a foot or more, lying close to the ground and putting down more roots.

Picking up the plants with the blade of the hoe was tedious, but many of the smaller ones came out with very short roots and could not be handled otherwise. When the roots were long enough, he bent down and picked up his harvest, trying to keep from being pricked. Some of the plants had long, stringy roots that were easy to grab. As he developed a knack for the different kinds of growth, he was still annoyed by uncut roots that had stayed hidden, plants falling off the hoe, and little needles sticking in his fingers.

When he picked up the plants by their roots and carried them to the wheelbarrow, they reminded him of dead birds—some like sparrows, some like quail, and some like dead chickens. The bigger ones flopped when he threw them onto the load.

He thought about prairie chickens, of which he had seen very few, and he wondered if the field scientist, Stevens, studied them. He doubted it. The man had said he studied migratory birds and didn't kill any.

Some of the prickly pear came out like large, rich treasures with all of the pads intact. Some were small and dry and miserable, tough to grub out. From time to time, he looked behind him and saw one he had missed—sometimes in the cover of a clump of sage-brush, sometimes in plain view.

Delaine was pushing the wheelbarrow up the slope after dumping a load in the gully when he saw a man in uniform silhouetted where the pasture leveled off up above. He was standing where Delaine had left the hoe. The sun had climbed to mid-morning and was shining on the light-brown tones of the man's clothing.

Closer, Delaine saw that he wore a clean hat, jacket, and shirt, with a leather vest. A dark-brown gun belt showed beneath his jacket, and he wore tan wool pants and shiny brown boots. As Delaine set the wheelbarrow down, the man moved his jacket aside to show his badge.

"Good morning," he said. "I'm Deputy Ted Blackmur from the Laramie County Sheriff's Office. I understand you were present yesterday when they found the body."

"That's right. I was at the rear of the convoy."

"Just to be sure, can you tell me your name?"

"Jess Delaine."

"How long have you worked here?"

"About a week."

"Oh, not long."

"I've been in and around Overton for about a year."

"Working."

"Yes."

"Well, I realize you weren't the first one to see the dead body, so you might not have much to add. Did you see him when he came by your hunting camp earlier?"

"Yes, I did."

"And you heard him state his business of looking for his runaway daughter?"

"Yes."

"Did you hear him state her name?"

"No, I didn't."

"That's what everyone else said. Just checking. Did you happen to see him again in the meanwhile, between that first visit and the time when your boss found him on the trail?"

"No."

"I think all of your hunters are accounted for. They were always with someone or close by. Did you see anyone else out on the range between the time of the man's visit to your camp and the time he was found?"

"During that time? Well, not on the range itself, but three men dropped by the camp when I was there with a hunter. They said they rode for the Big Eight, and they complained about hunters being out there."

The deputy nodded. "I heard they came by. Anything else? We're still trying to get the man's name. The most anyone can remember is that he was from Trinidad, Colorado."

"His name is Tiburcio Martínez."

The deputy's eyes widened. "You remember better than those others do."

"I happened to meet him before."

"You did? Where?"

"In Overton, the day before I came here. He was at the house of some people I know, through a woman I know there."

"I see. Did he say anything to you then that might have any bearing on what happened later?"

"He didn't speak to me at all. The people I know

there had invited me over to see if I might be able to tell him anything about the layout of the country, main-traveled roads and such, but he said he didn't need me."

"Were those his words?"

"No, he said it in Spanish, and he said it to the other people, but I understand it well enough."

"They say that he spoke good English when he came to your camp."

"He did. He spoke only Spanish the first time I saw him and only English the second time."

"And you saw him only three times."

"That's right."

The deputy put his thumbs on his gun belt and straightened up with a deep breath. "Well, I don't think I have any other questions at this time. You've been good help with knowing his name. Did you happen to hear his daughter's name when you were with those other people?"

"No, just that it was his...favorite one. Like his pet."

"I understand. Now that I've got his name, I can send a wire down there and get more information. Do you remember the name of the family in Overton?"

"Mendoza."

The deputy nodded. "That's all I can think of at the moment. I'll leave you to your work. It looks like you're doing a good job." He made a quick half-smile. "Thanks."

"Glad to be of help."

———

DELAINE HAD CLEARED LESS than half of the ten-acre pasture and was about to go out for the third day when Percy said they were all going to town to wait for the deer hunters to arrive. He told Delaine and Hiller to get the buckboard ready, saddle two extra horses, and saddle two for themselves. As was his habit, he would saddle his own horse. The train would not come in until late in the day, so they had time to clean up.

All the way into town, Delaine had the apprehension that they would find another body, but the trip was uneventful. The tops of the buildings on Main Street came into view, and life beyond the ranch and the rangeland seemed normal again.

As the group passed the intersection of Pearl Street and Main Street, a small jolt of recognition ran through Delaine. A man was standing on the veranda of the Dunfield Hotel. He was tall and slender, dressed in a pinstripe suit, a wool overcoat, and a dark hat. His watch chain flashed. He had a full mustache, light and dark in the shade of the overhang, and he had his chin raised as he watched the traffic go by. He did not show any recognition of the small group from the Lazy T.

Percy took out his watch and consulted it. "We got here with plenty of time to spare," he said. "If you boys want to go in and wet your whistle, I'll go down to the train station and wait. I can send someone up for you when they come in."

Delaine thought it was considerate of the boss not to make the rest of them wait with him. On the other hand, it was an easy way for him not to have to buy a round of drinks.

Percy rode on. Delaine and Hiller tied their horses and the extra mounts at the hitching rail as Meredith parked the buckboard. Delaine stood aside for the other two and followed them into The Lookout.

The place had not changed. Overhead lamps were shining. The two frontiersmen in the painting were looking out over the plain. A few patrons stood along the bar, talking and laughing.

Meredith and Hiller let Delaine buy the first round. Hiller said, "I'll buy the next one."

A full-bosomed woman with feathers in her hat walked by.

"Early in the day for her, isn't it?" said Delaine.

Hiller said, "It's Saturday."

"I suppose it is. I lost track of the days of the week."

Meredith tucked back the corner of his mouth. "If you're not Catholic, you can eat pork every day of the week."

Delaine paid for the drinks and handed them around. As they lowered their glasses from the first sip, a man in range-riding clothes and a hat with an upturned brim stopped and smiled.

In a gravelly voice and a jovial tone, he said, "Good to see you boys out of jail."

Meredith said, "We were never in there."

The man's yellow teeth showed as he smiled. "I heard they found a dead man out your way."

"Just a Mexican," Meredith said.

"What was he doin' out there?"

"Layin' in the road."

Hiller said, "He was looking for his lost daughter who ran away with her Romeo."

The corner of Meredith's mouth tucked back again. "Foolish old man. That's like tryin' to stop a train that doesn't have any brakes."

The man with the rough voice said, "Yeah, they're gonna do it one way or another. Too bad for him."

Delaine thought it was easy for them to talk that away about someone who didn't matter to them, but he did not like to be part of it. He allowed himself to move back a step.

A woman's voice said, "Be careful you don't bump into me, sweetheart."

He turned to find himself face to face with the woman in the feathered hat. "Thanks for the warning," he said.

"Didn't know if you needed it."

"Seems as if I did."

The woman had green eyes, dark hair, a light complexion, and shiny red lips. Her bosom was as prominent as before. "What brings you to town?"

"We're on the job," he said. "Waitin' for word from the boss."

"Oh." She raised her eyebrows, then touched his arm. "I'll see you some other time."

"Sure." He smiled and turned away. It seemed as if the meeting had taken place by itself without his having time to think about it.

Another man joined the group. Delaine recognized him as Meredith clapped him on the shoulder. "Brother Ben. Been to the rooster fights?"

"Not in a while."

"Where's Crawford? Has he got his finger in the pie somewhere?"

"He'd like to." Ben spoke to Delaine. "Are you done bothering that woman?"

Delaine frowned. "I didn't do anything."

"Don't lie to me. I saw you. I was watching you."

"I heard her voice in back of me, and I turned around. I didn't even touch her."

Ben had a hard look in his eyes. "Don't contradict me, or I'll clean your plow. It's as much as calling me a liar."

Delaine took a breath and said nothing. The flare-up seemed to come out of nowhere.

"I didn't like you the first time I saw you, and I like you even less now. What do you think you are?"

Delaine kept his eyes on the man.

"I asked you a question."

"I don't have an answer."

Ben had a cigarette in his right hand, which he raised to chest level. He made a spitting gesture, as if he was getting rid of a grain of tobacco, and he thrust his hand forward, flicking the cigarette.

Delaine batted it away, and Ben came at him, smashing him in the head with a left and then a right. Delaine's feet went out from under him, and his drink spilled on his shirt.

Ben stood with his fists doubled, looking down with his flinty brown eyes. "No one talks to me like that, you understand?" He glanced at his brother, said, "See you later," and stalked out of the saloon.

5

————

THE DEER HUNTERS ARRIVED ON THE EVENING TRAIN
with their luggage and gun cases, which went into the
buckboard. The hunters were similar to the first group,
well dressed and equipped for the excursion. Delaine
learned that they all came from a sporting club in
Chicago where Percy sent advertising materials, but
they did not know each other from before. Two of
them appeared to be in their forties, one in his fifties,
and one in his sixties. The two older men rode in the
buckboard, and the other two went on horseback.

The group arrived at the ranch after dark. Percy
set out a bottle of brandy and a bottle of whiskey while
Meredith went to work in the kitchen and Delaine and
Hiller unloaded the hunters' belongings. The two older
men were to sleep in the ranch house, and the other
two would sleep in the bunkhouse.

Percy did not encourage anyone to stay up late.
Not long after supper, he put the bottles away and
ushered the two older men to the ranch house. The
two younger ones opened their bags on their bunks.

The youngest, a man of about forty, was named George Dorn. He was of average height and build, with brown hair and a wreath-like brown mustache. His teeth showed when he smiled.

He set out his equipment to show Delaine and Hiller. He had a hunting belt that carried a knife, a compass, a folding saw the size of a large pocketknife, and a lightweight hatchet with a steel shaft and a varnished leather handle. In addition, he had a brown canvas hunting vest that held a coil of light rope, extra gloves, and a green stocking cap.

Hiller said, "You're pretty well set up."

Dorn smiled. "I happen to be the manager of a hardware store."

"Hardware?" said Hiller. "Crowbars and the like?"

"Anything from the smallest nails and tacks to steel vaults you could put your horse into. Plus all manner of ropes and chains."

The other man, who was about the same age, was named Walter Rumford. He was short and slender with dark, wavy hair and a bald spot like a monk's. He had dark eyes and a quick manner, and his voice had a quacking tone that Delaine associated with Wisconsin or Michigan. He showed the contents of his knapsack. Like Dorn, he had a heavy cord, extra gloves, and an extra cap. He also had a whistle. He carried a compass in a buttoned vest pocket and a bone-handled folding knife that he kept in a coat pocket. "Contrary to appearance," he said, "I don't manage a hardware store. I'm an accountant for a bottle factory. But now that I know where George is, I can improve my stock."

Dorn said, "You're one ahead of me with that whistle."

"It's for being lost in the woods. I hope I never have to use it."

Meredith had poured himself another glass of whiskey when Percy left, and he had sat at the table with it and a cigarette. He stood up, blew out one lamp, and waited by the other. His face took on a dull stare as Rumford put on a red nightcap before turning back the blankets.

"Everyone set?" Meredith asked. "I don't want anyone falling down in the dark."

Dorn said, "I've got a light if I need it." He set a small candle lantern on the upended crate next to his bunk.

Meredith said, "Everyone sleep tight," and he blew out the light.

———

PERCY TOOK the hunters past the barn to sight in their rifles while the workmen organized the equipment and supplies for the next outing. They would use the same wagon for camp, and all the hunters would go on horseback from here. Delaine and Hiller fitted out all the saddle horses and packhorses as usual.

Meredith served a lunch of beef stew and biscuits in the bunkhouse, and Delaine and Hiller washed and dried the dishes.

Percy and the hunters sat around the table. The two older men smoked tailor-made cigarettes. Meredith kept busy in the kitchen.

Percy said, "Well, I hope you men are all ready for a good hunt. With deer, I feel that I need to say something ahead of time, 'cause you can come onto somethin' all of a sudden. You want to be careful with what you shoot. Whatever you kill, that's what you get. We don't leave something lay there and go off and try to find something better. I say this because of things that have happened before, not anything I expect out of anyone here. And you know, they're startin' to pass laws that'll require everyone to have a license and to be able to shoot only so many of each kind of animal."

"I think we're used to it," said the man who was in his fifties. His name was J.M. Packard, and in addition to saying the evening before that he was an attorney who specialized in family law, he had said that he had hunted quail and whitetail deer.

"That's good," said Perry. "I don't know if any of the hired men have anything to add. Art?"

Meredith appeared at the doorway to the kitchen. "Just don't shoot any cattle."

"Ed?"

"I think the thing I see the most is buck fever. They either can't decide how to take the shot, or they get nervous and jerk on the trigger."

Percy said, "That happens, all right. You want to try to stay calm. How about you, Jess?"

Delaine had been considering the question. He said, "I think it's a good idea to decide what you want or will be satisfied with. Then that'll make it easier for you to accept what you get, like Percy said. If you decide ahead of time, then you're accepting your own decision when you shoot something."

"That's right," said Percy. "That's a good way to put it."

DELAINE AND HILLER were securing the hunters' bags and rifle cases onto the packhorses when a buggy rolled into the ranch yard. The vehicle had only one person, a large man who sat in the middle of the seat. Delaine did not recognize him.

Closer, the man appeared to have features that Delaine associated with the southwest. He had dark hair and a light-brown complexion, and he wore a light tan suit and white shirt with no hat. He brought the buggy to a stop, and he smiled. He was clean-shaven with a high forehead, trimmed hair, dark eyes, and a full, jowly face. He had a fold of flesh between his chin and his throat, and he sat with his legs apart and his large abdomen resting in his lap. He tugged at the soft leather gloves on his hands as he continued to smile.

"Good afternoon," he said.

Percy stepped forward and said, "What can we help you with?"

The man's voice was soft but clear. "It looks as if you're getting ready to go somewhere, so I'll try not to take up much of your time. My name is Pedro Cuenca. I come from Trinidad, Colorado. I have come a long way. I took a train to Cheyenne and then Wheatland, another train to Overton, and rented this buggy to come back this way. I have come to your ranch because I understand that this is where my uncle, in reality a cousin of my father, Tiburcio Martínez, was found."

Delaine noticed that the man pronounced the town and the state with an English accent but gave his uncle's name a Spanish inflection, which seemed normal.

Percy said, "We know who he was. We didn't quite

find him *on* this ranch, but we did find him, and we did meet him when he was alive and stopped in at our hunting camp. Which, by the way, we're about to go out and do again."

Cuenca smiled. "I'll try not to keep you. I would just like to find out any other information I can."

Percy looked around. "I can't say that we know anything other than his name and where he was from, which he did say. We don't even know the name of his daughter that ran away."

"Then you do know that he was looking for her."

"He did say that much."

"Her name was Guillermina," Cuenca said, hitting the Spanish inflection again. "Her family calls her Minita. And, to share a little more information with you, the young man is named Jaime Romero."

"Well, we don't know anything about either of them."

Cuenca said, "I just thought I would share it. To be clear, I am not looking for information about either of them. Just about my uncle. I have arranged to have his body sent home, and I will stay around for a little while to see what I can learn."

Percy said, "I believe the law is handling the case. A deputy named Blackmur has been out here to comb all the information he could."

"Yes, I know that. But I feel an obligation to the family to find out what I can. That is why I came this far."

Delaine felt that he should say something. "I don't know anything more than what's been said already, but I want you to know that I have sympathy for you, and I would help if I could."

Cuenca's voice remained soft, and he smiled in a

way that Delaine found condescending. "Thank you for your sympathy, though I was not seeking that, either. In truth, this is like a different country here. I do not expect you people to understand these things at their true level, but I thank you."

Delaine held his tongue. He did not see a purpose in saying that he had known the Mexican people and some of their language or that he knew the people in Overton. As with Don Tiburcio, it was easier not to bother.

Cuenca spoke to Percy. "I thank you and the others for your attention. May things go well for you in your hunting."

"Thank you. And the same to you."

"Very well." Cuenca shook the resins, and the buggy horse picked up its feet and went into a trot.

Delaine saw that Meredith had been standing by. When the visitor was well out of earshot, Meredith made a spitting sound as if he was getting rid of a fleck of tobacco.

He said, "These people aren't from here, but they bring their problems here. Like that foolish old man, just like a hot-headed Mexican. This one's more cool-headed, but just as high-handed. And you can imagine what that girl is like. Hot as a chili pepper, doesn't give a damn about her family."

Delaine flared up. "Say what you want, but she's somebody's daughter."

"Hah," said Meredith. "Her cousin doesn't seem to be worried about her, and he doesn't seem to care for your sympathy, either."

Delaine pulled himself in. He felt as if he had said more than he needed. He had been rebuffed by Cuenca and made fun of by Meredith. He even felt silly, as if he had shown a soft spot for a girl he didn't know. But the situation was bigger than that. He did feel an obligation to help these people, because there did seem to be an injustice, and because he should be capable of helping when others didn't seem to care. But there was no point in going out of his way at present.

Percy said, "Like I told him, this is in the hands of the law. This fella here seems pretty sure of himself, and he does seem to be able to do things on his own, so that's up to him, as far as what he does."

Delaine waited for Meredith to say something, but no comment came.

The spirit of the occasion returned as the men loaded the last of the gear and provisions. Meredith took the reins of the wagon, and Delaine and Hiller helped the hunters onto their horses. Percy and the hunters rode first, followed by the wagon and the rider-less horse, and then Delaine and Hiller with the four packhorses.

The ranch headquarters looked empty as Delaine gave a parting glance. No horses were in the corrals. All the spare horses were in the pasture, where they had grass and water. A ranch could be an austere place when it had no children, dogs, cats, or even chickens—slim pickings for coyotes or birds of prey.

———

PERCY LED the company northeast to an area where the ridge had pine and cedar trees on top and side canyons along the base. After more than two hours of travel, he stopped at the mouth of a canyon where a small stream flowed out.

As with the antelope camp, the place showed signs of having been a campsite on past occasions. The spots for the wagon, the tents, and the rope corral were all determined. Delaine could sense that it was the beginning of an adventure for the hunters, while it was one more segment in a series of job duties for the hired men.

The tents went up, and the hunters settled into theirs as Meredith and Percy got things established in the kitchen tent. Delaine and Hiller had to range quite a distance for firewood, but they dragged back some good pieces on horseback. By the time the sun went down, a pile of chopped firewood was visible in the glow of the campfire.

Delaine had a recurring memory of the man who had ridden into their first camp and of the man who was hoping to learn information about him. He told himself not to be concerned about them but to stay attentive to the tasks at hand and the affluent men who had come to hunt.

————

PERCY LAID out the deer-hunting plan as the campfire blazed in the dark of early morning. "We've gotten deer all along this ridge in the past," he said. "We start from each end with one hunter on top and one down below. The one on the ground tries not to get ahead of the one on top, so the deer don't run out behind him. If someone gets something, they dress it out there and wait. When we all meet, someone will go for packhorses to bring in what we get."

J.M. Packard, the attorney, said, "We have to dress out our own deer?"

"No. The man who's with you will do that. We'll go in pairs. You'll go with Jess, up on top." Percy turned his attention to the oldest hunter. "You'll go with Ed. The four of you will start out on foot from here and work your way north. Meanwhile, Art and I will take the other two a mile and a half north and work our way back."

"So you'll need four horses," Hiller said.

"Right. There's a place where we tie the horses, and we'll go back for them. You and Jess can saddle two for us before you leave."

The men shook their coffee grounds into the fire as the group broke up.

J.M. Packard was ready to go when Delaine returned from saddling a horse for one of the other hunters. Packard stood by the fire, with the flickering light playing on his dark eyes and sagging face. He was dressed in a charcoal-grey wool shooting jacket with pants to match. He wore a single-billed deerstalker cap of grey and black checks, and he had his rifle slung on his shoulder. He held the bipod in one hand and was smoking a cigarette with the other.

He said, "I might as well tell you at the outset that I don't want anything less than a ten-pointer."

Delaine took a second to register what the man said. "By that, do you mean four main points on each side as well as eye guards?"

"When they have four good points on each side, they have an eye guard as well, don't they?"

"As a general rule, I suppose. We just count the main points, and if there's a difference, we go with the best side. Or that's what I'm used to. What you describe would be a four-pointer to me."

"We count all the points."

"That's fine. As long as we have an understanding."

Delaine set off on foot, and the hunter followed. Within a few minutes, they were climbing the ridge in grey light. Delaine heard the man breathing, so he waited.

"Catch your breath," he said. "You don't want to be breathing hard if you see something."

Packard held the shooting stick forward. "If you carry this, I'll do better."

They reached the top after ten minutes of climbing and stopping. The sun had cleared the hills farther east, and daylight was spreading.

"It's light enough to shoot," Delaine said, "so be ready."

Packard put his thumb under the sling strap, swung the rifle down and around, and pointed it at Delaine in the process.

"You can go first," Delaine said as he handed him the shooting stick.

"I don't like someone in back, pushing me."

"All right." Delaine took the lead. Before he had taken two steps, he heard the clack-clack of a shell being levered in. He stopped and turned. "If you're going to hunt with a shell in the chamber, you're going to go in front."

Packard expelled a breath. "I've hunted before. When you're in the woods, you don't have time to put one in. Sometimes you're lucky if you get a snap shot."

"Then you go first."

"What if I don't know which way to go? You're the guide."

"Then you can ask, and I'll tell you."

Packard set out walking. The trees on top were

pine, not very tall or thick and not very close together. Packard followed a trail, and the going was not hard at all. From time to time, he rested his rifle on his shoulder, pointing the muzzle in Delaine's direction but higher.

The sun rose. Packard walked at a slow pace, stopping at intervals. He did not make much noise, as there was not a carpet of twigs and branches as there would be in a forest.

No sounds came from below. Delaine trusted that Hiller could keep track of their progress and wasn't getting ahead.

A thumping sound crossed in front of them, and Packard stopped. He raised his rifle but did not fire. When Delaine caught up with him, the Packard said, "Doe and fawn."

Hunter and guide walked on. The sun climbed higher, and the day warmed. Delaine felt that they were getting into that part of the morning when a hunter's attention relaxed. Packard seemed to be plodding now and not setting his feet down with as much care as before.

A scrambling sound up ahead caused Packard to stop. As Delaine took light steps forward, he saw three deer going uphill where the ridge rose ahead. The shapes disappeared behind a pine tree, then came into view again with a glint of antlers. As mule deer tended to do, they paused near the top of the rise and looked back. The middle deer had antlers.

Packard had moved ahead and now stopped again. His rifle went up, and a shot crashed, shattering the stillness of the morning. Two of the deer bolted, and Packard shot three more times.

Delaine moved up to stand by the hunter.

"He's down now," said Packard.

"Let's go take a look at him." Delaine led the way downhill through a kind of saddle that crossed the ridge, and he climbed the sagebrush slope on the other side.

The buck was laid out with its rack of antlers sticking up. Delaine counted four on each side and was glad for that part. Closer, he saw that the antlers were an inch thick at the base and had good beams, and the eye guards were an inch and a half long. The buck looked like an old one, as it had a heavy build and a grey coat. The tips of its ears were gone, as if they had been nipped off by some hard winter in the past.

Packard came laboring up the hill. He stopped and surveyed the animal as he caught his breath. "I don't like his ears," he said.

"You got a nice big deer. And these antlers will make a good mount by themselves."

"I don't like not having the option of mounting the head." Packard lowered the rifle from his shoulder, and in so doing, he swung the muzzle toward Delaine.

"Let's make sure that thing is unloaded."

"It is. It holds four shots, and I fired all four. If he hadn't gone down, I would have had to reload."

"Where's the shooting stick?"

"Oh. I dropped it when I shot. It's still back there. I didn't need it."

"We'll get it later." Delaine pulled the deer around so that its abdomen was downhill, and he went to work with his knife to open it up.

Packard lit a cigarette. Delaine stepped across the animal to hold a rear leg uphill with his thigh as he bent at the knee. He did not want to ask the hunter to do anything.

The shots had hit the deer in the hindquarters, the spine, and the upper shoulders, and nothing inside was shot up. Delaine cut out the colon and the bladder, then tumbled out the steaming entrails, loops of silvery green with globs of fat. He was reaching in for the heart and lungs when movement caught his eye.

Ed Hiller had come up the draw that became the saddle as it crossed the ridge. His brown hat, dark-blue shirt, and grey vest showed through the pine needles before he stepped into the open.

"I was hopin' you got somethin' with all those shots. When I didn't see any more movement from you, I thought I'd come up and take a look. That's a nice one." He smiled at Packard.

"The ears are cut off on top," said the hunter.

Hiller raised his eyebrows. "Yeah. Frostbite. He's got good horns, though."

Delaine said, "I'm glad you came up. I imagine the best way to take care of this thing is to drag him down the way you came. How is it?"

"A little steep in a couple of places, but I think we can do it."

When Delaine had the heart and lungs out, he asked Packard, "Do you plan to save the hide?"

"Nah."

"Then we'll drag it like I thought. Just wanted to make sure. We'll go first, in case he gets ahead of us. You can come behind at your own pace, and we don't want to forget the shooting stick."

"I won't."

Delaine wiped his hands on the grass and on his pants so as not to stain the antlers, and he and Hiller each grabbed a side. They leaned into their work and dragged the carcass down the slope.

The draw going down from the ridge was rougher, and the bulky body slid between them in a couple of places. When they came out at the bottom, the heavyset older hunter, Paul Edson, was sitting on a rock, smoking a cigarette.

The four men stood together by the dead animal. Hiller said, "The way Percy wants to do it is for us to keep hunting until we meet." He nodded at Packard. "You can stay here with your deer. We'll put it in a place where it'll stay in the shade." To Delaine, he said, "Jess, you can go back on top and haze anything down this way. Looks like you don't have a gun."

"I wasn't hunting."

"I always carry one in case someone needs help bringing one down. If we shoot one down below here and he's still running when he reaches the top, you could drop him." Hiller glanced at Packard's rifle.

"I'm fine the way I am," Delaine said. "I'll carry a rifle tomorrow."

Hiller hesitated. "Well, here. I'd better stay with the man Percy put me with, but there's no point in you being up there if you can't stop a deer that's been shot. You can use mine."

"I'd rather not," said Delaine. "And you might need it just as much down here. I'll go up by myself, and if I see any draws that are thick with trees, I can throw rocks down to run the deer out to you."

Hiller drummed his fingers on his legs. "All right. But don't throw any rocks. Just keep an eye out."

"Good enough." Delaine had caught his breath, so he turned and walked away. He found the drag marks where they had come down, and he followed the same route to the top.

The sun was high and warm. He had to remind

himself to walk at a hunting pace, which meant to take soft steps, stop, listen, and go on. He did feel bare without a rifle.

The trees on top became thicker in number, but he still found trails easy to follow. He came across dried cow pies as well as deer droppings, some of them darker and not so dry.

About an hour had passed, and he walked along, feeling idle. He heard commotion ahead of him, and he stopped, then moved ahead to see the last tail end of what he guessed to be three or four deer going down the slope on his left. He did not think it was the two does from earlier. They would not have let him get that close after what had happened.

A minute later, the blast of a rifle carried up from below, and after about ten seconds, two more shots sounded.

Delaine waited another long minute until he heard Hiller's voice.

"Come on down!"

Delaine found a cleft that looked passable and made his way down. He assumed he missed the deer's route, as he saw no tracks. He came out into an inlet or shallow canyon, and he saw Hiller and his heavyset hunter standing by a low heap on the ground.

As he approached, he saw that the dead animal had at least three points. He looked at the hunter and said, "Got one, huh?"

No one spoke as Delaine came to a stop. He saw nothing wrong with the deer. It had three good points on each side, and it was good-sized, though not as big as the one Packard had shot.

The hunter, Edson, stood with his rifle upright, resting with the butt plate on the ground. He had a full face with heavy eyebrows and prominent brown eyes. He wore an outdoors sporting outfit like the others, of a dull brown wool, with leather suspenders pushed out by his upper body. He was breathing hard through his nose.

"He shot more than one," Hiller said. He pointed at another low mound some twenty yards away, where a pale forked horn stuck up.

Delaine wanted to ask how it happened, but he held his tongue. He turned his attention to Edson, who had been looking down and now raised his eyes.

"I thought someone could use it," he said.

Hiller huffed out a breath. "I don't think Percy will like it, but that's between the two of you." He looked at Delaine. "Looks like we have two to clean. I'll do the first one, and you can do the second. You can hold a leg for me, and I'll do the same for you."

Delaine nodded. "Sounds all right."

Edson said, "I'll stay out of your way." He picked up his rifle by the end of the barrel and walked away.

Delaine waited until he found a shady spot in the canyon and sat down. "How did that happen?" he asked.

Hiller glanced at the hunter. "I'm not sure. He wanted to hunt ahead of me, so I let him. He came to the edge of this little canyon, and I couldn't see past him and the wall. I think you might have sent these deer down to us. He shot once and then twice more. I think he shot the little one first, then saw the bigger one, and shot it."

"Just like Percy said not to do."

"He's been bossy with me all along, so I'm not surprised. He can have it out with Percy. But this isn't any good. In a way, everyone in the group has to be a part of it."

Delaine shook his head. "I know. But we might as well get to work."

———

Percy and Meredith and the other two hunters showed up not long after Delaine and Hiller had finished cleaning the two deer and dragging them into the shade.

When he heard the news, Percy drew his hand down over his mouth and chin and said, "Always somethin'. No one in our party fired a shot. Looks like you two have got work for the rest of the day. We might go out again for an afternoon hunt."

6

————

DELAINE AND HILLER TRANSPORTED THE THREE DEER to camp in one trip, tying each one onto a packhorse and lashing the antlers to a crossbuck. In camp, they skinned the animals, salted the capes, and put a clean game bag on each carcass. Dusk was drawing in when Percy and Meredith returned with their two hunters, who reported seeing deer but nothing with antlers.

Percy was having a drink with the hunters when Delaine and Hiller arrived at the fire, having put away the last of the horses. Full night had not fallen, so the firelight was thin.

Whinnying from the rope corral was followed by the sound of a horse's footfalls and the squeak and rub of wheels. A buggy stopped at the edge of the light, and the body of the carriage tipped as a large man let himself down. He was dressed in a wool overcoat and muffler and a floppy wool hat, and when he turned toward the group, he presented the face of Pedro Cuenca.

"Well, good evening," he said. "I did not know

whose camp this was, but I should not be surprised. I remember that you were getting ready to leave your ranch when I saw you."

"How do you do?" said Percy. "Your travels seem to be taking you quite a ways off the main trail. The temperature drops when night falls, and you're likely to get a chill before you make it back to town."

The man was wearing thick wool gloves, and he waved his hand down the front of his coat. "I bought these things. They are quite warm. And we are used to the cold where I come from."

"What brings you this far out?"

"Oh," said Cuenca, lifting his head with a discreet expression. "Certain information I was able to obtain. And this country is not hard to get around in."

"I hope you have a safe trip back, if you're going tonight."

"Thank you. I have a lantern if I need it."

"We're a little ways from suppertime, but you're welcome to join us if you'd like."

"Thank you. I'll be on my way. It's just that I saw your fire, and I thought I would see who was here. Good evening." He gave a slight bow.

"And a good one to you," said Percy.

The large man returned to the buggy, hauled himself up, and adjusted the skirts of his coat as he settled himself on the seat. He raised a gloved hand, turned the horse, and drove away into the night.

Percy said, "I hope he goes armed."

"He'd be a fool not to," said Meredith. "But he might be a fool for coming out here at all, not to mention by himself in the dark."

J.M. Packard said, "He appears to be quite sure of

himself, but he seems to me to be a bit of a... greenhorn."

"You never know," said Percy. "Trinidad is not a soft place."

———

DELAINE AND HILLER were washing and wiping the dishes on the tailgate of the wagon when Percy gave the plan for the next day.

"Ed and Jess, I think I'll have you take these two men out in the morning. You'll need to go farther north. We've hunted this whole part of the ridge enough for right now. Ed, you know the way. Go north of where we started this morning. You know where that is. Hunt north along the ridge, one on top and one below, and if you don't get your two deer, you can hunt those breaks that go across to the west. You'll be a long ways out, even at the beginning, so take two pack-horses with you." He spoke to Delaine. "Jess, you'll have your rifle on your horse, won't you?"

"Yes, sir."

"You'll want to carry it when you go on foot. If nothing else, you've got a second gun if your hunter's rifle jams or doesn't fire."

"Right."

The boss spoke to Hiller again. "Our two men took turns hunting on top today, so they can do the same tomorrow. Just to make things easy, so you don't have to draw straws when you're out there, Walt can hunt with you, and George can hunt with Jess. Any questions?"

Hiller said, "I think you covered everything."

"Jess?"

Delaine shook his head. "It all sounds clear to me."

"Good. I hope you see some deer."

———

THE PINK SKY of morning was turning yellow when Delaine and his hunter, George Dorn, reached the top of the ridge. The air was cold, and their breaths showed.

"Do you want to go first?" Delaine asked.

"I don't mind."

"Have you practiced aiming with the shooting stick?"

"A couple of times. I haven't used one before, but it seems like it could be a good help."

"If you have time to get set up, you may not have to shoot your animal so many times."

Dorn smiled, and his teeth showed in the morning light. "Packard was telling us how he didn't need his, but even when you hunt in the woods and you don't have many long shots, you get a rest on a tree trunk when you can."

Delaine nodded. "Even in country like this, with trees and draws, you'll get shots of a hundred and two hundred yards and more. Shooting across a canyon is deceiving in itself. You need to bear down. But in any situation, you want to make your first shot a good one. Don't feel that you have to hurry. If your deer gets away before you can shoot, we'll hunt until we find another one."

"Good." Dorn hefted his rifle and set out.

The ridge did not have a smooth, level back, and it went up and down more than it did in the stretch that Delaine had covered the day before. The pine trees were fifteen feet at the tallest and sparse in their foliage. The smell of dust was stronger than the smell of pines.

Dorn walked like a practiced hunter, watching where he put his feet and stopping at intervals. Birds flitted in and out of the trees, including one blue jay that reminded Delaine of the field biologist. A magpie came soaring over the ridge and veered away.

The whole setting seemed smaller and more spare than the mountains, where huge pines and fir and spruce grew thick together and where squirrels chittered, blue grouse flushed, and snowshoe hares huddled in the white shade. But Delaine knew that big deer could be found in this country. He recalled one occasion, in country more open than this, when he had seen four big bucks grazing together in late summer. He had stopped his horse to watch them, and a fifth buck, also a four-pointer, had appeared farther down the slope.

Delaine kept his eye on his hunter as well as on the broad ridge top that sloped off on either side. He had caught up with Dorn and was waiting behind him when the crash of a rifle carried up from below and made them both flinch.

"Be ready," Delaine said.

A minute later, a scrambling of hooves sounded ahead of them on the left. By reflex, Delaine knelt. Dorn did the same, set up the bipod and his rifle, and levered in a shell.

Dull brown shapes came into view, slowing as they reached the ridge top. They separated into one, two, three does. Delaine's pulse jumped when he saw antlers on the fourth. Dorn was set, and he fired.

The buck lurched and bolted as the does scattered.

The buck ran with his head lowered, and he disappeared over the edge.

Dorn said, "I think I hit him."

"I think you did. Let's hope he didn't go too far over on that side."

Dorn worked in another shell and picked up the spent casing. The two men stood at the same time.

"You go first," said Delaine.

They walked about sixty yards until they came to the spot where the deer had crossed. The trail was evident where their hooves had kicked up debris. Delaine stood in back of Dorn and to one side as they took slow, careful steps to the edge of the ridge.

Dorn started to make his way with sidesteps, and he stopped. Twenty yards down the slope, where thin spears of grass grew up around flat, dark rocks, a set of antlers showed from the downhill end of a fallen deer.

Dorn's upper body settled as he breathed out. "That's him."

Delaine said, "I'm glad he didn't go any farther."

They made their way to the deer and stood for a moment. It was a good-sized buck with four points on one side and three on the other.

"Are you happy with this?" Delaine asked.

"Oh, yes."

"Good. Then let's think about how we're going to get him out of here. I'll gut him where he is, and then we might be able to drag him up over the top. If we can't, I can go for the horses, but it will take a while, and I'd rather not have to come back up here a second time if we don't have to."

"Whatever you think."

"I'll dress him, and then we'll see. We can set our

rifles aside, and you can hold a leg as I need it. Be sure to take the live one out before you set your gun down."

"Right."

Delaine dragged the deer around and went to work.

The sun rose higher, and warm air lingered on the side of the ridge. A bird screamed, and Delaine thought it was a blue jay. No one had come up from below, so he imagined that Hiller might be working on a downed animal as well.

When Delaine had the deer dressed, he wiped his hands on the grass and stood up to straighten his back. The hunter stood waiting.

Delaine said, "I'd like to get this fellow up and over the edge, and even down the other side if we can. I think they may have gotten another deer down below. If they did, we can have everything together when someone goes for the horses. This is a good buck, and I don't like to leave him here in the sun, even if you're with him."

"That's all right with me. How do you want to do it?"

"Ed and I dragged that one yesterday by the antlers, and we could do the same now, but your arm gets tired, stretched out and twisted like that, and we're each carrying rifles." Delaine paused. "What would you think about sacrificing some of that light rope you have?"

"You mean cut it up?"

"Yes. Take a couple of ten-foot lengths off it, to make pull ropes."

"That would be all right. I've got a hundred yards of it on a spool back home, any time I need it."

"How thick is it?"

"It's half-inch hemp."

"Oh, that should be good. And if I could borrow your saw, I can cut a couple of handles."

Delaine cut two pieces of dry pine about an inch and a half thick and a foot long. With each one to serve as a handle, he tied one end of the rope around the middle, and he tied the other end into a three-inch loop. Passing the slack through the loop, he made a much bigger loop, which he passed over the deer's antlers and down the neck, where he snugged a front upper leg against the neck, took a couple of wraps, and tied a knot. He did the same on the other side and had two drag ropes.

"This is easier on the arm," he said, "and it keeps you farther away from the body, so you don't kick your foot against it. If you make one of these at home, you can bore two holes and make a 'D' or a triangle with the rope, so you don't have it going between your fingers, but this is good for now. The length is good, and we can keep the front end up and not have so much weight dragging."

They each took a handle, and with a drag in one hand and a rifle in the other, they leaned forward and pulled the deer up onto the broad area on top of the ridge.

"That wasn't too bad," said Delaine. "What do you think about dragging him down the other side?"

"I think I can do it. I'm not done in yet. I've dragged a deer by the horns with another fellow before, and this is easier."

The descent on the other side had a couple of rough spots with washouts, but they made it to the bottom and dragged the deer across a grassy area like a boat in easy water.

Hiller and his hunter, Rumford, came to meet them. Hiller had dried blood on the backs of his hands and fingers and a smear of it on one cheek.

"We thought you might have one," he said. "When Walt shot the big one, we saw another good buck go up the ravine with the does."

"Well, this is good." Delaine looked up at the sky, where the sun was overhead. "We should be able to get everything done by dark again. How big is the other one?"

Hiller said, "A little bigger than this one, and four on each side."

"That's good. Everything neat and clean. Shall we go back and get the horses? Leave these men with their deer."

"Might as well." Hiller's gaze pulled away to the west. "Who's this?"

The two hunters, Dorn and Rumford, were shaking hands and congratulating one another. They broke off to see what had caused the interruption.

Three riders were approaching at a trot, raising a low cloud of dust and debris.

Delaine recognized the wide-brimmed dark hat, sand-colored shirt, and brown vest of the man in the middle. He was riding a bay horse.

Hiller answered his own question. "Big Eight."

The other two riders were in the same position as the first time Delaine saw them. He recognized the beard on one and the mouse-colored hair and protruding nose on the other.

The horses slowed to a walk but did not come to a stop until they were within five yards of the four men on foot. Delaine could see the blue eyes, flushed complexion, and stubbled face of the man in the center. He evened his reins with his big hands, looked down on the group, and said, "What have we got here?"

"Just what it looks like," said Hiller. "We're out hunting. These two men have each gotten a deer."

"We heard shots."

"That was a while ago. There's nothing to worry about."

"There's cattle out here."

"Not many, and not in the direction where these men were firing."

The Big Eight leader gave a contemptuous glance at Rumford, dressed in his grey wool outfit and matching deerstalker cap. "Dandies. Come out to buy a little bit of Western adventure."

"They're honest men," said Hiller. "Leave 'em alone."

The man with the beard spoke. "You boys look funny, out here on foot, with two dead deer."

"We've got horses, as you well know," said Hiller.

The man in the middle spoke again. "This is cattle country. We don't like namby-pamby outsiders who come out here and shoot all over the place. Last week, you were way the hell over there."

"That was antelope," said Hiller.

"Sure. And this is deer. Next it'll be coyotes, and you'll be chasin' 'em all over like Englishmen after foxes." The rider drew his six-gun, a Colt. 45 with a long, shiny barrel, and showed it to Dorn. "See this? This is a gun. It's not for sport. This is for business. We learn early on out here that a gun is not a toy."

Dorn met him with a resentful expression but did not answer.

The rider put his pistol in its holster and gave his attention to Hiller again. "If we find one dead head of beef, and if it even *looks* like it's been shot, we're comin' to talk to Mr. Pussy Calvin. And you can tell him."

Dorn's chest went up and down. His patience seemed to have lapsed. "Are you pleased with yourself? You take out your gun and intimidate me with it."

The man with the beard stood in his stirrups, swung a leg over, and dropped onto the ground. He took off his hat with the flat brim and rounded crown and set it on his saddle horn, then took the pistol out of his holster and tucked it in his saddlebag.

He said, "I don't need anything but my bare fists to intimidate you, mister."

"To what purpose?" said Dorn. "I'm an American citizen. I pay my bills. I pay my taxes. I'm responsible for the incomes of a dozen working men. I don't need to bully anyone. If you think you want to thrash me, go ahead. But I'll warrant there's some kind of law in this country for unprovoked assault."

"Don't make me mad, mister. And don't call me names."

"I didn't call you anything. Now if you want to hit me, go ahead. I've got witnesses, and I've got an attorney, and we'll go to court." Dorn took a breath. "And if you're doing this as part of your work, we'll have your employer in court as well."

The man in the center said, "Put your hat on, Nate."

"I don't like him to—"

"Unless he throws the first punch, you don't—"

"Aw, hell. Let him talk that way. What do I care? But it's like my old man told me. I worked under a son of a bitch like this in the brewery. Always lordin' it over me. My old man said, 'Catch him off shift.'" The man doubled his fist and brought it up short in front of his chest. "And that's what I did." He turned to his horse, put on his hat, collected his pistol and put it in his holster, and stabbed his foot in the stirrup as he swung up into the saddle.

The leader of the Big Eight riders leaned forward and put his two big hands on the saddle horn. He bore down on Hiller and said, "I'll put it this way. We're fed up with you and your hunters. I knew of a hunting party one time that had a herd of cattle run right through their camp."

"Is that a threat?"

"I wouldn't think of it. Just a story I heard." He reined his horse around and said, "Let's go."

The other two touched spurs to their horses, and the three of them took off at a gallop.

Hiller faced the two hunters. "Sorry about that little encounter. As you can tell, these fellows are used to throwing their weight around. They ride for a bigger outfit, and their boss has money. I don't know how much he knows about or approves of these kinds of visits. I don't even know him, as far as that's concerned."

"What is his name?" said Dorn.

"Albert Marcus."

"Doesn't mean anything to me, but if he's got money, I'll bet he doesn't want to lose any of it."

Hiller said, "They sang a different tune when you mentioned goin' to court."

"I wasn't bluffing. You can't let some ruffian get away with things like that. What was his name?"

"The man who got down from his horse is Nate Jonas. The man in the middle is Ross Mitchell. And the third one, who never does much, is a fella named Arnold Hand." Hiller cast a glance in the direction where the riders had gone. "I don't think they'll be back. Do you two mind waitin' here with the deer while we go for the horses?"

"I don't mind," said Dorn.

"Neither do I," said Rumford. He gave a short laugh. "We're armed."

"Good. We'll drag the two deer into the shade, and we'll be back."

When they had left the hunters a couple of hundred yards behind, Delaine said to Hiller, "That was an interesting face-off between Dorn and that Jonas fellow."

"It sure was."

"If it had been you or me or any other workin' man, he would have gone at it, fists flyin'. But he sees a man who looks like he might have a little bit of money, or station in life, and things change."

"And the idea of draggin' his boss into court. You could see he was done, and Mitchell saved face for him."

"That was how I saw it, too. By the way, didn't Art Meredith say his brother worked for that same outfit?"

"He did. I'll have to ask him about that."

———

THEY HAD the two deer skinned and hanging in camp by dark, as Delaine had hoped. They had the capes salted and rolled, and the second two hunters seemed satisfied at showing their trophies to the other two. As the group gathered around the fire, Delaine waited for Hiller to mention the run-in with the Big Eight riders. He thought that if Hiller did not mention it, he would. The boss deserved to know, and the hunters might well have talked about it already among themselves.

When the whiskey was poured in the tin cups, Hiller told the story. He did not draw out the part about Dorn threatening legal action, but he included it.

"That's the way they always are," said Percy. "They act as if they own the whole range, but they know they don't. We stay on public land. And if they were over where you boys were huntin', they were well off their own range. Sounds like you might have put them in their place a little. I don't know how much of this will get back to their boss. I think it might be one of those deals where he lets them do as they please as long as it doesn't get back to him. I don't know him, but I have heard that in the long run, everyone does things his way."

Hiller said, "That reminds me. Art, didn't you say that your brother works for them?"

Meredith tucked back the corner of his mouth. "I said he *used* to." He waved his hand. "He works for another outfit now, a hardscrabble ranch out north that's got four or five sections spread apart from one another, so he spends all of his time goin' from one pasture to the next."

"But he knows these others."

"So do you and I. You mentioned Mitchell and Jonas by name."

"Wal," said Percy, "we're done with huntin' for this

season anyway. Like an old fella that used to work for me would say, eat a can of oysters and let the hotheads cool down a bit."

Meredith said, "Was that old McDermott?"

"Yep. He's gone now. Everyone wears out, sooner or later. Just like a machine."

———

A CHEERFUL MOOD was on the air as sunlight spread over the camp in the morning. Delaine and Hiller took down the tents, packed up the gear, and loaded the wagon. They fitted out all the horses and loaded the items that went on the packhorses, plus two of the deer carcasses. The hunters helped with their bags and gun cases. At one point, J.M. Packard offered to hold a packhorse for Delaine. He draped the lead rope around his neck and shoulders while he lit a cigarette.

Delaine felt that he had to say something. "I hope you don't mind my mentioning it, but you don't want to put a rope around any part of you when it's attached to a horse. Not even around your hand. If the horse spooks and the rope tightens—well, you get the idea."

Packard unwrapped the rope and held it by his side. When it was time to move on to the next pack-horse, he left.

He did not seem put out, however. He offered to ride one of the horses to the ranch, to have less weight in the wagon. Paul Edson, on the other hand, remained surly and said he wasn't going to ride no horse.

The procession set out as before, with Percy and the hunters in front, the wagon and a saddle horse in tow in the middle, and Delaine and Hiller in the rear with the rest of the horses.

When the group was strung out, Delaine spoke to Hiller. "What's eatin' on that oldest fella? You'd think he'd be more apologetic, shooting an extra deer."

"He acts like someone peed in his porridge. What happened was that Percy told him in front of the others that he wasn't welcome to come back."

"Oh."

"He said he didn't plan to, anyway. But I'm glad Percy told him."

"So am I. You can't let the other hunters think it's all right, after they all follow the rules. If you think about it, it's a better experience for them if someone protects the quality of it."

"That's it. Percy might be tight, but he knows his business."

"What are they going to do with the extra deer?"

"Percy knows someone who can take it. An old fellow who can't hunt anymore. No one will say a thing. That is, what's-his-name that shot it."

"That's good."

The sun rose in the sky as they traveled toward the ranch, where they planned again to leave off some stock, transfer the meat and capes to a lighter wagon, and go on to town.

The tone of the day changed when they rode into the ranch yard. A horse and a buggy stood in front of the bunkhouse. By the time Percy rode around in front and studied it, with his three hunters on horseback behind him, Delaine and Hiller passed up the camp wagon and came alongside the buggy.

"What is it?" said Hiller.

"See for yourself." Percy gave a backward wave of the hand.

Delaine and Hiller, still leading horses, rode around in front to take a look.

A large man in a wool overcoat, muffler, and floppy hat sat in the middle of the seat. His face was pale, and his eyes were closed. A dark seam of what looked like dried blood showed between his lips.

Percy said, "This is no good, whether someone left him here or whether he made it on his own after someone got to him. If someone left him here, they knew we were gone."

Hiller said, "You don't think he, um, had some kind of an attack on his own? Big people are susceptible to that."

"Not with that blood in his mouth. I think that if you open up that coat you'll find a bullet hole, but I'm not going to. That's for the law."

Meredith had parked the wagon and had made his way around on foot. "What is it?" he asked.

Percy said, "It's that second man from Trinidad, come to see what he could find out about the first one."

Meredith raised his eyebrows. "And this is all the good he could do." He looked at the boss. "What do you want to do?"

Percy gazed at the body without showing any reaction. He rubbed the stubble on his chin. "No reason to leave him here, I guess. We're goin' to town. We've got the means to transport him, with his own rig. Ed, what do you think about leading this horse?"

"I'd rather do that than sit on the seat beside him."

Delaine had been observing the body and did not have any definite feelings. He remembered how self-assured the man had been and how he had brushed away Delaine's offer to help. Still, it did not seem as if he deserved to come to this end.

Percy said, "You can ride along, Jess. Take turns leading. Make you feel better if you're doin' somethin'." He let out a heavy breath. "Damn it all. If it isn't one thing, it's two."

7

As the procession made its way into town, people on the street did not pay much attention. Delaine and Hiller and the buggy were in the latter half, so most people had already glanced and looked away. Delaine was glad not to see anyone on the veranda of the hotel. When the group turned right on Main Street, Percy put Meredith in charge of delivering the meat to the butcher shop and the heads and capes to W. Olejnik, tanner and taxidermist. Percy and Hiller took the rented buggy, with Cuenca's body out of sight on the floorboard, to the small office between the bank and the barbershop where the deputy spent time when he was in town.

The deer carcasses were much heavier than the antelope, but no one seemed to mind as Delaine hefted one after another onto his shoulder and carried them into the butcher shop. The butcher helped him hang each carcass on an overhead track and then weighed it and put a ticket on the shank as Delaine went for the next one. The fifth and smallest carcass stayed in the buckboard. Meredith said Percy would deliver it. As before, Delaine collected the game bags, folded them, and stacked them in the wagon.

At the tanner and taxidermist's, Delaine carried each head with its rolled hide into the shop. On each trip back to the wagon, he brushed off the front of his shirt and hoped he had not caught any fleas.

At the hotel, he untied the hunters' bags and gun cases. A pall had settled over the group from the time they found the body at the ranch, and the hunters did not linger as they collected their belongings. Only George Dorn stayed long enough to shake hands and to thank Delaine.

He said, "If you're ever in Chicago, look me up. I'm at the Great Lakes Hardware on Randolph Street. I'll show you the whole store."

"I'll do that," said Delaine.

"Cowboys marvel at the tall buildings. They call our streets canyons."

"Must be a sight."

"Meanwhile, there's this." Dorn took from inside his coat the hatchet he had carried on his belt during the hunting. He handed it to Delaine. It had a continuous head and shaft of polished steel, with a grip made of rings of leather shellacked into a solid handle.

"Well, thank you," said Delaine, taking it and admiring it. "This is too nice for me. It's part of your set."

"I can get another in a minute. I would have given you the leather cover for the head, but it's attached to the belt."

"This is a treasure by itself. Thank you again."

"You're welcome. It's a small thing."

Percy and Hiller returned from leaving off the

body and the rented buggy. Percy said, "The deputy's not in, so we left the body in the back room of the barbershop. It was a full job for the three of us. Wish you'd been there. I suppose all the hunters are inside."

Meredith said, "Gettin' checked in."

"I need to go in and settle accounts with them. You boys can go to The Lookout if you want, and I'll come and get you when I'm done."

Delaine made sure all the horses were secure as Hiller tied his and Percy's to the rail. Meredith parked the buckboard and climbed down.

"I'm ready for a drink," said Hiller. "I've had enough of dead bodies."

Meredith said, "At least you didn't have to sit with one out in the country this time with no one to talk to."

"Huh," said Hiller. "That was no pleasure. A barber told me once that it was lonely work, shavin' dead men, because there was no one to talk to."

Meredith said, "That's barbers. They talk a lot."

On the way across the street, Delaine said, "It just occurred to me that I could stop in at the post office and see if I have any mail. I'll catch up with you boys in a few minutes."

"You could see if there's any mail for the ranch," said Meredith.

"I will."

Delaine found the post office where he thought he remembered seeing it, across the street from the deputy's office and the barbershop. Inside, the clerk told him there was no mail for the ranch.

"What did you say your name is?"

"Delaine."

"I thought you said Delaney. Let me see. Oh, yes,

here's one that came in a few days ago." He handed him an envelope with familiar handwriting on it.

Delaine felt a lift in his spirits as he took the letter outside to read it.

Dear Jess—

I hope this letter finds you safe and in good health. The sad news about Don Tiburcio arrived here. I am sure you know more about it than we do.

Also there has arrived here a nephew of Don Tiburcio, also from Trinidad. His name is Pedro Cuenca. It is possible that you will meet him as he says he intends to go over there and see what he can learn about what happened to his uncle.

It seems to me that you might be in a dangerous place but I am sure you can see things for yourself and I know you can take care of yourself but of course I worry.

I do not know when you will have a free day but if you do I hope you can find time to come here.

May everything go well for you and may God protect you. Think of me when you see the stars at night.

Yours truly,
Rachel

Delaine folded the letter and put it in the envelope. He was not sure how to answer. Across the dusty street in this peaceful town, Pedro Cuenca was in the back room of the barbershop. That news would reach the people in Overton before long. Delaine did not feel that he had to write about it. He could wait a couple of days, and when he had the chance, he would write to Rachel and let her know he was all right.

The days were getting shorter, and the late afternoon sun was making its way toward the Laramie Range. The last plunge would not take long.

Delaine went into the lamplit world of The Lookout. The oval mirrors, the varnished pillars, and the painting with the two frontiersmen were the same as before. Delaine found Hiller standing by himself and joined him. Hiller called for a drink and handed it to Delaine.

"Thanks."

"Don't mention it."

"Where's Art?"

"He's down the bar, talking to his brother."

"Brother Ben. He was here the last time I was. He seems like a bad-humored sort. I didn't do a thing, but he saw fit to pick a fight with me and knock me down."

"What for?"

"Little or nothing. I had backed up and almost bumped into one of these painted ladies, and he accused me of bothering her. I think he was just looking for an excuse to hit someone."

"He always seems like a rough one to me. I try to stay out of his way." Hiller glanced past Delaine. "Uh-oh. Here's another one."

Delaine braced himself and turned. A short man stepped past the shadow of two other patrons. He walked in an uneven gait and had one shoulder lower than the other. He wore a wrinkled, loose-fitting, dull brown suit and a dingy white shirt. Delaine recognized him by the unwashed strands of hair across the top of his head and by his impassive brown eyes. He had a sallow complexion, and he needed a shave as before. The man was gazing at the floor in front of him. He raised his head, and his face showed recognition.

He stopped in front of Delaine. "I remember you. You're the puncher that takes out hunters."

"That's right. We just finished with a second bunch."

"Get everything killed?"

"They each got a deer."

Mardell's thin eyebrows went up, and his large mouth area drew down. "Paid well for it, I'm sure."

"Percy takes care of all that. We do the work. Do you know Ed Hiller?"

Mardell flicked a glance. "Oh, yeah." His eyes went down to Delaine's drink.

Delaine felt a sense of obligation. "Buy you a drink?"

"Why not?"

Delaine signaled for a drink. "I've thought about that story you told me last time."

Mardell's chin shifted to one side, and he gave Delaine a close look. "Which one?"

"About the hunters who kill all the antelope."

Mardell waved his hand. "Oh, that. You get that everywhere you go."

"Everywhere?" The drink came, and Delaine handed it to Mardell.

"Thanks. Maybe not everywhere, but I've seen it in other places. Or known of it. I don't go out and do it myself." He took a drink. "But out on the west coast, there's places where the salmon are runnin', and men stand on the banks and pull 'em out with pitchforks, toss 'em on the ground to die. Sell 'em by the hundred."

"That seems wasteful."

"They all get used. A lot of those fish aren't fit to eat, but they go for fertilizer."

Delaine tried to keep an unpleasant expression from showing on his face.

"You'll see it with ducks, too. They've got these big sloughs where the ducks some in by the hundreds. Thousands. There's men that'll set up a whole line of shotguns to fire at once, with strings on the triggers. They wait until enough ducks have settled on the water, and then they jump 'em all at once, and fire all the guns together. They'll kill a hundred, easy, and go out in a boat and pick 'em up."

Hiller said, "What do they do with that many ducks?"

"Sell 'em to the Chinamen. Just another business." Mardell leaned with his left jaw forward and drew his head up straight. "I wouldn't do it, go out there in the damp and the cold."

Hiller said, "I've heard those Chinamen sell opium."

Mardell raised his eyebrows in an ominous expression. "That ain't all. They say those Chinamen'll sell their own daughter. I don't know about that, but I know they'll sell someone else's. Shanghai 'em."

"I've heard that, too," said Hiller. "You wonder how they can do that. Sell 'em, that is."

"Someone's got to buy 'em, and there's always someone that will. There's an old saying about what somethin's worth. It's worth what you can sell it for. If you can't sell it, it's not worth anything." Mardell rubbed his thumb against his fingertips as Delaine had seen him do before. "But you take that thing, and you can always sell it." He swirled his drink and took a swallow, then settled back on his worn heels.

The loud sound of a man clearing his throat caused them to turn and look in the direction of the piano. A man in worn, dusty clothes and a cloth cap stood with a bundle at his right foot. It was tied at each end with a thick cord and looked as if he had just slipped it off his shoulder.

"Excuse me, gentlemen," he said. "I don't want to interrupt your enjoyment, but I'm a poor travelin' man. I've run out of money, and I'm up against it for somethin' to eat. Not to be a beggar, but I'm going to sing a song I made up myself. Then I'll pass my cap around, and if anyone could spare me a small coin, I'll appreciate it."

A man called out, "Enough talkin'. Just sing it, and we'll see if we like it."

A couple of others laughed.

"Good enough," said the traveler. It's called "Lost Angel," and it goes like this. He held out his hand like a Shakespearean actor and sang in a slow, steady voice.

> *I rode the lonesome country*
> *Hoping some day I would see*
> *The golden curls of a woman*
> *Who had turned her back on me.*
>
> *Without a word or letter*
> *From our home in Omaha*
> *She had met a passing stranger*
> *And had packed a bag and gone.*
>
> *The days of darkness followed*
> *And the months stretched into years.*
> *My hopes had all gone dormant,*
> *And my dreams had turned to fears.*
>
> *Until one day an old friend*

Who had traveled in the west
Told me he'd seen my lost love
And had taken her request—

Just this, to say she was sorry
And now lived her life alone,
She hoped I had forgiven
And found happiness on my own.

Far from it, I awakened
Hopes that just as well had died,
But I had to find my angel
Who was on life's other side.

And I became a traveler
On the lonely trails out west,
With hopes that I could salvage
Some small portion of the past.

In a town in far Wyoming,
In the shade of barroom light,
I thought I saw my angel,
Now a lady of the night.

Her face was drawn in creases,
And her hair was dull as dust.
She saw me as a stranger,
But she answered as she must.

No, thanks, she didn't know me,
And her name was Beth, not Rose.
Her friends and kin in Kansas
Had forgotten her, she supposed.

> *But she was used to punchers*
> *Who after a drink or two*
> *Would say they thought they recognized*
> *A woman they once knew.*
>
> *I left that town in darkness*
> *And set out upon the plain*
> *Where coyotes howled at moonrise*
> *And my mind suppressed the pain.*
>
> *I was sure the woman I talked to*
> *Was the one from long ago—*
> *Indeed a fallen angel*
> *But not a forgotten rose.*

A round of applause sounded as the man took off his cap and bowed. He handed the cap to the man closest to the door, and the cap made its way down the bar. Delaine put a nickel in it and passed it on. Mardell raised his thin eyebrows and let Hiller take it. Hiller put in a nickel and handed it to the next man.

Faded daylight showed as the front door opened and closed. The traveler picked up his bundle, slung it on his shoulder, and went to the far end of the bar to retrieve his cap.

"Thank you all," he said, waving his cap as he walked to the door.

Mardell seemed to be making his drink last. He raised his chin and surveyed the room. He said, "Well, that's our friend who came in."

Delaine looked to his left and recognized Stevens, the field scientist. "Good afternoon," he said.

Stevens raised his hand. "Good evenin'." He was

wearing his battered brown hat, loose canvas jacket, and canvas trousers.

Delaine said, "I've thought of you when I've seen birds out in the field."

"That's good."

"I saw a blue jay, and I think I heard another one."

"This is the time for them to be here. I've seen a few myself." Stevens raised his hand in greeting to Mardell. "'Lo."

"Afternoon, professor."

Stevens returned to Delaine. "Have you seen anything else interesting out on the range?"

Delaine motioned with his hand toward Hiller. "We just finished with a group of deer hunters. We saw some nice deer, but I suppose from your point of view it's not so nice, seein' as how they're now in the butcher shop and the taxidermist's shop, in separate pieces."

Stevens gave a backward wave. "That's someone else's business. And there's something to be said for thinning the population. Did you shoot all antlered deer?"

"The hunters did."

"Well, I hope it was all a success."

"It was."

"What else did you see?"

"Nothing else to mention. Oh, how could I forget? There was a man found dead in a buggy he had rented."

"I heard about that."

"So did I," said Mardell.

Delaine said, "It doesn't take long."

Stevens frowned. "What was he doing out there?"

Delaine shrugged. "From what I understood, he

was hoping to learn something related to the death of his uncle."

"Oh, yes. The one who was looking for his daughter. Was this one looking for the girl as well?"

"He said he wasn't. Just wanting to know about his uncle."

Stevens shook his head. "He must have gone afoul in some way. Poor fellow."

"I agree. He seemed so sure of himself."

"I heard he had a loaded .38 but it was still in his coat pocket."

"Huh," said Delaine. "I didn't even know that much. Sometimes, the less you know, the better."

"Isn't that the truth?"

Mardell followed the conversation, his large brown eyes moving from one man to the other.

Stevens said, "Have you got more hunters coming in?"

"I think we're going to work on roundup next." Delaine looked at Hiller, who nodded.

Stevens smiled. "Well, maybe you'll see something interesting there as well."

"A stork," said Hiller.

Stevens laughed. "Do you think that girl's out there?"

"Oh, no," said Hiller. "You know how it is. The farther away you are from girls, the more you think of them. By the way, my name's Ed Hiller." He tipped his head toward Delaine. "We work together."

"My name's Anthony Stevens. I'm a field biologist. I study migratory birds." They shook.

"Ducks and geese?"

"And quite a few others."

JOHN D. NESBITT

"That must be nice. Just watching, and not feeling that you have to kill any of them. Or do you?"

"I don't. But others do, for science or for sport. That's up to them."

Mardell's mouth had fallen open, and he followed the conversation with an expression of little interest.

Stevens said, "Don't let me take up your time. I can talk all day. That's what comes from spending so much time in the field. What do you think, Mason?"

"Every man knows his business."

"Ha-ha. You sure hope so, don't you?" Stevens looked at his glass.

Mardell took a sip and said, "Is this your boss?"

Delaine stood up straight as Percy approached.

The boss came to a stop and said, "I need someone to help me deliver that deer."

Delaine recalled the one remaining carcass beneath the tarpaulin in the buckboard. He figured Hiller had done his extra duty for the day, and Meredith was busy talking to his brother. "I'll go," he said. He downed the rest of his drink and set his glass on the bar. He remembered he needed to pay for Mardell's drink, so he set a quarter on the bar as well.

"See you all later," he said.

Stevens, Mardell, and Hiller hoisted their glasses.

Outside in the gathering dusk, Delaine said, "Do you want me to drive the buckboard?"

"I think a packhorse will be easier."

Delaine untied a packhorse, led it away from the other horses, and tied it to the rear wheel of the buckboard. He folded back the tarpaulin, lifted out the carcass in its cloth bag, and flipped it onto the packsaddle. In a couple of minutes, he had it tied down.

He untied his horse and led it into the street,

untied the packhorse, turned his horse so that he would not swing his leg over the lead rope, and mounted up.

Percy was on his horse, waiting. He led the way east, and at the edge of town, he turned north. Half a mile later, he turned east, took them over a dirt bank, and continued across an excavated area. The horse hooves crunched on scattered stone.

"This is the shortcut," Percy said. "If we took the wagon road, we would have to go around, about two miles more." He went up and over another embankment. "That's the old gravel pit. The new one's up ahead." He led the way around a hill, and the trail led into an open area with a shack, an equipment shed, and a set of corrals. Hooves thumped on the corral planks, and shapes moved. Night was falling. As Delaine came close to the corrals, he saw that the closest animals were mules.

Percy said, "He lives in this shack. He's kind of a watchman."

A light showed in the window of the small building. As Percy led the way, a door opened, and a soft light flowed out. A stooped figure appeared in silhouette.

"Is that you, Hamp?" Percy called out.

"It is. Who's there?"

"It's me, Percy."

"Well, come on in."

Percy rode up to the door and dismounted. "We brought you some deer meat if you'd like it."

"I'll say I would. What did you bring me, some hocks and rib meat?"

"No, we brought you the whole animal. Young buck."

"Well, bless your bones. What made you do that?"

"I had a group of hunters, and they ended up with an extra one. We were coming into town, so I thought of you."

"That's mighty thoughtful."

"Where do you want us to put it?"

"We can hang it in the shed. Let me get a light."

The old man went inside, came out with a lantern, and led the way with a halting step.

At the shed, Delaine swung down, untied the deer, hefted it onto his shoulder, and carried it in. The older man had tossed a rope over a rafter and was fumbling with it to make a loop. In the imperfect light, Delaine saw that the man's hands were gnarled and swollen. Percy was holding the other end of the rope, so Delaine set down the carcass to lean against his leg, took the rope, and made a slip knot to tighten on the deer's shank. He wondered how well the old man could handle a knife.

"How about we hang it by one leg, and I'll cut out the other hind leg and hip joint for you and take it inside before we leave."

"Oh, that would be just dandy."

Percy pulled on the rope, and they hoisted the deer carcass. Delaine went to work trimming the hindquarter loose.

The old man said, "It's hell to be all bunged up. If I'd known I was going to live this long, I might have taken better care of myself. But I don't know what I could have done about this arthritis."

"That's the way it goes," said Percy. "Just be glad you make it as far as you do. That's what I hope for."

"I should say so. It's hell to be old and feel worthless, but if there's anything to be glad for, it's that I've outlived a lot of sons of bitches."

"Ha-ha," said Percy. "That's a good way, for sure."

———

BACK IN TOWN, Percy said, "I think the deputy might be in by now, either in his room or having supper. If you want to go back to the saloon, I should be along in a little while."

They tied their horses with the others and went their separate ways.

Delaine found Hiller by himself. "We got that little job done," he said.

"Did you go to the quarry and meet Hampton?"

"Yes. Percy's looking for the deputy right now. He said he'd be here in a little while."

Hiller seemed to exert an effort to open his eyes. "It'll be late when we get back." He yawned. "Too late to eat."

"That's all right," said Delaine. "We'll eat good tomorrow." He ordered a drink, and as he sampled it, he saw in the mirror that the woman in the feathered hat had moved up to him on his left side.

He turned and met her green eyes.

"Remember me?" she said.

"Oh, yes. I almost bumped into you, but I didn't."

"That's true." She smiled, and her eyes played over him. "What's your name?"

"What's yours?"

"Lenore. Now tell me yours."

"Jess Delaine."

"Did you just come in?"

"I was here a little while ago. I had to help the boss run an errand."

"Are you the ones who brought in the body?"

"Yes. That was earlier. We found it on the ranch where I work."

She gave a sad expression. "It's too bad when things like that happen."

"It is."

Her face brightened, and her bright red lips formed a smile. "So what are you up to tonight?"

"Just having a drink until the boss comes back and says it's time to go home."

She pouted. "You look like you could use some sugar."

"Not now, at least."

"Do you have a girl somewhere?"

He met her eyes again, and he did not think she would make fun of him if he told her the truth. "Yes, I do. In Overton."

"Oh. That's a little closer than Okanogan."

"Is that where you're from?"

"No, but some of these boys say they have a girl back home, and when they go home for the winter, they find out different." She wrinkled her nose.

Delaine wondered if he smelled of hides and blood. To change the subject, he said, "Did you hear the fellow sing the song earlier?" As soon as he said it, he wondered if it was a good topic.

"That must have been before I came in."

"Said he was passing through, and he looked like it."

"You see all kinds. You said your name is Jess?"

"That's right."

She raised her hand in a small gesture of farewell. "I'll see you later, Jess. Nice talking to you."

"Yes, it is." Delaine returned to his drink. He imagined she left so she could find someone who was more interested.

Hiller said, "Did you resist temptation?"

"I did. Do you know where Okanogan is?"

"Sounds like a place in Wisconsin. Why?"

"She mentioned it like it was a place far away. I thought it was a place in Washington, near Canada. Maybe the name of a river."

"Could be."

Delaine caught movement in the mirror, and a man crowded close to him and shoved him. He regained his footing and turned to see Brother Ben Meredith.

The man was wearing his brown hat with a high, dented crown. The tag of a Bull Durham sack hung on a yellow string from the pocket of his dark blue shirt, and he had a cigarette hanging from his lips. It bobbed when he said, "Look out, buster."

Delaine frowned. "You had to go out of your way to push me."

Ben put out his chest and hung his thumbs in the pockets of his leather vest. "Don't make me mad again."

Delaine wondered if Ben had seen him talking to the woman. He tried to keep track of the man's hands without looking down as if he had been intimidated.

Ben raised his hand and took the cigarette from his mouth. His glance flickered, and he turned to his brother. "So long," he said.

"See you later."

Delaine relaxed his vision as Ben moved away, and

he saw that Percy had come in. Ben must have seen him in the mirror. Percy and Ben passed each other, almost touching shoulders, and they exchanged a minimal greeting.

"Percy."

"Ben."

Art Meredith had a drink in his hand. He raised it to chest level and said, "Time to go?"

"I think so," said Percy.

The three hired men tossed down their drinks and followed the boss outside.

Percy said, "I talked to the deputy. He'll be out tomorrow, I think."

The four men crossed the street and made ready for the trip home. Delaine led his horse into the street and tightened the cinch. The stars were out, and a sliver of a moon showed in the southern sky. He thought of Rachel and the Spanish word for the moon. *Luna*.

Percy took the lead, and the procession, smaller than before, turned left on Pearl Street and headed out of town. When the lights were behind them, and the clip-clopping of hooves was punctuated by the huffing and snorting of horses, Delaine settled into his own thoughts.

Somewhere out in the sage, the traveler who sang the song might be bedding down for the night. In town, in the dark back room of the barbershop, a man lay dead before his time. Not far from there, a much older man, happy to have outlived a few sons of bitches, was pleased to have fresh meat in his kitchen and the rest of it hanging one-legged on the end of a rope.

8

Percy shaved as the haze drifted out of the kitchen into the bunkhouse area. His bald head shined in the lamplight, and his pale blue eyes were clear. He pitched the water out the back door and put on a clean white work shirt with a full row of buttons, then his brown wool vest. He had put on a clean pair of grey wool pants before he came to the bunkhouse to shave.

"Hah," he said, as he sat at the table and took the cup of coffee that Meredith handed him. "It's good to be done with the hunting. We got it all done sooner than I thought, or sooner than I could plan for. The extra hands for roundup won't be here for three more days, so we're not in a rush. Ed 'n' Art, you can go back to workin' with those horses. Jess, you can go back to work on the cactus. You made good progress on it the first time."

Meredith brought a smoking skillet of crisp bacon from the kitchen and forked two strips onto each plate. "Seems late in the season for roundup. Other outfits are under way."

"They've got more cattle," said Percy. "Bein' able to fit in those hunters helps."

Delaine wondered why Meredith's brother wasn't out on a roundup crew.

Meredith came back with a skillet of fried potatoes and divided them into four portions. "No complaint about the hunters. They all pay their own way."

"Nice to have the company, too," said Percy. "Talk to people who come from other places. That fella Edson was a little sour, but even he had some interesting things to say when he stayed at the house. He's got a printing business, and he does bills and posters for the big shows that come through."

Hiller said, "I still think he shot the little deer first. Then saw something better."

"I don't doubt it," said Percy. "But once it's done, it's done. And he won't be back."

Meredith said, "And he paid his bill. Or I assume he did."

"Oh, yeah," said Percy. "By the way, we'll all stay round the place here until the deputy has come by."

———

DELAINE FOUND himself back in the routine of grubbing out cactus—dragging with the blade of the hoe against the body of the plant, cutting with the corner of the blade, lifting the thorny little plants with the handle upright like a staff, using the stringy roots to lift the larger plants like dead chickens. He had the illusion that no time had passed since the last time he had been engaged this way. The pile where he dumped his harvest had not shrunk, and the pads had not withered.

On one return trip uphill with the wheelbarrow, he found the deputy waiting, again as if only a day had elapsed. The lawman was dressed in his shades of light brown, with a clean hat, jacket, shirt, and pants, and a shiny star pinned to his leather vest.

"Deputy Ted Blackmur. I imagine you remember me."

"I do." Delaine set down the wheelbarrow.

"I'm sure it's no surprise that I'm here to talk to you about the man you found dead right here on the ranch. Pedro Cuenca." He pronounced the name in flat syllables. "That's the name he gave at the hotel where he was staying in town, and your boss says that's the name he gave here."

"As I recall, it was."

"Had you met him before, like you met his uncle?"

"No. He was new to me when he showed up here at the ranch."

"And you saw him again at your camp, when the others did?"

"That's right."

"Did you see or hear anything of him outside the company of the others?"

"No. I think we all heard and saw the same thing."

"Of course, people have different impressions. What were yours?"

"Of him? Oh, it's hard to say. I didn't like him or dislike him. That is, he didn't do anything to make me want to be friends, but he didn't do anything to the contrary. I felt that he talked down to me a little when I said I would like to be helpful, but I think he didn't know that I had friends among the Mexican people and knew something of their language. But I didn't blame him. He was up here among people who treated

JOHN D. NESBITT

him like an outsider, or that was what it seemed like, and as far as talking down to me, it was different but no worse than these hunters who come in from Cleveland and Chicago. From the way he acted, I had the impression that he came from a little bit of money or status."

"Not your typical coal miner from Trinidad, Colorado."

"I've only been through there a couple of times, but I've been to other places in southern Colorado, and a great number of places in New Mexico, and I've seen people at all levels—or, at least several levels. I can't say I've known people at the very top."

"I understand. So you saw him as well-to-do?"

"Comfortable in his place in society. And sure of himself in his ability to get around. I think they were related."

"Not one of those fellows with his hat in his hand."

Delaine paused. "As a general rule, Mexican people are polite. If they have a business, they say things like '*Para servirle*' or '*A sus órdenes.*' Here to serve you, at your orders. White people tend to misinterpret that, or some of them do. So they treat Mexicans like a servant class. And some of them, in return, aren't having any of it. At the same time, people are people, and some of the Mexican people might feel a little superior to others in their own society. Also, down that way, you meet people who say they're Spanish, not Mexican, as if that was maybe better. So there's a little of everything."

"No one I have spoken to has said anything about Mr. Cuenca seeming prosperous or flashing money. Do you think that might have been a motive for someone doing something to him?"

"I have no idea. How I saw him was based to some extent on my experience, but also, as I say, on how he acted. For example, he made a comment about buying some clothes for the weather here, and that muffler and wool coat did not look like cheap items."

The deputy pursed his lips. "Do you have any idea of why someone would want to do him harm, or any idea of who might have wanted to?"

"As for the *why*, I can't think past the obvious, which was that he was looking into the death of his uncle."

The deputy leveled his gaze. "How about the *who*?"

Delaine raised his eyebrows. "I don't know very many people around here. And it would be hard to say *who* without having a *why* to go along with it."

The deputy nodded. "The last time I talked to you, you mentioned some riders for another outfit. I understand they came by and harassed you and your hunters the other day."

"They did. If you know that they came by, then you know that it was quite a ways north of here, in the middle of the day. You know better than I do at what time of the day Mr. Cuenca might have died, but he was in a buggy, so it's hard to know where. I have thought of them, because two men have died out on the range, and the Big Eight riders I've met are the only trouble-makers I've met out there, but I don't have any idea of why they would want to do something to him. Their big gripe is about trespassing on their range, which we didn't do, and shooting in the direction of their cattle, which we also didn't do. Mr. Cuenca wasn't running cattle on their range or shooting deer or antelope, so I don't know why they would have it in for him. I've thought about it, but I don't see a reason."

"Anyone else?"

Delaine thought of Ben Meredith, but the only trouble he had seen there was directed at himself, and in town. He also felt a warning signal that if he mentioned the man, the deputy might repeat it, as a way of priming the pump for more information from someone else, and he did not want to seem as if he was naming someone else out of spite. "Not that I can think of," he said.

"There's always more than meets the eye. If you think of anything else, or see something suspicious, let me know. We've sent word to Trinidad, Colorado, and we've sent word to Overton where he rented the buggy. We'll see what's next. Thanks for your help."

"I didn't do much."

"I know. But you cooperated. And your impressions were interesting."

Delaine did not know if the deputy meant his comments about Cuenca, the people farther south, or the Big Eight riders. "Glad to help," he said.

———

THE PILE OF CACTUS GREW, but there seemed to be no end of the thorny, dull-green plants. Time and again, Delaine found stragglers he had missed. Some would have been out of view when he was on the other side of a clump of sagebrush, but some were out in the open. He admitted to himself that his method of working back and forth across the pasture, up and down little slopes, lent itself to oversight. Rather than move the wheelbarrow for one little cactus, he walked twenty or thirty yards to root out the fugitive, only to find another that required a separate trip. He thought he had cleared about half of the pasture in the first two days, but after another two days, he saw that he had at least another day's work ahead of him.

He put away the wheelbarrow and the hoe, and feeling a bit discouraged, he trudged to the bunkhouse.

A horse was tied at the hitching rail. Delaine wondered if one of the roundup hands had arrived a day early. His spirits picked up at the prospects of a change in routine.

Inside, a man sat at the table with his back to the door. Delaine did not place him at first, but when he turned around, Delaine recognized him as the field biologist, Stevens. His battered brown hat was sitting on the table in front of him, and his canvas jacket was draped on the bench next to him. Across from him at the table, Ed Hiller was smoking a cigarette in a relaxed posture.

"Hello," said Stevens. "They said you were out working."

"What brings you out this way?" Delaine asked.

"Work. Sometimes it doesn't seem like much, sitting in a cover of weeds with a pair of binoculars, and sometimes there's not much to see, but that's the nature of the work."

Hiller said, "A different kind of hunting."

"That's a way of describing it," said Stevens. "In school we learn how to observe out in the field and how to observe specimens up close. In the laboratory, we learn to observe by drawing."

"With a pencil?" said Hiller.

"Yes. As a professor once told us, a pencil is a good pair of eyes."

"Are you a professor, too?"

"No. People like Mason Mardell call me that, but I'm far from it. I make my observations, and I take my notes, and maybe I'll publish some of my findings, but I'm a long way from standing in front of a class in a lecture hall or having an office in an ivy-covered brick building."

Delaine said, "Are you looking for the same things as before?"

"Of course we're always on the lookout for everything, but, yes, right now I'm interested in the sandhill cranes and the blue jays. Two separate things, and you'd think I wouldn't find them in the same place, and to some extent that's true. But the blue jays stop over in the trees around ranch and farm houses, and the sandhill cranes land in the fields. And as you know, even when you're out in the middle of a big open pasture, you'll hear the sandhill cranes, flying way high overhead."

Meredith passed through on his way to the kitchen, and he glanced at Stevens.

Hiller said, "You can't see much from that far away."

"No, but it's still a sighting," said Stevens. "You have a date and a time and a place."

"I've heard of that," said Hiller. "Some people do it for a hobby. They keep a bird book and write things down."

"Yes, and they have a field guide with illustrations, to help them identify what they see."

"What's to separate an amateur from yourself?"

Stevens laughed. "Sometimes not very much. That's one thing a person can learn. Modesty. And I don't want to say anything about professors. I had some good ones. But one thing we come to understand is that no one owns the knowledge. It's the same with other fields. Literature, for example. Everyone has a right to learn about it. As I heard another person say once, 'I have a right to know about these things without being certified.' He was talking about insects, but it could just as well apply to salamanders or sand-hill cranes or Shakespeare."

"Every man knows his business," said Hiller.

Stevens laughed again. "Oh, yes. I remember who said that, and that could be true as well."

Meredith appeared at the doorway from the kitchen. "Do you think you'll be staying for supper?"

"No, thanks," said Stevens. "I want to make it back to town before it gets too dark. Some people in town are afraid, what with these things that have happened."

Hiller said, "They don't happen to everyone. Things happen for a reason."

"That's true as well. Has anyone heard a reason for the two deaths that have occurred out here?"

"Nothing definite," said Hiller. "Not that I know of."

"Well, it's beyond me. But now that we speak of it, I'd better be going." He ran his hand across the top of his molting head, picked up his hat, and put it on. He spoke to Meredith, who was still standing in the door-way. "Thanks for the invitation. Maybe I'll take you up on it some other time."

"You bet."

Stevens stood up, said good evening to all, and walked out.

When the footfalls of the horse had died away, Meredith said, "I wonder what kind of a bug hunter that fella is."

Delaine said, "He says he studies birds."

"He might."

Hiller said, "What's your doubt?"

Meredith tucked back the corner of his mouth. "I wonder if he's one of those amateurs he talked about."

"You think he's something else?"

"I wouldn't be surprised if he was some kind of a dick."

"What makes you think that?"

"The questions he asked earlier, about what-all we had seen."

"Oh, he asked the same questions the other night in the saloon."

"Uh-huh."

Hiller frowned. "Do you think he's one of those range detectives that work their way into the company of workin' men to see if they're conspirin' against their boss?"

"Not that kind," said Meredith. "They come in as ranch hands to begin with."

"Do you think he's lookin' into the deaths of those two fellas from Trinidad?"

"Nah. Like Percy says, that's in the hands of the law."

"What do you think he's lookin' for, then?"

Meredith rubbed his forefinger across the bottom of his nose. "Nothin'. Just birds."

———

DELAINE DID NOT ROOT out the last of the cactus by the end of the third day, or the fifth in total. As the sun went down and dusk took over, the plants became harder to see, so he had to give it up. In the fading light, it seemed as if there was not that much left, but he knew that if he came at the beginning of the day, where the pasture sloped downward to sunlight from the east, he would find more than he could see now. He put the hoe in the wheelbarrow and pushed his way uphill.

The barn was dark inside, but enough dim light came in through the door for him to put his equipment away.

The bunkhouse was bright and warm when he went inside, and he caught the aroma of baked biscuits. He hung his hat on a peg, washed his hands and face, and sat down. Percy and Hiller were already seated.

The crack of a spoon on the lip of a pot was followed by a shuffle of feet, and Meredith came out of the kitchen carrying a steaming pot of beans.

"Here it is," he said. "Dig in. We're out of butter for the biscuits, and it looks like we won't have any more until after roundup. So this is what we have. There's bacon rind in the beans, so it's better than you'll get in some places."

Delaine had taken a warm biscuit and had sampled the beans when a knock came at the door.

"That might be our two hands now," said Percy. "Just in time for supper." He looked over his shoulder and hollered, "Come in!"

The door opened, and two men stepped inside. They took off their hats. Delaine's first impression was that they were not from the area. They had dark hair and bronzed complexions, and the larger of the two bore a resemblance to Pedro Cuenca.

Percy had turned sideways on the bench. "What can I help you with?"

The larger man spoke in a deep voice. "Am I speaking to Mr. Calvin?"

"That's right. I'm Percy Calvin. What do you need?"

The man held his hat with both hands. It was dark brown and new-looking. He was wearing a light-brown wool overcoat with a fur ruff or collar that had been dyed a darker brown. He had a full face, perhaps a little darker than that of the man he resembled, and his voice was deeper. "My name is Miguel Cuenca, and I am from Trinidad, Colorado. I have been told that my brother was found here on your ranch. This is my nephew." Cuenca wore brown suede gloves, and he made a smooth motion to indicate the younger man, who wore a sheepskin coat that had not seen much wear.

"Come in and have a seat," said Percy. "We just sat down to eat. You're welcome to join us."

Meredith gave a look of expectation but did not rise from his chair at the end of the table.

Cuenca made a small wave of the hand. "No, thank you. we have just made a long trip, and we got here as soon as we could. But we had a full meal in town."

Percy said, "Ed, get them a couple of chairs."

Hiller rose from his seat and moved two chairs from the wood stove to the open area between the table and the door. The two men sat down.

Cuenca said, "This is my nephew, Francisco Gutiérrez." He gave the name a Spanish inflection.

Percy said, "Pleased to meet you both." He directed his attention to the older of the two and said, "I was sorry about what happened to your brother."

"Tell me how you happened to find him here."

Cuenca unbuttoned his coat. He had an ample mid-section, but it did not rest in his lap as his brother's had done. A dark pistol rode in a small holster by his side.

"Well," said Percy, "he was just sitting here, in the buggy, right outside, when the whole bunch of us came back from our hunting camp. I had a group of four hunters, and my three hired men, and we all went out and came back together."

"So there was no one here at the time?"

"That's right."

"And you had met him before?"

"Also correct. He came here to begin with, looking for information about your uncle. We talked to him right outside. We saw him again when he dropped by our hunting camp, several miles out on the range from here."

"I see. And all of your men and your hunters, you have a clear idea of where they all were, during that time?"

"Oh, yes. Each hunter was with a guide, so there weren't any stray shots fired out there. And all my men were on the job the whole time, I can account for everyone. I have no doubt about that."

"My brother died of a bullet to the chest."

"That's what the deputy told me. I was sorry to hear it. When we first found him here, the thought came up that he might have had a seizure or a stroke or a heart attack, and might even have come here for help, but that didn't seem to be the case."

"How could you tell?"

"We saw a little bit of blood."

Cuenca sat up straight and took in a breath. Still in his deep voice, he said, "So the question remains. Who shot him, why, and even where. They must have brought him here for you to find him."

"That seemed to be the case. Any number of people might have known we were all gone. I have hunters in here every year at this time."

"You are quite an impresario in that way," Cuenca said, with a rise at the end giving a tone of a question.

"I'm not sure what that word means."

"A business man," he said, separating the two words. He smiled. "It's close to the word we use in Spanish."

"Yes, it's a business for me. We went out to one area with the antelope hunters, and another area with the deer hunters. For that matter, your uncle came by when we were at antelope camp."

"And he, also, was left where someone would find him."

"Seems that way."

"Which was you, by coincidence."

Percy stiffened. "I'll tell you, it was no pleasure either time. And on top of that, it takes up time and interferes with our work. We're about ready to go out again, to do our fall roundup, and I hope to hell we don't find someone else."

"I will try not to be an inconvenience in that way. To become a stone in your road."

Delaine was familiar with the expression in Spanish, but he thought Cuenca was making a morbid literal joke as well.

"At least you have the good sense not to travel alone. Those other two, they'd get way off the main trail, all by themselves. A man ought to be able to travel alone, and we do it all the time, in our work, but at least we know the country."

Cuenca raised his head and gave it a slight toss. "Don't you think it's a matter of motive, Mr. Calvin?" The deep voice was almost patronizing.

"Of course there's some kind of a reason. But your uncle said he was looking for some scoundrel who took his daughter. I don't think they were out here on a honeymoon. So I don't know what the motive was. As for your brother, and I don't mean to make light of it, the motive is a little more understandable, if he happened to come across something related to what happened to your uncle."

"You and the deputy seem to think very much alike."

"I don't know what else to say. And again, I don't want to make light of any of it. Men die in this country, but we like it to be in a fair way—if they fall off a horse, or they did something wrong."

"I have no doubt that somebody did something wrong here, but not either of the two people who died."

"I'm of the same mind. And I hope someone comes to account for it."

"I have had the impression that there is still not very much law in this territory."

"This is a state," said Percy. "New Mexico is still a territory, but this is a state. We have officers of the law, and courts, and judges. It's just that things are spread out, and sometimes the law is a long ways away. But there is such a thing as the long arm of the law, and it can reach here."

Percy had taken on a flush, and it was the first time Delaine had seen him depart from his calm, matter-of-fact manner.

"I hope so," said Cuenca. "And it has not been my

intention to say anything that you would take in a personal way."

"I didn't."

"To the contrary, it seems as if we both hope for the same thing, which is some kind of justice. One of my purposes in coming here is to let you know that I am offering a reward for information and discovery of whoever is responsible for the deaths of my brother and my uncle."

"Did you say 'information and discovery'?"

"Yes. I think they say 'information leading to the discovery' or 'information leading to the arrest,' or 'arrest and conviction.' Information by itself may or may not be useful."

"And you assume the same party is responsible for both deaths?"

"Perhaps it is not good to assume anything, but if we could place the guilt for one of the two, we would be in a good position."

Percy's flush had faded, and his business sense seemed to have awakened. "And how much of a reward do you have in mind?"

"A thousand dollars."

"Well. That's a lot of money comin' from...so far away."

Cuenca gave his slight toss of the head again. "Not all Mexicans are poor people. I come on behalf of my family, and we want to see something done."

"Well, that's a good intention. Who knows if it'll get any results, but I'll be glad to see it if it does."

"So will I. But I also know that intentions and results do not always match. But enough. We have taken up much of your time, and your dinner is getting cold."

Cuenca stood up, as did his nephew. The younger man had unbuttoned his sheepskin coat, and now it fell open to reveal a tooled leather holster and an ivory-handled pistol.

Percy stood up and shook hands with both men. "These are my hired men," he said, with a wave of the arm.

Cuenca nodded to each of them but did not step forward. "We'll be on our way," he said. "Thank all of you for your attention."

"Our pleasure," said Percy. "I'll hold the door open to show you a little light."

The sounds of the horse and buggy receded, and Percy closed the door. He took his seat at the table and said, "That was interesting."

"It sure was," said Hiller. "A thousand dollars. That's not chicken feed."

Meredith said, "I didn't care for the fat party myself."

Hiller shrugged. "You don't have to like him to like his money. I wouldn't turn my back on a thousand dollars."

"Would you go after it?" said Percy.

"I've got my work to do. But if the opportunity came up, I wouldn't ignore it."

9

————

MEREDITH SERVED FLAPJACKS AND BACON, AGAIN WITH no butter but with a jar of molasses. The men had finished eating and were drinking coffee when human voices and the snuffle of horses could be heard outside the bunkhouse door. Hiller rose from his seat, crossed the entry area, and opened the door a crack.

"It's them," he said.

A minute later, a middle-aged man and a younger man came through the door as a buckboard turned around and disappeared. Hiller closed the door as the newcomers each set a duffel bag on the floor.

"You made it," said Percy. "We were expectin' you."

The man had greying hair, a flushed face, and grey eyes that were a little bloodshot. Delaine guessed him at about forty-five. He took off his wool cap, and his voice was rough as he said, "We couldn't get anyone to bring us out here last night, but I was able to hire a ride for the first thing this morning." He took off a canvas overcoat and draped it on his bag. He was of average height with slack shoulders and a bit of a paunch. He wore a striped grey collarless cotton shirt, charcoal-colored suspenders, tan trousers, and lace-up work boots. He coughed and said, "We're ready to go to work."

"Have you eaten?" said Percy.

"We ate some crackers on the way."

Percy said, "We just cleaned the skillet, but Art could fix up some more."

The man looked at the lad and back at Percy. "We're all right."

"Just fine," said Percy. "Pick out your bunks and put your bags there. We're about ready to get started for the day. Oh. This is Jess Delaine, another hand. Jess, this is Pete McGrath."

Delaine nodded. "How do you do?"

"Not bad, in spite of a chilly ride out here."

Percy said, "And this is Hal. What's your last name, Hal?"

The young man had taken off his coat and had his cap in his hand. "Needham."

"That's right."

Hal was about eighteen, with a lean build. He had dusty brown hair, a filmy complexion, muddy eyes, and a soft mustache. He wore a light-brown flannel shirt, a darker cloth vest, denim pants, and dull black boots.

Delaine said, "Pleased to meet you, Hal."

The young man had large hands that he didn't seem to know what to do with. He waved at chest level and said, "Same here."

As the new arrivals found bunks and stowed their belongings, Percy spoke to Delaine.

"It looks like we've got enough help for this morning. Do you want to finish that last bit of cactus that you seemed to have hangin' over you yesterday evening?"

"I wouldn't mind it."

"That's good. Ed 'n' Art can work on gettin' the wagon ready, and Pete and Hal can work on the grub. They know our whole way of doing things."

Delaine went out for one last round with the cactus. As he had expected, the morning light was a great help, and he dragged and chipped with a light spirit, knowing that he would finish this drudgery and be done with it.

———

THE AIR WAS calm and dry as Delaine wheeled his way up the slope through the clean pasture and made his way to the barn. He put the wheelbarrow and the hoe in their places and went to join Hiller and Meredith.

The two men had finished greasing the hubs of the camp wagon, now the chuck wagon. Meredith handed Hiller a cloth and began to roll a cigarette as Hiller wiped his hands.

Hiller said, "We'll go through the equipment and make sure everything we need stays in the wagon and the stuff we don't need gets left out. The chuck box is the same, of course, but we don't need the field box with all the huntin' stuff. We'll just use one tent, the kitchen tent, because it's too much bother to set up and take down the other one every day or two. We'll take along the same tarpaulins. There's a canvas fly for the front of the kitchen tent, and a couple of lighter poles for it. We'll take all the ropes, but we use a picket line rather than a rope corral because we don't have trees in most places where we camp, and we have more horses, so they graze in a herd most of the time. Hal is the wrangler, and Art is the day herder."

"Three riders in all?"

"Art will ride until we have a gather. All we gather is what we're going to ship and what we need to brand, anything that didn't get branded in the spring or that was born in the meanwhile. And all that we hold is what we're going to ship. Percy doesn't have a huge amount of cattle to begin with."

Delaine nodded.

"So we can begin by sortin' things out. We'll take all of the canvases and ropes out of the wagon, to make sure we don't have any mice. Unfold the canvases to see if anything needs to be mended. Then we'll get things packed away neat, and leave room for the grub. Hal is grinding coffee and bagging it, and they'll put the flour in smaller bags. Double-bag everything in case the bags wear out. You know how that is. Beans and rice, too, and dried apples and raisins. Pete's a good cook, and Art's glad to have someone else do it. Isn't that right, Art?"

"It's all work."

"How many horses do we bring?" Delaine asked.

"Twenty-two in all. Those ten horses that have been in the pasture and that we've been workin' with, plus the twelve we've been using all along."

Delaine did some quick figuring. With four riders, that came to five each, plus something for the wrangler to ride. In other places where he had worked, a rider had seven or eight in his string and on the average rode two a day, one in the morning and one in the afternoon. Even for three riders, if they took out the wagon horses and had the wrangler and herder ride them, they still had fewer than seven each. Most outfits had a day wrangler and a night wrangler. Delaine gave a light shrug. Hiller had said the Percy was tight but knew his business, so he must know how to make everything come out even.

The three men worked through the rest of the morning, with a comment here and there about how things should be put in order or how Percy or Pete wanted things to be done. Delaine wondered if Meredith harbored any jealousy or resentment about another man taking over, as the chuck wagon cook had authority over everything that was done in and around camp, and that included bossing around the wranglers and the herders. Meredith seemed not to care, but the more Delaine came to know him, the more he was convinced that the man kept his cards close to his chest.

As they walked to the bunkhouse for noon dinner, Delaine noticed a glaring white area near the woodpile by the back door.

"What the hell is that?" said Meredith. He led the way around the corner of the bunkhouse and kicked at the white powder that lay on the ground, on the grass, and on the leaves of the sagebrush. "Looks like flour," he said.

He led the way in through the back door. Percy looked up from the table, where he was looking at a sheaf of papers with a coffee cup at hand. "What's up, boys? Is the front door locked?"

Meredith's voice had an angry edge to it. "What the hell's all that white stuff that someone threw out?"

"I don't know," said Percy.

McGrath appeared at the kitchen doorway and spoke in his rough voice. "It's flour. I had Hal throw it out. It was full of weevils."

"All of it?" said Meredith.

"Yes, the whole thing. Both sacks. I wasn't going to feed that to anyone."

Percy frowned. "What about that, Art? Did you see any weevils in the flour?"

Delaine recalled the flapjacks they had had for breakfast, the biscuits the night before, gravy before that, and biscuits off and on almost every day in the recent past.

"A few," said Meredith. "But I picked 'em out. It's not like they were mouse turds."

Percy had an unpleasant expression on his face. "Was it very bad, Pete?"

"To me it was. Half a dozen in a cupful. You'd get at least one with a tablespoon."

"Wal," said Percy. "Flour costs money, and I don't like to throw it out. But I agree that you don't want your men to be eatin' bugs or the remains of bugs. So I can't complain about what you did. You might have said somethin' to me first, but it's done." He paused. "I was in a camp once where the cook's helper threw out the fresh coffee by mistake, and he was out there trying to collect the grains off the leaves of the sagebrush. You can go without just about anything if you're stuck for it, but there's no need to if you know about it ahead of time. And flour is one thing we don't want to have to do without for the whole time we're on roundup. Flour or coffee."

"I hope not," said McGrath.

"Then someone'll have to go to town this afternoon. I want to roll out of here in the morning."

Meredith had hung his hat on a peg and stood by the cold wood stove with a sullen look on his face.

Percy said, "Art, I'll let you help Pete and Hal, kind

of oversee things." His voice became more jovial as he said, "And Pete, don't let Hal throw out the raisins unless they've got maggots in 'em."

McGrath answered in his rough voice. "Everything else looks all right. It was just the flour. Most of the time, the weevils are in there already. It's just that the longer it sits, the more they breed."

"I know." Percy shifted in his seat. "Ed, you 'n' Jess can go. Take a packhorse. Get three twenty-pound sacks. And let's get, let's say, four pounds of butter. We'll have clean hot biscuits and butter to go with 'em." Percy rubbed his chin. "I assume you got the rest of the cactus, Jess?"

"Yep. Got 'em all."

"That's good. We won't have any little things pending when we go out."

———

DELAINE AND HILLER tied up at The Mercantile, which was the general store in town. It sat on the southwest corner of the intersection of Pearl Street and Main Street. The sun was crossing over in the afternoon sky, where thin, high clouds contributed to a light haze.

Inside, Delaine slowed his pace at the sight of Miguel Cuenca and his nephew standing at the counter. Hiller slowed with him.

The men were wearing the coats they had worn the evening before, in spite of the mild day. Cuenca held his suede gloves in his left hand as he handed a coin to the storekeeper. He and his nephew each picked up two wrapped chocolate bars and an assortment of gum drops. They were putting the candy in their pockets as they turned around.

Cuenca's face broadened with a smile, and he spoke in his deep voice. "The men from the Lazy T. What a surprise to see you again so soon." He finished putting away the candy and shook hands with both of them.

Delaine recalled that it was not unusual for Mexican men to shake hands each day when they met, so he did not suspect Cuenca of giving them a glad hand. "Good to see you again. I hope you're enjoying your day."

"Oh, yes. We've been out for a ride, and we're back. And yourselves?"

"We're fine." Delaine nodded toward Hiller. "We came in to pick up a couple of things before we go out on roundup."

"Oh, yes. Mr. Calvin said you were going to do that. I hope that it all goes well for you, that you are able to get your work done, and that no mishaps come your way."

Again, Delaine recognized the standard courtesy, along with Cuenca's remembering the name of the ranch and its owner. "Thank you. and I wish you well in your own undertakings." He did not want to speak in explicit terms in front of the storekeeper.

Cuenca said, "And thanks to you as well. Yes, we hope to find out about these things that have happened. And of course, I have not changed my mind about the reward I mentioned."

Delaine could see that Cuenca had no reservations about making his purposes public.

Cuenca went on. "We're staying at the hotel. So if you hear something or see something, don't hesitate to let me know. If someone earns the reward, it goes straight to him."

"Thanks for mentioning it. We'll keep our eyes open, won't we, Ed?"

"You bet," said Hiller.

"Very well." Cuenca touched his hat. "We'll see you later."

The nephew, Francisco Gutiérrez, nodded as he followed his uncle.

Hiller placed the order and had it put on Percy's account. A boy who worked in the store carried out the third bag of flour and butter. Delaine and Hiller put their bags in the panniers on each side of the packsaddle, and they divided the butter into two portions. They wrapped the third bag of flour in a manty, or sheet of canvas, and tied it on top.

Hiller looked around and said, "It was interesting to see the gent from Trinidad again so soon."

"It was. He seems pretty open about looking for information. I guess he has to be if he's offering a reward."

"No reason to try to keep it a secret. As out of place as they are, they might as well wear a sign. Not that I'm criticizing them, mind you. That reward money is still nothing to be sniffed at." Hiller patted the top of the pack. "What do you think? Shall we have a drink? Percy doesn't mind, as long as we don't stay too long. He knows we're likely to anyway, and it's no money out of his pocket."

"Sounds agreeable to me," said Delaine. "I'd like to check the mail, though, and I might take a minute to drop a note, so I can meet you there."

"All right. If there's any mail for the ranch, of course, get it, too."

THE POSTAL CLERK scrunched his face and drew envelopes out of a couple of pigeonholes, then put both hands on the counter and said, "None today."

Delaine said, "I'd like to write a letter if I could." He put a nickel on the counter and said, "I'd like a sheet of paper, an envelope, a pen, and ink. Then I'd like to send it."

The clerk nodded. "It'll be three cents when you're done."

Delaine received the materials and moved to one side. He prepared himself to write with care and try not to make mistakes. He already had the contents of the letter in mind, but when it came to writing the salutation, he hesitated. He did not know whether he should use "Dear." Remembering Rachel's letter, he decided he would. He focused his attention and wrote.

Dear Rachel—

> *I received your letter a few days ago and have just found the chance to write back. I imagine by now you have heard the news about Pedro Cuenca, and I would guess that you may have had the opportunity to meet his brother. He and his nephew are over here now. I haven't heard the nephew say anything, but Miguel Cuenca is pretty forward. He is offering a reward. I have not found either of these men, the two brothers, to be the kind of person I would be natural friends with, but I still think that these people from Trinidad deserve help if I saw a way to do it. Still, I am trying not to be tempted by the reward, as I would rather not get into any difficulties if I can avoid it. So please don't worry. I am doing my work and staying out of trouble.*
>
> *I hope everything is well with you and your work. If I get a free day, I will try to go over your way for a visit.*

Sincerely,
Jess

He clenched his teeth. It was not the first time he had written the cold closing of "Sincerely" before he thought about it, but the letter was written, and in ink, so he put the pen by the inkwell. He blew on the page, and when he was sure it was dry, he folded it and put it in the envelope. He addressed the letter, then had to wait so he would not smudge the ink, and he jotted his return address. He licked the envelope, pressed it, and handed it to the clerk.

"Everything all right out your way?"

"For now," Delaine said. "We're getting ready to go out on roundup."

"That's good. Some of the others have already started."

"That's what I've heard."

"Tell Percy to let me know when he's done. Outfits that stay out for a while have mail come to 'em on the range if someone's goin' out that way."

"I'll tell him."

"Good luck. You never know when the weather will change."

———

ON THE WAY to The Lookout, Delaine had the taste of glue in his mouth. It was still better than folding a sheet of paper at home and having to seal it with wax.

His thoughts changed to an image of Miguel Cuenca as he had seen him in the general store. Delaine had a feeling he had had before, of seeing a person and perceiving that person as someone who was mortal and vulnerable and subject to not living long. Delaine realized he had had that feeling about the first Cuenca, and he hoped his premonition was wrong this time.

————

INSIDE THE SALOON, music from the piano mixed with the flow of voices. Hiller was talking to a man who looked like a range rider, so Delaine took a place at the bar and ordered a drink. As he waited, he heard the melody of the music, which was slow and not accompanied by words.

> *da-dum, da-dum, da-dum-dum,*
> *da-dum, da-dum, da-dum*
> *da-dum, da-dum, da-dum-dum,*
> *da-dum, da-dum, da-dum*

The third line rose, and the fourth line fell. After hearing the tune for a few stanzas, he realized it was the same as in the song that the traveler had sung about the lost angel.

In a small wave of motion in the crowd, a space opened for a second, and Delaine caught sight of a man near the back door. He was tall and slender, in a dark hat, with a full mustache going grey that matched the tones of his tweed overcoat. When Delaine had seen him earlier, in the café and then on the porch of the hotel, he had been wearing a pinstriped suit with a gold watch chain. At present, Delaine could see only the chest, shoulders, and head. His line of vision closed, and after he received his drink, he stepped back to see if he could catch another glimpse, but the man was gone. He must have left through the back door.

A feathered hat appeared in the mirror, and Delaine turned to his left. Green eyes, rouged cheeks, and red lips combined for a pleasant effect. Her name came to him. *Lenore.*

"Good evening," he said.

"The same to you. What are you up to?"

"In for a quick drink. We came to town on an errand, and we're about to go back."

"Same as before."

"You could say so."

She touched his arm. "Some day when you're not so busy, we could talk longer. Get to know each other. Wouldn't you like that, Jess?"

He smiled. "It's hard for me to disagree with someone who puts things in such a pleasant way. And there's no harm in talking."

She pursed her lips. "Of course there isn't." She patted his arm. "So maybe I'll see you when you're not on your way somewhere."

"It's good to see you, if only to say hello."

"Yes, it is." She raised her head, as if she saw someone she knew, and moved away.

Delaine sipped from his drink. He glanced at Hiller and saw that he was still engaged in conversation. Closer, a man moved into the clear, a shorter man with an uneven movement. *Mardell.* It occurred to Delaine that the man's loose-fitting suit might have belonged to someone else in better times.

Mardell took a step toward Delaine, shifting his jaw to one side and maintaining an unapologetic, almost insolent air. "Evenin'. In town for Saturday night?"

"I guess it is, but, no, we just stopped in for one drink. Ed Hiller and myself."

"I saw him."

"We came in to pick up a couple of things for the chuck wagon. We roll out in the morning."

"No God in Gomorrah, no balm in Gilead."

Delaine frowned. It seemed like a remark about working on Sunday, which was the next day.

"Just a couple of phrases I picked up."

"Did you study at one time?"

"Either too much or not enough. For all the good it did me."

Delaine was used to Mardell disparaging himself. "Buy you a drink?"

"I wouldn't turn it down."

Delaine signaled for a drink, waited, and handed it to Mardell.

"Thanks." Mardell took a sip, lowered his head, and seemed to be staring at the floor. The top of his head was visible, with unwashed strands combed across a top that sometimes saw the sun, for it was not pale.

Delaine said, "What do you think of the two deaths we've had?"

"It doesn't pay to think."

"Not much."

"Not in coin of the realm." Meredith twisted his mouth.

Delaine waited a moment. "You said something a while back that has made me think a couple of times."

"Have you gotten any pay for it?"

"No. I've had more than one job where I've been told I wasn't being paid to think, just to do my work. Even at that, some jobs leave a man free to think."

"Philosophers mucking out the stable."

"I've done some of that, but I don't know how philosophical I've been. In the last few days, I've been grubbing out cactus. A thousand things go through your mind in the course of a day." Delaine drank from his glass. "I've wondered about your comment about men transporting women as a kind of commerce."

Mardell glanced around. "I don't know that I said anything that definite."

"We had been talking about men who shipped antelope meat."

"I know. I remember. Men make money by dealing in different things. Hides, meat, what we could call horse flesh. Even information."

Delaine thought he understood. If he wanted information out of Mardell, he would have to pay. Buying a drink was just good will. It might lead up to the door, but it did not open it. Delaine returned to his earlier topic. "There's a third relative that has come from Trinidad, Colorado. He brought a nephew for company."

Mardell said, "I've heard of him, and I've seen him, but I haven't talked to him."

Delaine wondered if Mardell had talked to either of the other two, but he did not want to ask and be turned away. "What do you think of this weather we've been having?"

Mardell stared with his large eyes and shrugged. "Good for the kind of work you'll be doin'. But it'll get cold and wet, sooner or later. Not so good for your work, as I understand."

"No, it's quite an inconvenience, even dangerous, if a horse slips on a wet hillside."

"They say, good weather for ducks. I don't like it."

Delaine noticed a newspaper tucked into Mardell's pocket. "I haven't seen an almanac predicting what kind of winter we're supposed to have."

"Neither have I."

Hiller appeared out of the crowd. "About ready to go?" He nodded to Mardell.

Delaine looked at his glass. "I need to finish this." He drank the rest of his whiskey, set the glass on the bar, and left a nickel and a quarter to pay for the two drinks.

"So long," he said to Mardell.

"Thanks for the drink."

"You bet."

Delaine and Hiller walked out of the lamplit saloon into the evening, where dusk was giving way to dark. They walked a few steps to the hitching rail where they had left the horses tied in front of The Mercantile. Hiller offered to lead the packhorse for the first stretch, so Delaine mounted up and waited as Hiller put the two horses in position and swung aboard. As they were about to move out, a man came running up the street from the south.

He bumped into a man on the corner, who grabbed him by the coat and said, "What's the matter, Earl?"

Breathless, the man heaved out his message. "There's been a man found dead on the tracks, next to the train station."

"Run over?"

"Not yet. Someone needs to go for the deputy."

Hiller brought his horse alongside Delaine's and said, "We might go take a look before we leave town. I doubt that it has anything to do with us, but I think we should know before we ride off to be gone for more than a week. I think Percy would want to know, as well."

"Shouldn't take long," said Delaine. He laid the reins on the horse's neck and nudged it to turn the corner.

The train station sat on the south side of the street, north of the tracks, two full blocks from Main Street. Men came from different directions, a couple of them carrying lanterns to join the one lantern that was already there. Voices rose in short comments and exclamations.

Delaine and Hiller rode two blocks, dismounted, and led their horses toward the small crowd that had gathered.

"Give me your reins," said Hiller. "I'll wait."

Delaine reached the half-circle of men and worked his way around. Lanterns swayed, and shadows moved, but he got a view of the man lying face down on the tracks.

The man wore field boots, canvas trousers, and a tan canvas jacket. His hair was thinning on top, and a flat-crowned brown hat lay on the gravel between the tracks, a foot away from the man's outstretched hand.

A man at the front of the crowd said, "I've seen him around."

"So have I," said another. "He said he was a scientist. Studied birds."

"You wonder what he's doing here. He couldn't have had much money on him."

A voice from behind said, "Move aside. Let us through."

The crowd parted, and Deputy Blackmur pushed forward with another man behind him. The second man wore a dark hat and suit and carried a satchel.

The doctor knelt by the fallen man, felt for a pulse at his wrist and at his neck, and turned to look up in the lantern light. Speaking to the deputy, he said, "I'm afraid he's dead."

"Can you tell what caused it?"

The doctor indicated with the backs of his fingers in the direction of the man's head. "It looks like a blow to the back of the skull."

The deputy said, "Where's the station master?"

"Right here." A man in a cap and jacket, holding a lantern, stepped forward.

"Who found him?"

"I did. I came down here to open up, before the evening train came in, and I saw something lying here."

Another man said, "That's pretty cold-blooded, to hit a man in the back of the head and leave him to make it look like the train hit him."

"We don't know that yet," said the deputy.

"The train could have mutilated him."

"I know that, and we're glad it didn't happen. Let me make sure I have accurate notes about the position of the body, and we could use a little help to move him before the train gets here."

Delaine returned to Hiller where he held the horses. "Did you catch all of that?"

"Yes, I did. Poor fellow. I wonder who would do something like that, and why."

"So do I." Delaine tensed his shoulders and relaxed. Stevens had seemed like an inoffensive sort, with his professed interest in migratory birds. But he did have a tendency to ask questions.

10

———

THE WIND WAS BLOWING AS THE CREW MADE READY FOR the first day of fall roundup. It seemed late in the year to Delaine, and it was, as Percy had had to allow a certain number of days for each set of hunters. He did not show any worry, but everyone was short on humor as they tipped their heads into the wind and squinted as they stacked bedrolls in the wagon and pulled cinches.

Delaine mulled things over as the group set out. A bigger outfit would have two wagons—a chuck wagon and a bed wagon. A bigger outfit would have two wranglers, more horses, a second man in charge, and on and on. Percy was not poor, but he was cheap. Delaine offered to use his own horse, but that would have entailed another twenty-five cents a day, so the brown horse stayed in the pasture with a couple of old swaybacks and a horse with a bad hoof.

Hiller and Meredith had been working with the horses, and Delaine did not know which ones were in his string. He was used to riding his own string at least once or twice before going out, but the assignment was not fixed, due in part perhaps because Meredith would ride out to gather at the beginning. On the other hand, Delaine did not know of any horses that were unruly. In a larger herd, there were always a few.

The plan was to make a broad sweep of the country, something like an oval, given the ridge on the east and some of the fenced sections on the west. Most of Percy's cattle grazed north of the ranch headquarters, as there was a natural barrier of alkali flats to the south. For the first hour, then, the crew followed the same path they had taken for antelope hunting.

"We'll split up here," said Percy. "Art and I will ride a circle on the east, and you two'll do the same on the west. We'll meet about a mile and a half to the north. You'll see where the wagon will be stopped. That'll be our first camp. We'll gather stock north of the camp in the afternoon. See you there."

Hiller and Delaine rode west and split up. Delaine had heard the plan more than once, so he knew what to do—bring in any cows that had unbranded calves, and bring in any steers that looked big enough to ship. When in doubt, bring 'em in, and Percy would decide which ones to send to market and which ones to turn back onto the range.

Delaine was riding a horse he had ridden before, but he did not know how good it was at working cattle. A good horse did not need constant directions. Once it knew which animal the rider wanted to cut out or herd, it went to work. Some horses were almost too good, however, as they could make quick turns beneath a rider and leave him off balance. Delaine practiced with a couple of cows he did not intend to bring in, to get a feel for the horse and to be prepared when they came to an animal he wanted to keep. Range animals were not herded often, and some of them were wild and devious, so he wanted to be prepared.

Delaine found that the horse was smooth and not full of surprises, so he was off to a good start. His first candidate for the day was a brown steer with dark legs that looked like it weighed about a thousand pounds. It had pointed horns about ten inches long and not very beefy hips, as if it came from older Texas stock. He pushed the steer in the direction where camp would be, and he rode out to each side to see about any other cattle to join his gather.

The wind kept up and did not make his work any easier, but he stayed with it. He found a second steer, and the two paired up all right. The wind was dry, and it picked up bits of grass and flung them. The steers wanted to keep their rumps to the wind, but Delaine needed to drive them at an angle. The sorrel horse huffed and grunted as he went back and forth, keeping the steers on track.

The location of the camp did not have much to distinguish it. The wagon was parked with its tongue on the ground, out on a spot on the prairie with no trees or cover. The tent was pitched near it, rippling in the wind. Hal was on horseback, riding around the horse herd about a quarter mile south of camp. As Delaine brought the steers in, he went over a swell of ground and saw a muddy waterhole between the camp and the horse herd.

Three hundred yards north of camp, Art Meredith was slouched in the saddle not far from a cow and a calf, the first of the gather. Delaine hazed the two steers to become part of the herd. He stopped his horse near Meredith.

"You can go in," said Meredith. "Percy's there. He brought these in. I didn't find anything."

The tent and the wagon made something of a windbreak. The horse Percy had been riding that morning was tied to a rear wheel, so Delaine tied his horse to the other wheel. In warm, still weather, no one liked horses in camp because of the manure and the flies. The wind that would help keep flies away at present carried debris each time a horse shifted its feet, but no one had set up a picket line, and Delaine did not know if he was expected to take the same horse out in the afternoon.

McGrath came out of the tent, buttoning his coat. In his rough voice, he said, "It's cold grub at noon today. What with the wind, and not much fuel, we'll have a fire at night and in the morning until things get better. But we'll have coffee when you need it the most. Right now, it's cold meat and biscuits. But the flour is clean. You don't have to worry about that."

"Glad to hear it."

"You can eat in the tent. Percy's there."

The light was dim inside the tent, but Delaine was glad to be out of the wind. Percy was seated on a wooden box that held camp supplies.

"Sit here," he said. "There's room." He moved to one side.

Delaine had just enough space to sit down, with his elbow close to his ribs.

McGrath came into the tent and said, "I'll get you your grub." A minute later, he handed Delaine a tin plate with two biscuits, two slices of beef, and half a dozen slices of dried apple. "I've got beans soakin' to be cooked for tonight, and I'll have a mess of speckled puppy for this time tomorrow, so things won't be so glum."

Delaine had a pleasant image of cooked rice with raisins. Meredith had not prepared anything like dessert, even with the paying hunters. Jam for the biscuits and molasses for the hotcakes were as far as he went.

Delaine spoke to Percy. "Do you want me to use the same horse this afternoon?"

"If you didn't work him too hard this morning. These horses have been takin' it easy, so if we get a full day out of each one to begin with, it'll stretch things out better." Percy yawned. "I'm glad you boys went for more flour yesterday. I was sorry to hear about the man they found on the tracks. I didn't meet him when he came to the ranch. Art says he was a bug hunter or at least said he was. What do you think?"

Delaine took a couple of seconds to swallow the dry food. "He said he studied birds, and he seemed to know enough about them."

"Well, it's not good that things happen like that, but at least it didn't happen out here again. Did anyone think it was related?"

"I don't know. We didn't stay around long enough to hear what everyone had to say."

"Just as well. With some of these deals, you can wait until things get sifted out and you get the grain of it later. This wind is somethin'. You notice it more when the weather has been so good for so long. I saw tumbleweeds blowin' in two different directions, fifty yards apart."

"Means the weather's gonna change," said McGrath.

"That's the way," said Percy. "I don't doubt it."

Hal was still riding around the horse herd as it grazed when Delaine rode out in the afternoon. The wind had a cold edge to it, and the sky was bleak. Once he was away from camp, however, the world opened up, and the wind felt normal. Riding the broad country made him feel free again.

A familiar sound, sharp and repeated, caused him to look up. A flock of geese was flying crossways in the wind. Geese were another sure sign that the weather was changing.

The geese flew over, and the honking faded. Delaine wondered if Stevens had ridden over this same stretch of country. He wondered what parts of it Tiburcio Martínez had seen, or Pedro Cuenca. The elation he had felt a few minutes earlier gave way to a forlorn feeling that had come to him on other occasions, a sense that life and the natural world went on, and that the deceased would not see it again. Whatever Stevens had been, whether he was a true scientist or a pretender, he had known enough of nature to appreciate it, and now his term was over.

Delaine tried to brush the empty feeling aside. He needed to pay attention to his work and to his surroundings. He was on that side of the broad, oval-shaped campaign where he could expect to cross paths with one or more of the Big Eight riders.

———

DELAINE BROUGHT in another steer that afternoon. Hiller and Percy each brought in one as well. Hiller, like Meredith, had found nothing in the morning, so the herd they were holding consisted of six animals.

Percy said that when they had a fire in the morning, they would brand the calf and let it and its mother go.

McGrath had a fire that evening, as he had said he would, and he had a pot of beans and a pile of warm biscuits. The wind died down at nightfall, and the men sat around the fire rather than have to huddle in the tent. The mood was cheerful.

As always, some of the crew was out. Hal was the night wrangler, and he seemed to be the day wrangler as well, catching snatches of sleep when he could. Meredith was now the day herder, and with few cattle, he watched the horses for short periods when Hal slept beneath the wagon. Now in the evening Percy laid out the plan for watching the cattle at night.

With larger outfits, Delaine was used to having two night herders, who rode around the herd in the dark, each covering half the circumference. When they met, they would each ride back the other way, meet again, and so on. By tradition, there were four shifts or watches in the night—from supper until ten, from ten until twelve, from twelve until two, and from two until daybreak. With a typical crew of twenty or more riders, a man did not have to go out on shift every night.

As in other areas, Percy skimped on night herding. He had three shifts instead of four, and because the herd was so small, he had one man per shift. The same three men—Percy, Hiller, and Delaine—would ride one shift every night. To Percy's credit, he took his shift, in the spirit of the boss who would not ask his men to do something he wouldn't.

Delaine had the third shift, from half-past-one until daylight, so he turned in early. Percy, Meredith, and

McGrath were to sleep in the tent, so Delaine and
Hiller rolled their beds out on the ground.

———

DELAINE DID NOT HAVE a sense of having slept long
when he felt the toe of a boot in his ribs and heard
McGrath's gravelly voice. "Your turn to go relieve Ed."

Until the herd became larger, all three men would
ride the same night horse, poking around the small
perimeter and stopping for periods long enough to get
down and walk around. The moon was bright, and
Delaine did not have to do much more than stay
awake.

He walked with the horse plodding along behind
him. The cattle were all bedded down. Faint noises
came from the horse herd, and although horses stayed
on their feet a good part of the time and moved
around in the night, everything seemed to be calm
there.

Delaine's thoughts wandered, and he came to a
line of thinking he had entertained before, about how
much work it took to make a living off of animal life.
Some people might think that all livestock owners had
to do was let the animals graze and then go out and
gather them up for market. He did not know of
anybody, with cattle or sheep or even with donkeys and
goats, who could get by on so little effort. Those who
did ignore their animals were subject to lose a bigger
percentage through one hazard or another.

Even those who lived off the fat of the land, as the
saying went—hunters and trappers—had to put in
long, hard hours. Hunting for sport, or managing sport
hunters, required sustained work. None of it was easy.

Most of the time, he assumed that everyone had to make a living at something, and he left it at that. But when he had the leisure, or the idleness, to think as he did now, sometimes he pondered the phenomenon of men exploiting animals. It wasn't just the great chain of being, as he had heard the idea expressed, in which a man ate a squab like a coyote ate a mouse. Men raised or hunted animals, or caught them in other ways, with fish hooks and leg traps, in greater numbers than their immediate needs, and often for purposes other than need. They exploited for luxury, for items such as mink and ivory. Or for the pleasure itself, of feeling a tug on the line or seeing an animal fall. And what gave one man pleasure would give another man commerce. Business. Every man knew his business, Mardell said. Men had been doing it for centuries, collecting and selling everything from tea and oranges and silk and ostrich feathers to elephant tusks and elk's teeth and bear claws and Chinese girls.

Delaine shook his head. He had almost dozed off, wandering the regions between sleep and wakefulness. It was as if he had touched on something and had come back to solid ground.

Here he was, in the dark, but part of the broad, daylight world of men making a living on cattle, just as they had been making a living on deer and antelope a week and two weeks earlier. At the same time, men somewhere were making a living on the traffic of women, and it wasn't the free adventure of a young man running off with a pretty girl.

———

McGRATH WAS PUTTING little mounds of biscuit dough in a Dutch oven when Delaine returned to camp.

"Grub's on the way. Coffee's in the pot."

Delaine poured himself a cup from the one-gallon coffee pot and felt the warmth of the fire on his face. McGrath had been right about having coffee when Delaine would need it.

The cook came to the fire in a bustle and set the Dutch oven on the coals. "I'll get two batches and then start frying bacon," he said. He reached inside his coat, drew out the makings, and began to roll a cigarette. "We'll see if the wind picks up again today."

Delaine sipped his coffee.

McGrath finished rolling his cigarette, stuck it in his mouth, used the short-handled shovel to lift a live coal, and lit his smoke. He shook the coal into the fire and laid the shovel on the ground. "Nice and peaceful," he said. "You get a bigger herd, and they're bawlin' all the time."

Delaine wondered about a man giving up the comforts of town to live in the elements and be short on sleep. "Do you miss town?" he asked.

"Not much. Not yet. Give me a few days of cold, wet weather and drivin' wind, and I might wish I was back in town, listenin' to men talk about their ailments and hard luck."

"Are you a barber?"

"Close to it. Most of the time, I work the early shift at The Lookout. I'm a bartender. I work those hours when men come in and have one drink, which sometimes becomes three. They talk about why they can't sleep, or why they can't piss, or why some woman left 'em. On and on. What they need so they can get back into makin' good money. A better job, one good business deal."

"You don't get the ones who sleep well, have wives that bake apple pie, and make enough to put some of it in the bank."

"It wouldn't be fair to say I don't ever, but those aren't the things I hear about the most."

Delaine drank from the warm tin cup. He was the only one at the fire, except the cook. He was confident that Meredith was well out of earshot, tending to the herd, as he had gone out when Delaine came in. "Something I was wondering about," he said. "You've heard a lot more talk than I have, but one thing I've heard about a couple of times, or got a hint of, is men who make a living off women."

"You hear all kinds of things. In towns bigger than this one, you've got pimps and whoremasters, just as common as gamblers."

"I'm familiar with that. But what I was referring to was, I guess you could call it a kind of gossip, but more secret-like, about men transporting women for purposes of putting them to work in places like logging camps and mining camps."

McGrath lifted his cigarette to his lips and took a puff. "Oh, I suppose that goes on."

"Have you heard about it around here?"

McGrath looked at him sideways. "You're not the first one to ask me about that."

"Oh?" Delaine thought he might have in mind someone like Mason Mardell, who would be a good one to wander through the saloon at mid-morning with a newspaper in his pocket.

"That fella who went by the name of Stevens. Said

he studied birds that were migrating. He was curious about it, too, that kind of business."

Delaine felt his eyes widen. "Do you think that might be related to how he died?"

The cook's rough voice was non-committal. "I have no idea."

"Let me go back to my other question. Did you hear about that kind of commerce going on around here or through here?"

McGrath held his cigarette between his thumb and forefinger at mouth level. "Let's put it this way. When you work in a saloon, you hear a lot of things, and sometimes you don't know how to separate the fly shit from the ground pepper. More than that, you learn to be careful about when and where you repeat it, which, for the most part, is better if it's not at all."

———

DELAINE STILL DID NOT KNOW which horses he was to ride or whether he had a definite string. When he asked Percy, the boss said to ask Art, but he thought the grey horse would be a good one to ride next. As the morning sun was clearing the rim to the east, Delaine went with rope in hand to ask Meredith, who said, yes, the grey horse would be a good choice.

Delaine made his way to the horse herd, where Hal looked down from the saddle, bleary-eyed, and nodded.

Delaine roped out the grey horse, which had a dull white coat flecked with grey, set off with a dark mane, tail, and hocks. He led the horse close to camp, where he had his saddle and bridle.

The horse did not tremble or flinch as Delaine

brushed him and combed the mane and tail. Still holding the neck rope, having no place to tie the horse unless he wanted to shovel manure later, Delaine laid on the double blanket and smoothed it. After draping the cinches over the saddle, he swung it by the horn, high and clear, and let it settle on the horse's back. The grey horse remained calm the whole time.

Delaine reached under, took the cinch ring, and brought it up. He ran the latigo from the cinch ring to the D ring and back twice more until he had it snug enough to put the spoke in a hole. He buckled the rear cinch, which he did not always use but had attached for roping and dragging if necessary.

He patted the horse on the neck, and still holding the rope, he took the headstall in his right hand and the bit in his left. He laid the bridle on top of the horse's head, from its ears to its nose, used his thumb and second finger like a broad hook to open the horse's mouth, and worked the bit in over the horse's tongue. He worked the headstall over the ears, saw that the bit was snug enough to make the horse smile, and straightened the bridle. He gathered the reins, took the rope off the horse's neck, coiled the rope, and tied it onto the saddle with its thong.

He led the horse out for a half-dozen steps and put his first three fingers between the cinch and the horse's warm body. He pulled the cinch to tighten it another notch, felt again, and set his reins around the horse's neck and onto the saddle horn.

He pulled the left rein to turn the horse's head inward, so that it would be discouraged from bolting, and he held the reins and a hank of mane with his left hand as he grabbed the saddle horn with his right, put the toe of his boot into the stirrup, and swung aboard.

As he brought his right foot around to catch the other stirrup, he was prepared if the horse wanted to buck, but it didn't. He held the reins even, patted the horse on the neck, and let it walk.

Hiller, meanwhile, had saddled his horse for the day and was ready to go. Delaine joined him, and the two of them rode west out of camp. Hiller would make a circle around to the south, while Delaine would ride around to the north.

The wind came up at mid-morning, as it often did in the fall. Delaine rode to his farthest point west and did not see anything to bring back. He had a sense that he was close to Big Eight range, but he did not see any of their cattle. He imagined they had come through on roundup earlier and may have driven their stock closer to home. Some outfits had winter pastures, and some put up enough hay to feed for the winter. He did not know how the Big Eight did things, and he did not know if he would find out. Some punchers liked to keep up with the business of other outfits, down to how many holding pens and haystacks they had, but Delaine did not try to know that much.

Some men were like that in the high country, too. They kept track of how many men were in each camp, how many horses they had, and how many deer or elk they had hanging. Some of that would be going on now. There would be snow in the higher elevations, elk on the move, and here and there a black bear, such as one he remembered meeting on a shadowy trail one grey morning. The bear had risen up, dropped to all fours, and taken off down through the timber, past the beaver pond where beavers never came out when humans were around.

Delaine came back to the moment, to the clear

daylight and the wind on the side of his face as he rode around to the north in the open grassland.

He saw a group of six cattle, downhill, grazing out of the wind. As he headed toward them, he took down his rope in case he needed it. Closer, he read the brands. They were all Lazy T cattle—two cows, two calves, a yearling heifer, and a larger steer. He nudged the grey horse into a trot to cut out the steer, and the horse went to work. The steer ran one way and the other, and the horse kept after him. Delaine slapped the coiled rope on the shank of his boot, called, "Hep-hah," and drove the animal eastward. It was a good-looking steer, with a blocky build and a reddish-brown color that looked like the newer stock that had been brought to the northern ranges. The steer wanted to go back, but Delaine and the grey horse kept pushing it.

The range thinned out, and Delaine saw only four more head of cattle—one cow-calf pair and then another, all of them with the Lazy T brand.

Delaine drove the steer in the direction where the next camp was supposed to be. The sun was close to its high point when he saw the wagon and tent, the horse herd, and the small beef herd. He brought the steer in, and Meredith nodded from his post on horseback. The cow and the calf from the day before were gone, so Delaine assumed that Percy had branded the calf and let the two animals go.

Delaine rode to the horse herd and dismounted. He loosened the cinch, took off the bridle, and hung it on the saddle horn so the horse could graze. He waved to Hal and made his way to the camp.

A horse was tied to a rear wagon wheel, and Percy

was sitting on the lee side of the tent, in the sunlight. "How did you do?" he asked.

"I brought in one steer. And you?"

Percy scrunched his nose. "Nothin'. We got to start doin' better than this, or we'll all go broke. The good thing is, we got grub. Cold beans and biscuits, but it's grub. Did you see anything else?"

"Of yours, I saw two cows with calves and a heifer, then two pairs, one after another."

"Not much. But this is big country, and they're scattered out. They come in closer as we get into winter. We feed some hay through the harder times, and they know it. Seen Ed?"

"Not since we split up."

"Well, he'll be in, and then we'll all go out again in the afternoon. Get yourself a plate."

Delaine saw that McGrath was not rationing out the food this time, so he served himself a helping of cold beans and took two biscuits.

Hiller came in as Delaine was getting the last of the crumbs with his spoon. "Two steers," he said. "One a little bigger than the other."

"That's good," said Percy. "Fella I worked for before I came out here used to say, 'Pennies make dollars.' We add these one or two at a time, and we'll have somethin' to ship after all. See anything else?"

"I saw a big buck antelope that any one of our hunters would have liked. He was running with a band of does, and in this wind, they stayed more than half a mile away."

"Hah. Any other cattle of mine?"

"Half a dozen. All branded. Four in one bunch, two in another."

"Seems to me my cattle should be in bigger

bunches. Maybe those other outfits have scattered 'em, goin' through and gettin' their own."

"Hard to say. I didn't see anyone else."

"Just as well. Go ahead and get yourself a plate."

Delaine drank half a cup of cold coffee and was chewing the grounds when he heard the footfalls of more than one horse. He and Hiller and Percy all looked up as three riders came around the north side of the tent. They stopped crossways to the wind and looked down.

They were not in formation as they had been the first two items Delaine had seen them, but he knew them as the Big Eight riders. Mitchell, the one in the wide-brimmed hat, was wearing a long denim coat, unbuttoned, with a blanket lining. As usual, his gun and holster were in view.

"Looks like you're gettin' around to gatherin' a few head of beef."

Percy's pale blue eyes were narrowed as he looked up. "'Bout that time of year."

"You're not a big enough outfit for us to have a rep with you, but we'd like to look over what you've got, since you've been workin' the range over on our side."

"We got nothin' to hide, and it won't take you long to look," Percy said.

Mitchell's eyes roved over Delaine and Hiller. Delaine was sure the man remembered them from the deer hunting incident, and he detected a glare from the bearded man as well. Mitchell glanced at McGrath and came back to Percy. "We'll do that."

He reined his horse around, and the other two followed. Delaine stood up to watch them. They did not ride to the small beef herd but went first to the horse herd, where they rode around the animals that grazed over an area of an acre or more. After that, they took their horses across the stretch of bare ground, rode close to the small bunch of gathered steers, and paused long enough for an exchange with Meredith.

Percy and Hiller were standing and watching as well.

"That's just the way they are," said Percy. "Ride right into your camp, push their way around. They know they're not goin' to find anything, but they do it because they know they can, and their boss lets 'em. Marcus. You don't ever see him out here gettin' dirty, but he gets things done his way."

"Oh, to hell with them," said Hiller. "We do our work and mind our own business."

"That's the best way," said Percy. "They don't make a penny by this, and they know it."

11

Dark, grey clouds began to pile up in the west, thick accumulations that looked like sodden wool blankets. Delaine buttoned his coat and ducked his head as he rode northwest out of camp. He could smell moisture, and he recognized the kind of weather that was on the way. The cattle were in bigger bunches now, half a dozen to a dozen, huddled, so that he had to ride among them to read the brands. On the third day of roundup, he brought in three steers.

On the fourth day, Delaine and Hiller stayed together. The outfit had moved far enough north that they would have to work the breaks, an area of draws and canyons that they would have gone to if the hunting had lasted longer. A slow, cold rain had moved in, so they both wore slickers that Percy provided.

Delaine expected more cattle to have taken shelter in the breaks, but the weather was not that severe. It was wet enough, however, to make the going slow and slippery. Delaine never knew what to expect around the next turn in a canyon. Once he jumped a group of seven big-eared does and fawns, their grey coats rough and darkened with the moisture. The deer bounded away, farther into the canyon. On another occasion, his horse spooked at the sudden movement of a four-point buck, also dark and wet, that whirled and raced out of sight.

They brought in four steers in a long, slow walk that lasted into the early afternoon. They did not go out in the afternoon.

McGrath and Hal had covered the chuck wagon with tarpaulins and had made a shelter on one side. Pungent smoke from the nearby fire rolled in under the canvas, but the ground in the center of the sheltered area was dry.

Hiller had expressed his opinion more than once, out on the range, that if they had started a week or ten days earlier like the other outfits, they would be done by now. The other, larger crews that had more area to cover would still be out, but some would be back at the home corral, playing cards and checkers in the bunkhouse.

In the morning of the second day of rain, Percy suspended riding out. Too much chance of getting hurt, he said. He re-scheduled the shifts so that Meredith and Hal would not have to stay out all day in the rain.

On the third day, the rain tapered off and the clouds moved east as the outfit stayed in the same place.

The next morning broke clear, with a heavy frost everywhere, including on the canvas sheet that covered Delaine and Hiller's beds in the middle of the sheltered area. McGrath was fanning the fire with a folded flour sack, trying to get flames to rise out of the low clouds of smoke.

Percy spoke in his loud, cheerful voice. "Time to get back at it, boys. In a few more days, we'll be back in the parlor, eatin' bread an' honey."

Delaine and Hiller rode out to the breaks again. The world was quiet, and the footfalls of the horses on damp ground were muffled.

They found the new campsite in the early afternoon and added three steers and a cow and a calf to the herd. Meredith looked over the animals with a sullen gaze, and Delaine wondered if another calf to brand represented unwelcome work. It shouldn't be so bad. In the routine they followed, Meredith roped the calf, Delaine and Hiller or Hall and one other held the calf down, and Percy placed the brand. The men on the ground might get muddy or even smeared with manure, but Meredith didn't.

Delaine and Hiller continued to work together as the group worked its way around the north. Delaine and Hiller went into the breaks each day. The beef herd was growing, and the ground was drying out. The afternoons were pleasant. This was Indian summer, the period of shorter, warm days after the first frost. Every morning was cold, and the riders' ropes had gathered enough moisture that they froze, and the men had to thaw them out at the morning fire.

In the broad, methodical sweep, the outfit was moving south, in the direction of the clear sky where the sun crossed every day. Delaine felt as if they had left the clammy weather behind them for the time being, but he knew that the days were getting shorter and becoming chilly sooner.

———

DELAINE AND HILLER rode out of camp as a vermilion sunrise lit up the sky on their left. Within a short while, the grassland in front of them had a sparkling glow from frost on dull grass, with tiny spots of shade from clumps of sagebrush. No cattle were in sight. They rode on. Delaine was on a dun horse that he had ridden a couple of times before, a bit of a laggard that he had to spur from time to time.

The two riders headed southwest toward a rise where they planned to split up and ride their separate circles. The dun horse gave a burst of energy to climb the slope, and Delaine let it go until he topped the rise and reined the horse by habit.

On the plain below, a carriage was moving in a west-northwest direction. Delaine backed the horse, slid off, and turned it as Hiller on a brown horse came trotting up the hill.

Hiller stopped, swung down, and pulled his horse by the reins as he faced Delaine. "What is it?"

"A carriage of some kind. I don't think it's a stage-coach, and this isn't a place for one."

"We'll take a look and see." Hiller went to his saddlebags and took out a leather binocular case. Delaine recognized it as one of the newer sets that had been in the field box during hunting season. He wondered if Hiller had borrowed the binoculars since he had taken an interest in Cuenca's reward.

The two men leaned forward as they led their horses at full length to the crest of the hill. The carriage had stopped, and three dark figures had gotten out. They looked like women wearing dresses and cloaks. Hiller watched through the binoculars as they formed something of a triangle with their backs to one another. He lowered the binoculars.

"I don't want to watch them when they're going pee," he said, "but it's three women. I wonder where they're goin'. This sure isn't a main route."

Nor was it the middle of the day. Delaine imagined the carriage had traveled through the night. Wherever it came from, it may have had to wait for good weather.

The women appeared to have finished their business, as they walked away together a few yards and stopped, facing northwest. Two men had gotten down from the front seat of the carriage, and they appeared to take turns holding the horses and making water.

Hiller raised the binoculars and held steady for a long moment, then lowered them and handed them to Delaine.

The three women all looked like white women. They were dressed in dark dresses and cloaks, as they had seemed at first. They also wore dark cloth hats of felt or wool, which contrasted with their light-colored skin. One woman had dark hair, and the other two had brown hair. The detail was not good, but the darker one appeared to have cloudy features, while the other two were plain. None of them was painted up, but they had a common, not very delicate way of moving around that suggested that they did not come from a church group. In Delaine's observation, they could be washerwomen or prostitutes.

One of the men came around to the women's side of the horses. He wore a large, light-colored hat and a sheepskin coat. He appeared to speak to them, and they walked toward the coach, again not in prim steps but leaning forward and holding their skirts. They helped each other up the step and inside. The man closed the door behind them and climbed up into the seat. His partner climbed up on the other side, a shorter man in a dark-brown hat and a long, dark coat. The carriage went on its way.

"Well, that's something," said Hiller. "You wonder what they're doin'."

"Hard to say," said Delaine. It looked like men transporting women, but he did not think he knew enough to say so.

Hiller sniffed, rubbed his nose, and put the binoculars in the case. "I don't know about you, and I can't tell you what to do or say, but I think I'd prefer not to say anything to Art or Percy. There's been strange doin's out in this country, and I don't know if this has anything to do with 'em, but I'm still interested in that reward, and I don't want to queer the deal by tellin' someone else what I know. Or think I know."

"I agree," said Delaine.

"There's always time to tell someone later. I don't want to say anything about Art, but I don't know for sure what his brother does. Neither of those two fellows was him. They're complete strangers. But you never know if there's a connection."

"Between him and them, or them and the men who were killed out here? These ones look like they're just passing through."

"Any of it, or none of it, I don't know. But I would keep this under my hat until I knew more."

"I'd go along with that," said Delaine. He had kept confidences before, only to have them spilled by the other party, and keeping a secret always entailed some kind of a risk. At the same time, he still felt like a newcomer here, and not saying much was a good practice.

———

DELAINE AND HILLER each brought in three steers that day. Percy brought in two. As they sat by the evening fire, Percy said, "We might make a beef herd after all. Not much longer, and we'll be done. Next thing you know, Ed'll be buying his girl a corsage."

Hiller shrugged. "If I had a girl."

"Ha," said Percy. "If I had one, I wouldn't tell anyone, either."

"Not around a bunch like this," said McGrath in his rough voice.

There were only four people present. Delaine thought McGrath's comment came out of habit, a kind of celebrating the rugged life they shared.

Percy yawned. "See anything else today, either of you?"

Hiller said, "Maybe a jackrabbit."

"Nothin' to mention," said Delaine.

"So much the better." Percy took off his hat, rubbed his pate, and covered up. "A few more days."

Delaine held his hands to the fire. He realized that for the first time in several days, his boots and all of his clothes were dry. His bedroll had been damp when he put it away that morning, but it was getting better, too.

———

PERCY WENT OUT on first shift, and Meredith came to the fire. Because of their separate jobs, Delaine had not spent much time around Meredith since roundup began. Now as he caught a glance of the man in his wool coat, collarless shirt, suspenders, cloth vest, and striped wool pants tucked into stovepipe boots, he had the impression that he knew him less than ever. Meredith had seemed humorless for quite a while, and Delaine wondered if he had some ill feeling toward McGrath for supplanting him or if he still felt criticized over the incident with the flour. Delaine noticed that McGrath and Meredith did not speak or even look at one another very much.

Hiller must have sensed the lack of good feeling. He said, "Are you glum these days, Art?"

Meredith held his hands out as he stood by the fire. He seemed to grit his teeth, and his face had hard lines. "I haven't had dry feet for over a week, and if you want to know the truth, I've had a little trouble with my piles. I've taken to walkin' half the day, and that seems to help."

"Sorry to hear that."

"Nothin' for you to be sorry about. I shouldn't have said anything, but you asked."

"I've heard of remedies."

"So have I." Meredith went into the tent where the eating utensils were kept.

Hiller stood up and stretched. "I might as well turn in. Seems like I barely get to sleep when my shift comes around."

"Me, too," said Delaine. He crossed paths with Meredith at the edge of the firelight and went to find his bedroll. He had the illusion that Meredith was put out because Hiller and Delaine were keeping information from him. But he knew it was just that, an illusion. He told himself not to feel guilty. He did not have any real friendship with Meredith anyway. The man acted as if nothing happened when his brother picked a fight, and as for sharing information, Delaine reminded himself that he also did not know with any detail where Brother Meredith worked.

THE CREW ENDED up at ranch headquarters on the last day of the fall roundup. The horse herd was in its pasture, and the beef herd was grazing in another fenced pasture, when Delaine brought in his last steer. Hiller had brought in a cow with a spotted calf that no one had seen during the season, and Percy was heating a branding iron so that he could turn the pair back out. He said he wanted to take the steers on in, starting in the morning.

"Where do we take 'em?" Delaine asked.

"To the shipping pens in Overton. I suppose you know where they are."

"Yes I do. I even worked on those pens at about this time last year."

"You may have said something about that earlier." Percy turned the iron where it rested in the fire. "I think it's ready," he said. He turned and called, "Hot iron!

Meredith was on horseback holding tension on the calf's neck with a rope. Hal was sitting on the calf's neck and shoulders, and Hiller was pulling on one hind leg with his boot against the other hip. Percy pressed the brand, and the smell of burned hair lifted on the breeze.

As Delaine put his horse away, he saw the wagon parked in the barn with some of the range gear to be unloaded later.

Inside the bunkhouse, Hiller was sitting at the table across from Percy and Meredith. McGrath was in the kitchen, frying beef. Hal was sound asleep on a bunk. Delaine washed his hands and face and took a seat on Hiller's side of the table.

Percy said, "We'll do it just like last year." He glanced in Delaine's direction. "If we cut across the alkali and come out on the trail east of town, we can make it in one long day. Hold the herd overnight just west of Overton, then drive 'em into the pens in the morning. Art takes Pete and Hal into town in the buckboard, and he joins in with us. So we have our bedrolls in the buckboard. Make a light camp, eat cold grub, and come back the next day. Jess, if you've got anything you need to do in Overton, you can have the rest of the day on your own. Come back the next day. I'll have a little more work for you and Ed before we're done."

Delaine nodded. He saw once again how Percy did things. Some outfits paid for a meal in town, even hotel rooms and the chance for a bath, but Percy was doing things cheap, as the saying went, right to the end.

"Hot iron," said McGrath as he carried a big skillet of sizzling beef from the kitchen.

"Ha," said Percy. "You boys won't have to hear that again until next year."

Hiller said, "The ones who brand in the off-season don't call it out."

"There's that," said Percy.

———

HAL WAS UP and at it in the morning, helping McGrath. He had his bag packed and sitting on his bunk. On top of his bag lay a pale deer antler. It was not large, consisting of a fork and a third point, plus a small eye guard. The knurled end showed that it had been shed, and its dry, bleached appearance was typical of something that had been lying on the rangeland with its matching half who knew where.

As Hal brought a plate of hotcakes to the table, Meredith said, "Why do you want to collect junk like that?"

Hal paused. "Like what?"

"A deer horn that's been layin' in the dirt."

"It's just somethin' to keep."

"If you wanted some real deer horns, you could get a full set. Hunt it like a man."

McGrath came in with a skillet of bacon with light smoke wisping. "Leave the kid alone. He's not doin' any harm."

Meredith held his knife and fork in his two hands, resting by his plate, as he raised his head. Resentment showed in his brown eyes. "Don't tell me what to do or not to do."

"Let's not bother with that," said Percy. "We've got one more bit of work to do. Art, you're gonna take them into town. I'll pay them before we all leave here, so no one's bossin' anyone."

Silence fell for a long moment until Percy said, "Maybe Ed's still thinkin' about that corsage, but he's not sayin'."

Hiller said, "What do you think if I stay the night in Overton as well? Ride back with Jess."

"That would be all right, too," said Percy. "If Jess doesn't mind the company."

"Not at all," said Delaine.

———

THE BEEF HERD consisted of forty-seven steers. Delaine asked Hiller if Percy was concerned about the animals losing weight if he drove them too fast.

"It's not that far," said Hiller, "and it's cool weather. He has 'em fed for a day in the pens and makes sure they have plenty of water. They put it back on."

Percy took the lead, riding point. Delaine and Hiller rode on the flanks, each dropping back to take up the drag. The bunch stayed together better than a mixed herd did. Not long after they met the trail to Overton, Meredith came up behind them in the buckboard and stayed in back of the herd.

They did not lose time, and they camped off the trail not far from Overton, as Percy had said they would. Two men at a time would take shifts riding around the herd, to make sure nothing strayed at that point. The horses went on a picket line. Meredith had brought grain, so he fed Percy's horse and the wagon horses as Delaine and Hiller took the first shift. They would feed their two horses later.

———

DELAINE WOKE to the sound of someone throwing something into the back of the buckboard. It seemed as if he had just closed his eyes after changing shifts at midnight, but the sky was beginning to show grey in the east. He rolled out of his blankets and put on his hat and boots.

Cold biscuits and water were better than no breakfast at all. Delaine saddled the same horse he had ridden the day before, the steady sorrel, and rode out to relieve Percy. Meredith was picking up camp, and Hiller was waiting to help him hitch the horses.

They drove the steers at a slow walk, down the main street of Overton, and on to the shipping pens on the east side of town. Delaine's boss from the year before, Al Portman, stood outside his little office. He was dressed in his usual sand-colored hat, canvas jacket, and pants, and he had a drover's cane in one hand and a cigarette in the other. He spoke a few words in response to Percy's greeting, and he nodded at Delaine as he rode by.

A larger herd than Percy's was already in the pens. Delaine understood that they would all ship together. When Percy was sure of the count and the pen worker had closed the last gate, he rode over to the spot where Delaine and Hiller stood by their horses.

"You boys are free to go," he said. "I've got to make sure all the brands are clear and the shipping papers are signed. Then Art and I'll go back to the ranch. We'll see you there."

That was it. He didn't ask if they needed money, much less give them any, and Delaine realized they would have to pay to put the horses in the stable for the night, in addition to their personal expenses.

As the two rode toward the center of town, Hiller said, "I suppose you know of a good place to put up."

"I do. There's a rooming house where I stay. No meals and no cooking in the rooms, but there's a place to take a bath. There's a place to eat not far away, and more than one place to have a drink. One is a tavern and serves just beer, while the other has all your poisons."

"I think I know the places you're talking about. Are those separate rooms?"

"Yes, they are."

"That's fine. If you want to go your own way after we get checked in, we can meet up later on."

———

AFTER A BATH and a shave and a clean change of clothes, Delaine left his bag in his room and walked downstairs. Outside, the pale sun had crossed over into the afternoon. He walked the short distance to the Sweet Auburn Café.

His spirits picked up at the sight of Rachel in a tan dress and white apron. She put her hand to her hair and met him as he stopped at a table.

"Well, look who's back in town," she said. "Are you done for the season, or are you just free for the day?"

"Just a day off, or part of one. We brought a herd of steers to the shipping pens, and another fellow and I are going to stay overnight. We'll go back to the ranch tomorrow. From what I understand, I've got a few days' work before I'm done."

"But you're free this evening?"

"Unless something unusual happens. For right now, I could use something to eat. The boss had us on slim rations on the way over."

"I think you're in luck. There should still be enough meat, potatoes, and gravy."

"Good. I'd better take it before someone else comes in."

———

DELAINE ARRIVED at the house with the little statue of a Dutch boy out front. He noted the white cap, yellow hair, blue jacket and pants, and yellow shoes as he walked past. He wondered if Mrs. Vanderhoven would open the door, and he was pleased to see Rachel in her dark blue overcoat.

"Shall we go for a walk?" she said.

"It's all right with me." He did not mind visiting in the living room of the house where she rented, but he felt freer to talk when they were out on their own.

He waited for her to speak. After they had walked a short way, she said, "I have been troubled by these things that have happened to these family members of Mrs. Mendoza."

"So have I," he said. "It has been very unsettling, even though, in the world of men where I work, everyone seems to make an effort not to say much about it."

"You have a law officer there, I'm sure. Does he not have an idea of who or what is behind it?"

"Well you know how law officers are. They ask questions but don't share much, unless they're trying to get information in return."

"Do you have any ideas yourself?"

"Not in a very definite way, but I have crossed paths with these men. Don Tiburcio, as you call him, stopped by our antelope hunting camp and let it be known that he was looking for his daughter and the one she ran off with. Not long after that, Pedro Cuenca came to the ranch, and he showed interest in the area where his uncle's body was found. Then he showed up at our hunting camp, quite a ways away and quite by coincidence, I think, where he was poking around on his own. And we know that he came to an end out there, too. We don't know where for sure, but his body was found in his rented buggy, in the yard of the ranch where I work."

"I have heard most of that."

"And then Miguel Cuenca, with his own nephew, young Gutiérrez, which I think is a good idea, not to go alone, has been in the area. I believe I wrote to you that I had met him. I think I also mentioned that he has offered a thousand-dollar reward. I don't know if he's still around, but I haven't heard of anyone collecting it."

"I think he is still there. He said he would come back through here, but I have not heard anything of him." Rachel took a couple of steps before she spoke again. "So you have met them, and you have been in the area. You say you do not have any definite ideas, but I would imagine you have some."

Delaine looked around. The night was growing dark, but he could see for a short distance, and no one was near. "There is something curious I have heard about, and I don't know if it's related. There's a fellow in town who likes to talk in mysterious ways, or drop a comment about sinister goings-on, and he has hinted that there is some kind of a business out there somewhere that deals in women, maybe not under their own will."

"I have heard of those things, also not very specific."

"And just the other day, this fellow I work with, he and I saw a carriage, out there in the middle of the rangeland, that looked like it was transporting three women. I don't know how it could have any connection with this other case we're both familiar with, but I'm not forgetting about it."

Rachel shook her head. "That *is* curious, but it doesn't seem related. Don Tiburcio was sure of who took his daughter, and no one else seems to doubt it."

"That's how I see it," Delaine said. "Meanwhile, this fellow I work with, his name is Ed Hiller, is interested in Miguel Cuenca's reward. As you will remember, the last time there was a reward, no one collected it, and a fellow who was interested in it came to grief, so I try not to be very excited about that prospect."

"Which I think is a good idea."

"At the same time, I feel that I should do something if I could. But if I don't, and my friend does, it might help bring some justice for the two men who have died."

"Yet you don't have much of an idea of what you could do yourself."

"No, I don't. On one hand, both Tiburcio Martínez and Pedro Cuenca gave me the brush-off, and on the other, Miguel Cuenca is offering money, which I feel I need to resist. And my work over in that area is going to end before long." He paused. "I still feel I should do something if I could. I'll see."

"That's good of you," she said. "But there's no need to put yourself in danger if you don't have to." She had her arm in his, and she gave him a tug. "I want you to come back her, so we can play checkers by the fire on cold winter evenings."

She had told him before that she didn't play cards or dominoes or checkers very much, so he took it in a spirit of humor. "You always have good ideas," he said.

"If I don't keep an eye out for you, who will?"

"You're right," he said.

"Did you think about me when you saw the stars?"

"On some nights. On others, the sky was cloudy."

The stars were bright at the moment, and he took her in his arms.

———

On the way back to the rooming house, he realized he had forgotten to mention Stevens, the man who appreciated birds, and the puzzle of whether his death was related to the deaths of the men from Trinidad or to the fabled commerce of women. If it was still important when he saw Rachel again, which he hoped was before long, he could mention it.

12

DELAINE AND HILLER RETURNED TO SAYERS IN THE early afternoon. Delaine said that even though he was not expecting any mail, he should drop in at the post office, as he had told the clerk he would let him know when they had come in from roundup. Hiller said he would wait at The Lookout, where they could have one drink before they went on to the ranch.

Delaine tied up at the post office and went in. The clerk appeared at the window and shook his head before Delaine could ask a question. Delaine said, "I need to tell you, anyway, that we've come in from the range, and Percy will be at the ranch."

"I know," said the clerk. "Art Meredith came in day before yesterday and told me. He picked up the mail, then, too."

"I don't suppose there was any for me."

"As far as I recall, there hasn't been any mail addressed to you at the ranch."

"I wouldn't expect it."

"Art said you knew the fella they found dead at the train station."

Delaine felt as if he had been set back on his heels. "No better than a number of people, I guess. I talked to him a couple of times and knew who he was, and he came by the ranch."

"Art said he asked a lot of questions."

"He may have."

The clerk shook his head. "People don't like it when someone gets killed for no reason. It makes 'em worried. They lock their doors, buy ammunition." The clerk lifted his chin. "If I was you, I'd be wearin' a gun."

"It's in my saddlebag."

The clerk shrugged. "And two men have been killed out there where you work. I'd be lookin' over my shoulder."

"We all try to be careful, but we have work to do."

"Workin' today, or did you get off early?"

"We're on our way back to the ranch. We delivered some steers in Overton."

"That's what Art said. You're from Overton, aren't you? That's where your mail comes from."

"I might go back there when I'm done here."

"There's not much to do here in the winter, that's for sure."

Delaine nodded. "I'll be on my way. Thanks."

"You bet. Take care of yourself."

A haze hung in the sky as Delaine led the sorrel horse away from the rail and mounted up. He came to the main intersection with Pearl Street and looked both ways. Movement on the corner at his right caught his eye, and he saw the tall man with the dark hat, greying mustache, and tweed overcoat going into the bank.

Delaine rode on, turned to the hitching rail on the south side of the street, and swung down. He tied the horse, thought about the pistol in the saddlebag beneath his duffel bag, and stepped up onto the sidewalk. Maybe people in town were worried, but it was the middle of the day in the middle of the week, and the biggest thing going on was a couple of horses swishing flies.

He reflected that this was the time of year when wasps came indoors and gathered on the windowpanes near the light and warmth. Flies became lethargic, but they were up and about in the warm part of the day.

Delaine found Hiller at the bar by himself. He had put on a clean blue shirt and red neckerchief in Overton, and he was wearing his buckskin-colored wrist cuffs with blue and red beads. His hat sat back on his head, and he seemed to be in a light mood.

"Get everything taken care of?"

"Oh, yeah. That fellow in the post office is a busybody."

"Comes with working with the mail. There was a woman who worked the window in Kaycee who was as bad as any I met. They said her eyes were weak from trying to read through the envelopes."

"He said Art had been in a couple of days ago."

"Art's a busybody, too."

"I gathered that they had a conversation."

Delaine ordered a drink and was laying a quarter on the bar when an image in the mirror sent a faint jolt through him. He held the glass and stepped back as he took a drink so he could see the two men who had just passed behind him. They stopped at an open space at the bar and were ordering drinks.

The taller of the two men wore a broad-brimmed, light-colored hat and a sheepskin coat. He had straw-colored hair and a blocky face. The other one had a dark-brown hat and a coat of similar color that looked as if it had been waterproofed with oil or wax. He had dark hair, a pinched face, and a mustache.

Delaine stepped forward and spoke in a low voice. "Those two that just came in. They look like the two fellas who were driving that carriage the other day. The one with the three women."

Hiller stepped back, made a slow turn of the head, and came back to the bar. "It sure does. I would have thought they had gone on through."

"Maybe they're on their way back." Delaine wondered again whether the men had anything to do with the enterprise that Mardell alluded to. It seemed likely, but he did not want to fall into believing dark theories without more evidence. Delaine glanced around. "Do you ever talk to Mason Mardell?"

"No more than I have to. Why?"

"He talks about things like secret commerce, or the black market."

"Yeah, he'd like you to think he knows all about opium dens, steam baths, and harems. He says he's been in San Francisco and Sacramento. Maybe he carried towels." Hiller finished his drink and drummed his fingers on the bar.

"We'd better just have one," said Delaine.

"Yeah, you're right."

Delaine did not want to hurry, but he did not want to give Hiller time to weaken. He knocked off his drink with two swallows separated by a short interval, and he set his glass on the bar.

The two strangers were talking to one another and did not seem to take notice as Delaine and Hiller left.

Outside, they had no sooner mounted up and ridden into the middle of the street when a voice called to them from the veranda of the hotel.

"Hey, boys. You boys."

Delaine thought he recognized the accent and was not surprised to see Miguel Cuenca walk out of the shadows and into the sunlight at the top of the steps.

Delaine and Hiller rode across to meet him as he came down the steps. He was wearing his dark-brown hat and his brown wool overcoat with the fur ruff, and he had his suede gloves in his left hand. He looked up and spoke to them.

"Hey, you boys. I thought you were done and gone."

Hiller said, "We were rounding up steers."

"That's what I thought. You know, I haven't heard anything from anybody. My reward is still good. And I ask around every day."

Hiller said, "I'm still interested. If I find out anything, I'll sure tell you."

Cuenca moved his hat forward to cut the glare of the sun. "You do that."

"Is your nephew still with you?"

"Oh, yeah."

"That's good."

"Well, don't let me keep you. it's good to see you boys."

Delaine raised his hand in greeting, and Hiller said, "Good to see you, too. So long. Maybe we'll see you later." The two of them turned their horses, rode to the corner, and headed north out of town. As Delaine thought about the brief exchange, he could not escape the earlier sense he had that Miguel Cuenca had a vulnerable quality to him and might be susceptible to not living long.

———

A HORSE WAS TIED in front of the bunkhouse. As Delaine and Hiller stopped to leave off their bags before taking their horses on to the barn, they found Deputy Blackmur seated at the table drinking coffee with Percy. The deputy had a neat and clean appearance as always, and Percy had found the opportunity to shave and to put on a clean white work shirt. He had no doubt had a bath as well, as he had a scrubbed look about him, and the top of his head was shining.

"I was just about ready to leave," said the deputy.

Hiller said, "Finding anything new?"

The deputy shook his head. "It's not the only thing on my slate, and as a general rule, the more time that passes, the harder it is to get useful information. And then I have Mr. Cuenca getting in the way. I can't blame him, and in a way I admire his willingness to stick with it. Maybe one of these days he'll have enough and go back home, but I doubt that it'll change anything for me."

Percy said, "They say you find things when you least expect 'em."

"We've already had enough of that."

"Isn't that the truth?"

The deputy stood up and picked his hat off the table. "I had better be going. It'll be dark when I get back as it is."

"Take care," said Percy.

"I will. Thanks for the coffee."

As Delaine and Hiller unsaddled their horses in the barn, Delaine said, "I wonder if we should have told him about what we saw that morning, with those women and the two other men."

Hiller shrugged. "I doubt that it has anything to do with what he's looking for. Who knows if those two birds are even around anymore. Now that I think of it, I didn't notice what other horses were tied up outside, but there sure wasn't any carriage."

"I didn't notice, either. But you're right about the carriage. I didn't see one."

———

Percy did not ask how they had spent their time. He said, "Glad you boys made it back all right. I've got a little more work that I hope we can get in before the weather changes."

"What's that?" said Hiller.

"Well, you know, we have to go farther and farther for firewood, and I'd like to lay in a supply before we get a snowfall. I want you boys to take the wagon and go up to Brown's Creek." He glanced with his pale blue eyes at Delaine. "That's the one where we camped for antelope." Back to Hiller, he said, "You know, that creek winds around to the northwest. You go another half-mile or mile in that direction, and you should find enough to fill a wagon."

Hiller said, "Then we can expect to stay out overnight."

"I think so. Take two axes, a saw, and a sledgehammer. Sometimes you cut partway through, and you can break the rest. A hatchet, too, I suppose, but that's part of the regular camp gear. It don't think you'll need a tent for just one night, with all the work it takes to set it up and take it down, plus the room it takes up in the wagon, but if you want to run a canvas sheet down one side of the wagon like we did, that would be all right. Art will have some biscuits for you to take along, and you can fry some meat in camp so you can have somethin' warm. Coffee, too, of course. Don't want you to suffer."

Hiller said, "Do you want us to cut it all up first, or bring in lengths to cut up here?"

"The firewood? Cut it all up. You'll get quite a bit more in the wagon that way."

"What are you smiling about?"

"I was thinkin' of Pete McGrath. He had a bottle he nipped on, until it went dry. He thought I didn't know about it."

"We're not inclined to do something like that," said Hiller."

"I know. You're good boys."

———

DELAINE AND HILLER were up early to get the wagon ready. They took out the chuck box, put in a smaller camp box with grub, and selected the tools they would take. Delaine had his own camp hatchet. After breakfast, they put in their bedrolls and duffel bags, hitched the horses, and rolled out of the yard.

Frost began to melt as the sun rose. A horse from the pasture whinnied, and a cow lowed. Delaine followed the sound and located a brindle cow with curved horns and bony hips. It was not the one with the spotted calf. Delaine assumed it was one of the first to come in close for the winter.

Hiller rolled a cigarette and lit it as he handled the reins. He had left his wrist cuffs at home and was wearing a drab wool work shirt and his vest underneath his blanket-lined canvas coat. He stored his tobacco and papers in his vest pocket and buttoned the coat, then put on a pair of leather work gloves. The cigarette bobbed in his mouth as he puffed.

"I can't get over how much Art resents Pete McGrath. I wouldn't be surprised if he snitched to Percy about the whiskey bottle. Did you see the look on his face when Percy was talking about it?"

"No, I didn't."

"It looked as if he was stretching his face tight to keep from saying something."

"I hope he's pleased that we're going out to fetch firewood for them for the winter."

Hiller took his cigarette with his gloved hand. "The more I get to know Art, the more I think he's never pleased about anything. I know it's not good to talk about someone else you work with, but that's my impression." After a minute, he said, "So, do you think you'll go back to Overton for the winter? Do you have work there?"

"Last winter I worked in the stable. I could do it again. It's not all inside. There's work in the corrals, and breaking ice on the water troughs."

"It's work, anyway. And I guess you've got a girl there."

"I don't have a claim on anything, but I do have an acquaintance."

"That's all right. Makes it easier to put up with a lot of other things."

———

THEY HIT the creek and followed it northwest as Percy told them. The small creek bed was picked clean of firewood for quite a ways, as Delaine recalled from the time they had their camp.

Hiller said, "There aren't any ranch headquarters anywhere near, so there's still deadfall along here. At some point, there won't be, except what little dies each year. We'll have to go to the ridge and bring it down with horses. Either drag the logs and branches or cut up the wood and put it on packhorses. More work. And that old dead pine doesn't last long. Cedar is better, but not much of it dies."

When they began to see dead branches and trunks, Hiller said, "We'll drive on a ways more and drag it from both directions, then cut it up in a pile. None of this is that big."

Delaine could see for himself that most of the deadfall was six inches thick and smaller—good for stove lengths, and it didn't have to be split. The mountains were the place for thick pines and fir, large fireplaces, and screens to stop all the popping sparks.

A few trees in the creek bottom still had yellow leaves, but most of them had shed. Hiller parked the wagon in a sparse grove. "This looks like a good place," he said.

They unhitched the horses and put them on a picket line where they could graze. Then they went to work. They walked back to the farthest substantial fallen branches and began dragging. The sunlight came through the bare trees, and the air was not cold in late morning. On the second trip, as Hiller dragged a good-sized branch on each side, he began to sing.

Bringing in the sheaves,
Bringing in the sheaves,
We shall come rejoicing,
Bringing in the sheaves.

Delaine enjoyed the exertion. It was not exhausting, and it warmed him up after sitting on the wagon seat for a couple of hours.

They did not bother with cottonwood logs, which were soft and not good firewood to begin with. Most of them had fallen long ago and were decomposing. The men found one that was still solid and about eighteen inches thick, with the bark gone, and they used it for a sawhorse. One man sawed while the other held the piece steady. They broke thinner branches by hand, for kindling. A large pile of branches made a small stack of wood.

They sat on the cottonwood trunk in the sunshine and ate a lunch of cold beef and biscuits. Now and then a small bird chirped, but the area all around was calm and quiet.

Hiller said, "It's interesting to think that not too long ago, no one lived here. Indians passed through. It won't be long till it's all fenced in. I've heard that with bigger cities, they've got the land surveyed for miles around, already plotted on maps for streets and such."

"Better than no planning, I guess."

"Sure, but how would you like to have your little farm of corn and beans, knowin' that men in offices were schemin' to cut it up into little pieces?"

"Maybe it's better not to know, or to take up land as far away from a city as you can. As I've heard it more than once, there's only so much land in the world. It seems unlimited, but it's not. The way they make more land is to divide it up into pieces. There's still not more land, but there's more pieces of property."

"Until you get down to the smallest one."

"Well, yes," said Delaine. "And in the older places, they have to re-use the graves after a long time."

"Good reason not to live there, but you never know where you might end up when you get too old to work."

"I try not to think too much about it, but you see it. Old men who never got married or made provisions, and they've got no family or place to go. Like that old fellow we took the deer meat to. He said that if he knew he was going to live that long, he would have taken better care of himself. But he's got arthritis. You can't plan against that. At least he's still getting by."

"Old Hampton. Well, there's others worse off. Old men tell you, enjoy life while you're young, and they're right. But you'd better enjoy workin'."

"I try."

"So do I. I'm glad I didn't end up workin' in the coal mines." Hiller smiled. "But enough of that. Maybe we'll think of another song to sing. 'Clementine' is a good one for sawin' wood."

"We'll sing it." Delaine recalled that Clementine drowned, but he figured they would just sing that stanza when they got to it.

————

THE STACK of firewood grew through the afternoon, and they transferred it into the wagon. Hiller said, "Now we'll cut some for our own fire this evenin', and some for the mornin'. Don't burn up our day's work.

We don't have to cut the pieces so short, but we don't want to be prodigal."

"What church did you go to?"

"Methodist. Our preacher was a short little man with a round belly, but he drilled the lessons into you."

They cut a pile of one- and two-inch pieces for their cook fire and picked up a couple of broken, thicker end pieces they had tossed aside. After they fried their meat, they tossed on the bigger chunks of wood.

A large moon was rising in the sky. The full moon had passed a few nights earlier. Chilly air drew in, and Delaine was glad to have the fire. A canvas over their two beds and another overhead would be good.

———

DELAINE WOKE in the middle of the night, and he could not see the stars. He remembered that there was a canvas sheet above him. The tarpaulin that covered their beds seemed to sag on Hiller's side, and Delaine did not hear any breathing. He turned, and in the faint light, he saw that Hiller was not in his bed.

Delaine thought he might be watering the bushes or might have heard something with the horses. Delaine lay on his back and listened with his eyes open. The canvas overhead was thin enough to let a little of the moonlight through. A horse snuffled and shifted its feet.

After a long while, maybe twenty or thirty minutes, he became more restless and decided to get up and take a look. He tossed the covers aside and put on his hat, coat, and boots. He crawled out from the shelter and stood up. Again he heard the sound of a horse moving its feet and letting out a breath.

The moon was not as bright as it had been when it was straight up, but his eyes adjusted, and he could see his way to the place where they had tied the horses. As he approached, he saw that there was only one horse.

He imagined that one of two things happened. Either a horse had gotten away and Hiller had gone to look for it, or Hiller had left with a horse. If one had gotten loose and had not strayed far, Hiller might have gone after it little by little, trying to catch it as it ran off a ways each time, as horses liked to do. If, on the other hand, one had escaped and Hiller had decided to try to find it, he would have said something. Or he should have.

Delaine considered the other possibility, that Hiller had left on a horse. They had not brought along a saddle or a bridle, so he would have had to ride bareback with a halter. Both of the wagon horses were docile, so it was not out of the question.

If he did, the question was why. Delaine had known of men who would sneak off in the middle of the night, from a bunkhouse or from a camp, to go into town or to meet a woman somewhere. They might even sneak off to help spirit away cattle or horses, but that was more risky and less common. Hiller had just been to town—two of them—and although he liked to have a drink, he did not seem to be drawn there. Delaine had not seen any hints of his carrying on in secret with a woman, and he could not imagine how far a man would have to go from here to meet a woman who could slip away in the night. Hiller had not seemed to be interested in any woman in particular, but Delaine also knew that if a man had a bond with a woman who was unavailable—married or engaged—he could keep his secret buried.

Delaine knew there was no point in going out in the dark and trying to solve the puzzle. If Hiller was not back by daylight, he would go look. Resolved, he went back to bed.

He could not sleep, and he could not stay in one position for long. He was more restless than before. His arms and legs would not stay still.

He rolled out again, put on his hat and coat and boots, and went to the campfire that was almost died out. With a thin branch he uncovered some coals, then put on some twigs. He leaned close and blew, and when ashes rose in his face, he drew back and fanned with his hat until he brought up a flame. He put on more twigs and went to their work site to gather up small, thin branches.

Before long, he had a fire going. It would keep him warm, and it would help Hiller find his way back. Delaine decided he would ask no questions. If Hiller had been off on a clandestine visit, he would not have to say anything. If he was off on some other purpose, Delaine would listen with interest.

The fire burned down, and Delaine found more scraps. He did not want to use the supply they had left for the morning fire, and he could not think of digging into the neat stack they had put in the wagon. He kept a small fire going. Any light would be visible from quite a ways off.

The sky in the east began to show grey at last. Delaine found the saw and went to work cutting more fuel. The air was often coldest at sunrise, and the exertion helped him stay warm. The sun was close to rising when he had an armful to take to the fire.

The coals were beginning to ash over, so he stoked them and laid on a half-dozen pieces up to an inch thick. Using his hat again, he coaxed a blaze.

The sun rose, and the area around the camp took on a normal appearance. No birds or small animals stirred, but the horse snuffled. Delaine found one of the feed bags they had used the night before, and he gave the animal some grain.

Delaine was hungry, but he did not want to eat. He would wait until he saw that Hiller was all right, and they would both eat. He had a little bit of firewood left, and he decided he would save it until later.

Daylight was spreading. Delaine had the tired, empty feeling of having been up a long time and then adjusting to the new day. He considered going to work until Hiller returned, but something inside kept telling him he had to go look.

He thought of what he should take with him, and he remembered his gun and holster, still in his saddle-bag, back at the ranch. When men went out on a work detail such as this one, sometimes one of them thought to put a rifle and scabbard in the wagon, but he did not remember Hiller doing so, and he did not see one now. He had been so used to letting someone else take the lead on this job that he felt inept for a moment.

He shook off that feeling and told himself he needed to tend to business. Hiller was somewhere out there, and it was hard to guess where.

Delaine went back to the question of why, and a suggestion began to move, like a small animal under a cover of leaves. Cuenca's reward. Hiller may have thought he was in the vicinity of clues, or he may have picked up some information on his own.

Now the question was which way to go. Hiller had

said that they were not close to any ranches, but there could be line shacks and other hideouts. Delaine was not familiar with the surrounding country, but he had a sense that the Big Eight was somewhere to the west. For other reasons he couldn't pinpoint, perhaps Meredith's hand movement when he mentioned it, Delaine thought that the place where Brother Meredith worked was to the north.

Delaine had to decide whether to go on foot or to ride the remaining horse bareback with a halter. A man could cover much more ground on horseback, even without the help of a saddle and bridle. He looked at the horse, a stocky, dull brown animal, and decided to give it a try.

He led the horse to the wagon and used a wheel spoke to give himself a boost. He squeezed his heels without spurring the horse, and they moved out.

As the weather had dried off, there wasn't much to track, but a few dents in the fallen leaves suggested that a horse had gone out of the creek bed to the north. Delaine let the brown horse pick his way, and they went out onto the grassland.

A crying sound caused him to look up. A "V" of nine or ten geese on each side was flying south. They seemed closer than they were, for he could not see their feet. He had never hunted geese in a blind, but he had heard that a person had to be able to see their feet in order to make a good shot. If they were closer, he would hear their wings whistling, but all he heard was their lonely call.

He had to nudge the horse, but it did not resist. It plodded on, sometimes to the left and sometimes to the right, across the rolling grassland. The sun rose at Delaine's back, but he did not feel much warmth.

The brown horse nickered as they went over a crest. Down in a swale, another horse was grazing. Delaine recognized the bay horse with the dull black mane. It was taking one short step at a time, and the halter rope trailed on the grass. Delaine steeled himself for what he might find.

He rode around and came up on the horse's left side, leaned as far as he dared without a saddle, and caught the lead rope. Worry gnawed in the pit of his stomach, and his hand trembled. He realized his hands were cold, and he took the chance of holding the two halter ropes with one hand as he drew out his gloves and put them on. He felt a shivering across his shoulders.

The grass was short, and he thought that if a man was lying on the ground, he would not be hard to find.

Delaine rode in a widening circle and moved up the far side of the small basin. He did not see anything in the next depression. He recalled which way the bay horse had been facing, and he decided to go in the opposite direction.

A breeze from the west chilled him, and his eyes were tired. He had to pay attention in case either horse made a quick movement, as it was easy to slip off bare-back. His upper body was tense, and his legs felt ineffective, hanging off the sides of the horse.

A change in color tone appeared in the grass some three hundred yards away, first a patch and then something more identifiable, the wheat-colored fabric of a canvas coat. A brown hat lay on the ground not far away.

Delaine knew the coat, and he knew the hat. He felt as if he was recognizing something he had felt beneath the surface for a little while, back to the moment when he had found the bay horse, and, in a fainter way, before that.

He stopped a few yards away. Both horses nickered.

He focused on what he had to do. He could not do anything with two bareback horses. It would not be a good idea even to get down and then have to climb back on and hold them both. He would have to go back to camp and hitch them to the wagon by himself. Meanwhile, he would have to leave his working partner. Hiller, who had spent several long hours keeping another man's body company, was going to have to stay here alone for a while.

13

By the time he returned to the camp, he had a plan, or at least a sequence. This was no time to be weak. There were some things he had to decide and carry out on his own.

He grained the two horses while he picked up the camp. He had an uneasy, almost guilty feeling as he rolled up Hiller's bed, but he pushed himself past it. He stowed the bedrolls and duffel bags in the wagon, along with the folded canvases. After loading the cooking utensils and the tools, he hitched up the horses and put the picket rope and halters with the canvas. Out of habit, he looked around the campsite to see if anything was being left behind, and he relented to an idea he had been considering. He took from his bag the leather-handled steel hatchet that Dorn, the deer hunter, had given him. It was almost pristine. He had used it once, to peg out the canvas shelter. He tossed it onto the short, dry grass at the base of a box elder tree. He would remember where it was.

The sun was climbing in the sky as he drove out on

the grasslands to find the body. He located it once again by the tone of the canvas coat. The body was becoming rigid, and it was as difficult as the dead weight of the deer and antelope Delaine had handled, but he summoned his strength and got it onto the tailgate. He climbed aboard, dragged it into place, and covered it with a canvas. Now for the drive to town.

He had decided to bypass the ranch. For one thing, it was a detour of two miles each way, and if he struck a straight line, he could make up for the slow travel of the wagon. It did not have a very heavy load, anyway. For another reason, he did not want to deal with Meredith. He did not think that Meredith had anything to do with what happened to Hiller, but he did not want to witness the man's lack of feeling or his pretended sympathy. Delaine was not so reluctant to deliver the news to Percy, and he thought it would be more difficult later to tell him he had gone around him, but he wanted to talk to the deputy by himself.

————

THE SUN HAD CROSSED over into late afternoon when he came to the main intersection in town. He stopped at the small office where Deputy Blackmur worked, and he was glad to see a lamplight inside.

The deputy paid attention and did not show much response as Delaine gave him the news and told the story. At the end, he said, "You might as well pull around in back of the barbershop, and we'll come back here to talk some more." He rose from his desk and took his hat from a peg.

Delaine felt a new pang of regret as he turned the

canvas to one side. He braced himself and helped carry the body into the back room.

"No blood," said the deputy. "I don't see where a bullet went in or came out. All of that can be determined by the coroner. For the present, I would say that those marks on the throat look as if he was strangled by a cord."

Delaine gave a hard swallow. "I have no idea. Even if someone had fired a shot, it was a long ways from our camp, and I could have been asleep."

"Let's go to my office."

Across the desk from the deputy, with his hat on his knee, Delaine told the story again, beginning from the time that they went out with the wagon.

"Just to be clear," said the deputy, "the two of you went out, and Percy Calvin and Art Meredith stayed at the ranch."

"As far as I know."

"And from the descriptions you've given me of where you were working and where you found the body, there's no other ranch nearby."

"Not that I know of, and that's what Ed Hiller told me, as well.

"So let's go through what you told me before about anyone who gave you trouble out there."

Delaine had to take a breath to steady himself and stay focused. "The main ones have been the Big Eight riders. Three of them. They came by the antelope camp not far from where we just were. I was there with an antelope hunter. They complained about trespassers and hunters and city people."

"Did they threaten you?"

"No, it was more just like throwing their weight around, or as Percy says, being pushy."

"And you saw them again?"

"The second time, they came by when Ed and I and two hunters had a couple of deer on the ground. They went through some of the same complaints about hunters shooting. One of them got off his horse and kind of threatened one of the deer hunters who talked back, but the hunter threatened him with a lawyer, and he drew his horns in."

"No one hit anyone."

"No. Their leader, who I think is named Mitchell, helped them save face, and they rode away."

"Did you see them again?"

"Yes. The same three came to our roundup camp. Same method. They stayed on their horses and looked down on us in their bullying way, and they said they wanted to look over our stock. Percy told them to go ahead, so they inspected the horse herd and the beef herd, and they went away."

"No flare-ups."

"No. The closest it ever came to that was with the deer hunters. The Big Eight riders exchanged a few words with Ed Hiller on that occasion, but nothing heated. The sharpest it got was with the deer hunter, and all he did was threaten them with legal action, and he's long gone now. Back in Chicago."

The deputy nodded. "Anyone else out there?"

Delaine raised his eyebrows. "There's the matter of Art Meredith's brother. I think his name is Ben."

The deputy gave a matter-of-fact expression and a slight nod. "Ben Meredith."

"He and a pal of his dropped by our first camp. No conflict or anything. Then I've seen him in town a couple of times, and he seems to have taken a dislike to me. He picked a fight with me on one occasion and knocked me down, and another time, he shoved me."

"But nothing with Ed Hiller."

"No. I never sensed any tension between them at all. The closest Ed came to that was by asking Art where his brother worked. And it was a vague answer."

"I don't have a clear idea of where he works, either. Is there anything else you can think of?"

"Well, yes. Ed told me more than once that he was interested in Miguel Cuenca's reward. If I had to guess why he left our camp in the middle of the night, I would say it was for that. To see if he could find out anything about how either of those other two men were killed."

The deputy moved his head back and forth. "This has been more trouble than it should be. I don't want to blame Miguel Cuenca, but it may have gotten another man killed. And it seems to me that I run up against a wall any time I try to find out about those other two. Or maybe I should say I end up lookin' at wide, empty spaces."

A thought crossed Delaine's mind. "Do you think any of this has anything to do with the death of that fellow Stevens, who said he was studying birds?"

The deputy shook his head. "I've thought of it, of course, and I can't make it fit. And that's what I don't want to do, try to make something fit. I haven't been able to turn up any reason why anyone would want to do something to him." The deputy folded his hands on the desk. "Anything else?"

"Just this. One morning, early, when Ed Hiller and I were riding out to round up steers, we saw a carriage out in the middle of the rangeland. It stopped long enough for three women to get out and then get back in. But we saw it from a distance, and I don't think anyone saw us. There were two men driving, and we were pretty sure we saw them again, later, here in town. But again, they didn't pay us any attention."

"People come through here all the time. And you say you didn't have any interaction with them."

"Not at all."

The deputy stared past Delaine and came back to him. "I gather that you worked with Ed Hiller and got to know him to some degree. Did he ever say anything about having a grudge with anyone?"

"Not at all."

"How about the other two men you work with—your boss Percy, and Art Meredith?"

"Percy gets along with everyone. Art Meredith is a little more of a sarcastic sort, and Ed might have been skeptical of him, but they worked together and got along well."

"I have to consider everything. How about yourself? Did you and Ed ever have a falling out about anything?"

"Me? No, never."

"Sometimes two men go out on a work camp, maybe they get to drinkin' too much, and one of them says something or does something."

"Not at all. We didn't have a drop. Everything was cheerful." Delaine paused. "I don't want to speculate on how I would have done things if I *had* done it, but I don't think I would have gone to all the trouble of bringing him in. I think I would have reported him missing."

"Sometimes people do what they think is least expected of them. But I have to consider everything."

"I understand."

"Are you going back to the ranch now?"

"I might stop to have a drink. I could use one now."

"I can understand that. I don't know how soon I can do this, but I'll need to go out to the ranch, talk to the other two men there, and have you go out and show me where you found the body."

"I don't know how much more work Percy has for me, but if he lets me go, I'll be sure to tell you."

"Thanks. And thanks for your help on this. I know it's not easy." The deputy paused. "As you know, I'm working on more than one thing. I'll get out there as soon as I can."

———

DUSK WAS BEGINNING to draw in when Delaine left the wagon on the street and made his way into The Lookout.

The evening was young, and only a couple of other patrons stood at the bar. Delaine found a place by himself and ordered a drink. In the painting above the mirrors, the two frontiersmen continued to look out over the plain.

The bartender served him and said, "Sorry to hear about your friend. It's got people worried more than before."

"Thanks," said Delaine. He set a quarter on the bar and divided his attention between the mirror in front and the entry door on his left.

Movement in the mirror caused him to turn to his right. The woman named Lenore was dressed for an evening's work but had a subdued expression on her face.

"I was sorry to hear about Ed," she said. "I'm glad to see that you're all right."

"Such as it is. I can't say it's good for the nerves, but I'm not the only one who matters. Things like this are more important than one bystander."

"This, and the other things that have happened, have a lot of people worried."

"With good reason." He lowered his voice. "You seem like a good girl to me, and I don't want to put you in an uncomfortable position, but I wonder if you can tell me who knows things around this town."

Her green eyes were calm. "By that I imagine you mean things that other people don't know. Even at that, I doubt that you'll find out here in town what happened to your friend way out in the country."

He considered how to answer. "I don't expect to. But I've decided that I need to know more than I do, if only for my own self-protection."

"I don't blame you."

He realized he had decided to do something, to take some action on his own, to look beneath the surfaces, as he had heard of people going underground in a more literal way, in the network of sewers beneath the streets of Paris. He thought there might be a lower, darker level of knowledge in this small town. He even had a hunch where, but this was his first chance to ask.

"Where is the underground here?"

Her eyes opened wide. "Do you mean like the Underground Railroad, during slavery?"

"There may be something like that, too. But I mean underground information."

In an even lower voice, she said, "If it's dirty, and secret, and shameful, it could be with Mason Mardell.

Some people might say he has no shame, but I think everyone has some."

"I thought of him. He's not in here yet, and I need to head back to the ranch. Do you know where I can find him?"

"He rents a room."

"Do you know where?"

"From the tanner."

"The tanner and the taxidermist?"

"That's right." Lenore pointed toward the west. "Go to the next cross street and turn left."

"I know where it is."

"His place is in the back." Lenore gave Delaine a confidential look. "He knows things. But if it's anything valuable, he doesn't give it out for free. Be prepared to have something in exchange."

"A bottle? Money?"

She smiled. "One and then the other, I would expect."

"Thank you very much."

"You're welcome, and good luck. I would say to think about me every now and then, but I can tell you've got more serious things on your mind."

"I'll remember you for being helpful." He wondered if he should give her money, but he thought that for the moment, she was above that.

———

WITH A PINT BOTTLE of whiskey wrapped in newspaper and tucked inside his coat, Delaine walked the distance to the tanner and taxidermist's shop. From the light inside, it looked as if Olejnik was at work. Delaine went around back and found an addition that had been built onto the building. A dull light showed through a small window high on the wall. Delaine knocked on the door.

A crack of light appeared, and the door opened wider. Mason Mardell said, "It's you. What do you want?"

"Just come to visit," said Delaine.

Mardell's large brown eyes showed little expression, and his sallow face was motionless. "Come on in." As he stepped aside and Delaine passed into the room, Mardell said, "No one comes by just for a visit."

The room was dim and dingy, about twelve feet by twelve. On one side, a couch with a worn cloth covering had a jumble of blankets and a pillow piled at one end. On the other side, beneath the small window, two plain wooden chairs sat next to a table where a clay ashtray sat next to an oil lamp. A stale odor of cigarette smoke hung in the air.

Mardell was dressed as always, in his shabby brown suit, unclean white shirt, and worn shoes. His unwashed hair lay in flat strands across his broad skull. He motioned with his hand and said, "We can sit at the table." As Delaine turned in that direction, Mardell said, "I heard about Hiller. Too bad."

Delaine took a seat and faced Mardell. "News travels fast."

"I was out." Mardell turned to one side and coughed. Turning back, he gave a small rotation of his head and jutted his chin forward. "Is that what you came to talk about?"

"Not in itself." Delaine drew out the package, unwrapped it, and set the pint bottle on the table. To match Mardell's cynicism, he said, "A token of my esteem."

"Never turn it down." Mardell reached across the table where it touched the wall, and he moved two filmy tumblers toward him. He set them right side up, and with no further words, he uncapped the bottle and poured two drinks. He sipped from his own, rolled a cigarette, and lit it. "Go ahead," he said.

"I'm looking for knowledge."

Mardell shrugged his uneven shoulders. "Everyone's looking for something."

Delaine tasted his whiskey. "I want to go back to this older hard-shelled fellow who came from Trinidad, Colorado, to look for his daughter. I'd like to know why someone would stop him. I can understand why they would want to stop someone else from finding out who did him in, and here I might be talking about his soft nephew and my working partner, Ed Hiller. I'm sure you know Miguel Cuenca has been offering a reward, and as you may know, Ed Hiller was interested in it."

Mardell tipped his head to each side.

Delaine thought of how to present his question in a different way. "One thing that is not apparent to me is why Tiburcio Martínez, the first one, was out there in that country, looking. Why he didn't stay on the main trail."

"Maybe he thought he had knowledge."

"I'll tell you something I told the deputy but I've not made a point of telling everyone I talk to. I met this man Tiburcio Martínez in Overton before I came here, and he didn't seem to have any knowledge of this area or why he would look out there."

"Maybe he acquired that knowledge."

Delaine thought Mardell might be mocking him for the use of the word to begin with. "Then I suppose I would like to know how he did that."

"Maybe he did what other people do when they want something."

"Which is?"

"Maybe he paid a small amount."

Delaine had a moment of illumination, an imagined scene in which Don Tiburcio talked to Mason Mardell. "How much is a small amount?"

"Some people would say five dollars."

Delaine put a five-dollar gold piece on the table. Mardell lifted an eyebrow but seemed to consider it a matter of dignity not to lay his hand on the coin.

"How did he know where to look?"

Mardell drank from his glass. "I know of a place where a dark girl was being held. Way north of town."

"Was it his daughter?"

"Puh. I never went out and asked. I just know there was a girl there, and that was what he was looking for."

Delaine considered what he thought he knew so far. He could imagine Don Tiburcio thinking he had some command, paying good money for information from a tawdry source. "Would it be reasonable for me to think that his nephew acquired information in the same way, for a small amount?"

"It might be."

Delaine felt as if the breath had gone out of him. On one hand, five dollars was a large amount of money, more than three days' wages, but compared to a man's life, it was a pittance. He said, "This strikes me as something the deputy should have been told about."

"He never asked me." Mardell rose in his seat. "People come to me, not the other way around. If I make a habit of going to the law every time I know something, I'm not going to last long."

"What about Miguel Cuenca, the one who's in town now? He's offering a hell of a reward."

"That's a hard one. Very tempting. But I'm waiting for him to come to me." Mardell wagged his head. "I thought he would have, before now. I could do a lot with that money. Get out of this hole. But I've got to be alive to do it."

Delaine went back to the sequence he had in mind. "What about this fellow named Stevens? The one who said he studied birds. You knew him. did he acquire knowledge that way, too?"

"For a small amount. I think he was some kind of a detective, but it doesn't matter very much to me. He was looking for something else, not the girl from New Mexico."

"Colorado."

"Right. Anyway, he was interested in an operation of men using women."

"Something like you mentioned to me."

"If I did, it was only in a general way." Mardell finished the whiskey in his glass. "He might have been working for another girl's family, a white girl."

"Don't be shy with that," said Delaine, waving at the bottle. "There's more where it came from."

Mardell poured himself another drink.

Delaine said, "Ed Hiller and I saw an interesting thing out on the rangeland one morning. It was a carriage transporting three women."

"Don't know anything about that in particular."

Delaine made himself stay on track. "That brings me to Ed Hiller. It seems to me that he may have known where to look—that is to say, where the two men from Trinidad knew to look."

"He may have."

"For a small amount?"

"That very well could be."

Delaine sank in his chair. Hiller hadn't quite lied to him, but he had kept things to himself and might have thought he was a little sharper than the two men from Colorado. Delaine sat up. "Can you tell me where this dark girl is being held?"

Mardell shifted his chin to one side, lifted his thin eyebrows, and stared at the table where the gold coin had been.

Delaine had not seen him take it, but he understood. He reached into his pocket and put another half-eagle on the table.

Mardell did not look at the coin. He said, "I can tell you where she was. I can't guarantee she's still there. And the information didn't do those others any good. This is all at your own risk."

"I'm well aware of that."

Mardell tipped the ash of his cigarette and took a drag. "You go out north of town about fifteen miles. It's about five miles out to the turn that goes to your place. A little more than five miles past that, and to the west, is the Big Eight. You keep going straight until you come to the breaks."

"I think I know where that is. We curved around to the east along those breaks when we were on roundup."

"Well, you go the other way, west. You come to an open area, and then another set of breaks. There's a line camp there, at the foot of those breaks. It's the only one out there for miles."

"And that's where this dark girl is, or was."

"There's no need to repeat it."

"Do you think someone might have taken her, put her young champion out of the way, and—"

"I have no idea. I just had it on good authority that there was someone of that nature being held out there."

Delaine took a drink of whiskey. "Then I suppose that's all there is to know at this point."

"I think you're right." Mardell smiled. The second gold piece was still sitting in plain sight.

Delaine thought the man was quite sure of himself. Maybe he had good reason. "So long, then," he said. He rose from his chair.

Mardell stood up and brushed off the front of his coat. He followed Delaine to the door and closed it behind him.

———

THE RANCH HOUSE WAS DARK, but a light showed in the bunkhouse window. Delaine stopped the wagon in front of the door, and light poured out as Percy stood in the doorway.

"It's late," he said. "Where's Ed?"

"I had to leave him in town."

"What happened? Is he hurt?"

"Worse than that."

"Is he dead?"

"I'm afraid so."

"What happened?"

Delaine walked inside, and Percy closed the door. Delaine summoned a breath and said, "I'm not sure. We worked through the day, had camp at night, and turned in. At some time in the middle of the night, I woke up, and Ed was gone. So was one of the horses. I didn't know if one got away and he went after it, or if he snuck away on one. I went back to bed, but I couldn't sleep, so I stayed up by the fire. When it was light enough, I went out to look for him. I found him out in the middle of the rangeland, face down."

"Dead."

"Yes. So I went back to camp, packed up everything, hitched the horses, and went out and picked him up. Then I took him to town."

"Why didn't you come by here?"

"I made a beeline. I thought it would save time."

"You should have come by here."

"I thought of it."

"Well, you should have. It's my wagon, my horses. You both work for me. I should know about something like this right away."

"I know." Delaine glanced around. "Where's Art?"

"He went to town. He said you two fellas had a holiday, so he asked for one."

"When did he go?"

"Today at noon. Seems like a long time ago, but that's when it was. You didn't see him?"

"He would have been way ahead of me. But I didn't see him in town."

"I think there might be a woman he lays up with."

Delaine allowed himself to be pleased with the thought that it wasn't Lenore, as she was out and about. "I guess he'll hear the news about Ed. It would be unusual if he came back and didn't know."

Percy gave Delaine a close look. "I think he went where he said he was goin'."

"I have no reason to doubt it. Meanwhile, I reported this with the deputy. He said he'll come out here as soon as he can, but he has a lot of things on his hands."

"I would guess he does."

"I told him I didn't know how much more work you had for me."

"I don't either, at the moment. This is a hell of a mess. Ed was a good hand. I don't know what he would have been doin', out there sneakin' around, if that's what he was doin'."

"It's had me puzzled. The only thing I can think of is that he was looking for evidence. You know, he was pretty interested in that reward that Miguel Cuenca is offering."

"Son of a bee. All those Mexicans are more trouble than they're worth. Did he say something to you about it?"

"Not when we were out there. But he did earlier."

"There's been nothin' but trouble since that first one came out here. You wonder if it was all caused by some young blade stealin' a girl."

"I don't know."

"And I don't suppose you got all that much firewood."

"Less than half of what we expected, I'd say. But I brought what we had."

"Well, I don't want you going out there to stay on your own. We'll wait till Art comes back and see what it looks like."

"I need to go out there on my own, anyway, but I can go on horseback."

"What for?" Percy frowned as he peered at Delaine with his pale blue eyes.

"I left my hatchet out there. Real nice one that George Dorn gave to me. I used it to drive some stakes to hold down the canvas, and later on, in the flurry of everything, I left it there."

Percy set his mouth in an expression of displeasure. "That seems like a stupid little thing."

"It was stupid on my part, I admit, but my head was spinning. I can ride out and get it tomorrow. Maybe Art will come back by the time I do."

"By God, be careful."

"I will. You can bet I will."

————

DELAINE SADDLED the dun horse and set out not long after sunrise. He thought the grey horse would be better for an errand like this, but the dun would be less visible at a distance.

He found his hatchet where he left it. He put it in his sadddlebag and went on his way. His gun rode on his hip, and as long as the weather was not cold, he left his coat open. He had thought about bringing his rifle, but he thought it would be extra weight for the dun.

After leaving the campsite, he veered northeast. His thought was to reach the breaks where he and Hiller had worked them for cattle, then circle around to the north. The most obvious way to approach the line shack would be from the south, and he imagined that was what one or more of the other men had done. He was not going to march up to the front door or do anything like it. Taking the long way around would require more time coming and going, but he told himself he could not worry now about what time he got back to the bunkhouse.

He went up through the breaks and found a trail that took him out and up on top. The sky above was hazy. From the bench land, the vast country spread away for miles and miles to the south. He rode to the west, crossed the gap that Mardell had spoken of, and climbed the high ground above the next set of breaks. After a mile or so, he saw a spot out on the plain. He stopped, dismounted, and took out the binoculars that he had transferred from Hiller's duffel bag to his own saddlebag.

Through the glasses, the object looked like the roof of a shack. Thin lines suggested a corral. He put the binoculars away and searched for a path down through the breaks.

Cow trails in country like this were not much wider than game trails, and at times, the slope fell away at a steep angle on one side. Delaine took it slow on the dun horse, dismounting for the last descent and digging his heels into the mixed dirt and gravel that had washed down in the continual erosion of gashes such as these.

He came to the mouth of the canyon and gazed out onto the plain. The grass was thin and dotted with sagebrush, prickly pear, and small, sand-colored rocks. The line shack was about a half-mile away. Delaine stood at the edge of a clay wall with the dun horse behind him. He took out the binoculars, focused them, and watched.

Two horses stood in the corral. A thread of smoke rose from the stovepipe. The door to the shack, which he saw at a narrow angle, faced east. Behind the shack was an outhouse he had not seen from farther away.

Delaine watched through the binoculars, relaxed, and peered again. At last, a figure came out of the shack. It was a man with a light-colored hat, blondish hair, and tan and dust-colored clothing. Delaine did not recognize him. The man stretched, leaned one way and another, and loitered.

A second man came out and stopped to talk. He had a brown hat, brown hair, a dark blue shirt, and denim pants. He squared his shoulders and appeared to be rolling a cigarette, then tipped his head back and blew away a small cloud of smoke. He shifted in a swaggering pose. Delaine adjusted the binoculars a little finer and saw the man's face. Delaine's pulse jumped. It was Brother Ben Meredith. The other man was his pal, Crawford.

Delaine thought of the danger of the sun reflecting off the lenses of the binoculars, so he took off his hat to shade the area in front. He found a posture in which he could lean against the earthen wall, brace his elbows, hold his hat and the field glasses, and observe the shack.

His pulse ticked again when a dark-haired person came out. It was a woman, in a dark dress, with long hair and no scarf or hat. She walked past the two men and went into the outhouse.

Delaine did not know if the person he had seen was Guillermina, or Minita, as Pedro Cuenca had called her. He did not know the name of the outfit that Ben Meredith and his pal worked for. He did not know if they were holding this woman or girl against her will or if they had anything to do with the deaths that had taken place out in this broad country. What he saw was distant and detached, and what he knew was imperfect. He was a long ways from anywhere. He had decided to do something, and he had come this far. If there was a way he could do it, he would talk to that girl.

14

DELAINE WAITED IN THE BREAKS THROUGH THE LATTER part of the afternoon. He took the dun horse farther back in and came to the edge from time to time to look through the binoculars. Nothing stirred. He did not think the men in the shack had seen him, or they would have made a move. With two against one, this far from anything else, they would have a good chance. He had a strong hunch that they had done in two if not three men already.

When he was not at his post observing, he was back in a small grassy area, reviewing over and over how he had come down from the top and how he would ride out if he had to. He told himself he had to avoid making mistakes others had made, although he did not know what those were. He wondered if Stevens had ever come out this far and whether he was indeed a detective and just an amateur observer of birds. It occurred to him that he himself could be called an amateur detective.

Clouds appeared to be forming in the west, but he

could not see the horizon very well from his vantage point. He kept his coat buttoned, and when he was farther in, he walked back and forth to stay warm. He tied the horse to a leafless chokecherry bush that grew where the walls narrowed.

In the late afternoon, Ben Meredith came out of the shack. He took a sorrel horse out of the corral, saddled it, and rode away all with no sign of hurry. Delaine recalled the two times he had seen Meredith in town by himself. Maybe he was going for supplies. Delaine did not like to speculate how two men would spend their time with a woman this far from everything else, but he imagined it was not without whiskey.

The sun went down and cast long shadows on the land. Delaine thought his one chance to talk to the woman would be when she went to the outhouse after dark. He had not seen her again all afternoon, and there was always the chance that she would come out before he could make his approach under the cover of night. In that case, he would have to ride back to the ranch and think about what he would do next. Percy would ask him why he had been gone so long. He would answer that question when he got there, depending on whether he had learned anything new and whether Art Meredith was present.

Nervousness set in. He had not eaten since morning, and his stomach felt hollow. His fingers shook. He had kept his spurs on all this time in case he had to push the horse hard in order to climb out of the canyon in a hurry. Now as the light faded, he took off his spurs and put them in the saddlebag, on the other side from the binoculars. After one last pat on the horse's hip, he set out.

The shack did not have a window on the north

side, so he could not see a light. The outhouse was northwest of the shack, so if someone came out, he could expect to see light from the doorway and movement away from the light. He kept his eyes on the shack as he walked across the open distance. The corral was on the east side of the shack, and he headed for the other side, hoping to stay away from the remaining horse. A snuffle would not mean much to the man inside, but a whinny might.

Delaine knelt in a spot where he thought he would not be seen by someone who came out. The moon was waning, and a thin cloud cover had formed. He hoped above all that Crawford did not come out to use the outhouse.

At about an hour after nightfall, the scrape of the cabin door was accompanied by a dim flood of light. The door closed. A person was approaching. Delaine thought he saw a female form and smooth, female movement. He heard the soft clearing of a throat. His heart was pounding, and his mouth was dry. His hands were shaking as he pushed himself to a standing position and moved so that he could see her shadowy form. He rubbed his hands on his coat, and in a low voice, he spoke the line he had rehearsed.

"¿Eres tú, Minita?" Is that you, Minita?

"No, soy Rosa Linda." No, I am Rosa Linda.

He had to regroup. He had considered the possibility that it was someone other than Guillermina, but he did not have a set of phrases ready.

Her voice came again. *"Quién eres?"* Who are you?

"Una persona que viene para ayudarte. Si quieres ayuda." A person who comes to help you. If you want help.

He wondered if he had taken too much of a liberty, addressing her as *tú* rather than *usted*, but she was young, and she had answered on the same informal level.

"*Dime,*" she said, in two soft syllables. Tell me.

"*¿Dónde está el hombre?*" Where is the man?

"*Adentro, dormido. Está tomado.*" Inside, asleep. He's had something to drink.

"Very well," he said, still in Spanish. "Tell me what you want me to know."

Her Spanish was clear and easy to follow. "Are you looking for someone named Minita?"

"What I am looking for is information, about others who were looking for a person with that name."

"I do not know anything about that."

"Then tell me how you come to be here."

Her pronunciation and inflection were familiar to him, and clear, not the slurred or clipped Spanish he had heard in some places.

"I did not think anyone had been looking for me. I have been gone from home for more than two years, when I was sixteen. In Albuquerque. I learned to work on the streets. And they took me, they made me work for them."

"These men?"

"No, others. They have taken me from one place to another, and handled me, and used me as a servant in places that were no more than mining camps, rude men, one after another."

"I am sorry."

"You may think I have no shame, telling you this, but if someone is going to help me, I cannot lose time, and I cannot act like a princess. I have to tell the truth. I have lived in places where a woman wrote '*Soy puta*' on the mirror with lipstick. Perhaps you know of those places."

"I have seen some things."

"They have taken me farther and farther away from Albuquerque. I think we are in Wyoming now."

"That's true. How did you get here, to this place?"

"Two other men took me to a ranch, and then these two took me here, to hide out until they brought others."

"How long have you been here?"

"I don't know. I have lost count of the days. Maybe a month."

"And no one has been looking for you?"

"I don't think so. I think my family has forgotten me. I was the bad one. The black sheep, the dark grain in the rice."

"Do these men keep you like a prisoner?"

"Something like that. To begin with, there was a promise of money, but never very much did I see. We are told that we work for our food and our room, and we see very little else."

"Do they hold you here against your will?"

"In that style. There is always at least one of them here. They do not tie me up, but they tell me that if I leave, I will be at the mercy of the weather, wild animals, Indians, and other dirty men who go about in these parts."

"And they are waiting to transport you with some others?"

"So they say. They move by night. They go from one place to another, and they wait until it is clear."

"Do you know where you are going next?"

"I think they are going to take us to a place that is like the mining camps but might be a woodcutter or lumber camp."

"And there is nothing you can do about it?"

"One learns not to resist. And they say we are getting paid. I have not been given a nickel here, and these two brutes have used me as they have pleased. Maybe in the next place, they will pay us a little."

Much of what she said was in a rush, and now she paused.

He asked, "Do you know of any men who have come out this way looking for someone else?"

"Not for sure. I understand English well enough, and I have heard these two make a comment about someone else not making any more trouble, but nothing in detail."

Delaine took a deep breath. He did not feel as shaky as before, but he had a clear sense that Crawford could stumble out of the shack at any moment, and there was no telling when Ben Meredith would return.

"Tell me," he said, still in Spanish. "Do you want to get out?"

"It would be worth the trouble," she said, which he understood to mean worth the effort. "But I don't know how I could leave now."

"Neither do I." Delaine could not imagine the dun horse carrying them both all the way back to town, and there was always the possibility of meeting up with Ben Meredith. "I will see what I can do, if I can find help."

"What is your name?"

"It is better that I not tell you. If they become suspicious, they could force it out of you. If I return, you'll know me."

"Oh, yes."

"Until later, then."

"Until later."

———

DELAINE STAYED on the main trail all the way back to the ranch, but he was alert for hoofbeats, and he was ready to turn off at any minute.

He went through the whole situation in his mind several times. It all fit together. It all made sense. Now that he knew that there was a girl being held by Meredith and Crawford and it was not Guillermina Martínez, it was as if, on some level, he had known it all along. The same went for the man who said he studied plovers, blue jays, and sandhill cranes. He was on the lookout for one of the women in the carriage. Mardell knew plenty all along, thought it was not clear how much. He did not go to Miguel Cuenca because he was sure Cuenca would go straight to the law, but at the same time, he thought Cuenca would know to come to him, as his relations had done, and Mardell was confident that he could do things his way. What was it that Lenore had said of him? If it was dirty, secret, or shameful, Mardell knew it. She was right. Delaine had known that kind of man before, who did not seem to have a guiding principle according to what was right or wrong. What others did was all the same to him. What mattered was what he could get out of it. That kind of person had an ingrained aversion to the law, yet he had given, or sold, information to Delaine that might crack things open.

No light was visible in either the ranch house or the bunkhouse when Delaine rode into the yard. He dismounted and led the dun horse into the barn, where he lit a lantern, took off the bridle and hung it on the saddle horn, and tied the horse with a halter. He pulled off the saddle and blankets all together, flipped the cinches across the seat, and laid the double blanket damp side up to air out on top of the saddle when he set it on the rack.

A narrow object poked him in the back on the right side. A voice in his ear said, "Take it slow," and a hand reached under his coat and pulled his pistol from its holster.

He was sure it was Art Meredith, maybe an inch shorter than himself, with his hands now full, with his own gun in his left hand and Delaine's in his right.

Delaine saw the field hoe leaning against the wall, five feet away. It was his one chance. He lifted his left elbow and drove back with it, hitting the man on the chin. As he did so, he lunged forward and to his left, laid both hands on the handle of the hoe, and brought it up and around. He hit the man on the side of the head with the heaviest part of the hoe, where the thick handle went through the iron shank. The man dropped, and the two guns fell on the floor where bits of straw littered the hard-packed dirt. The man's hat had spilled aside.

Delaine lifted the lantern from the nail, took a couple of steps, and leaned forward. With the good light, he saw for sure that the man was Art Meredith.

He knelt by the body, set the lantern on the ground, and felt for a pulse. There was none. He felt again to be sure, on the wrist and on the neck. The man was done.

Delaine recovered his own pistol and stood up to think. He had ridden in with the idea of going to town in the morning, after seeing whether Meredith had returned and, if so, what indications he gave. Things had moved forward, and fast. The idea of spending the night in the bunkhouse was impossible now.

Delaine decided to leave Meredith where he was, catch a fresh horse, and ride into town.

———

THE NIGHT CLERK in the hotel said that Deputy Blackmur had turned in for the night and did not like to be disturbed unless it was an emergency. Delaine said he thought he could wait until the morning, and he asked for a room for himself. After he signed in, he glanced around the lobby until he saw a newspaper on a small table next to a chair in the sitting area. He asked the clerk if he could take the newspaper, and the clerk said it would be all right.

Delaine went up the stairs and found his room. Once inside with the lamp lit, he locked the door and put the key on the dresser. He looked out the window and saw no way that someone could get in. Trying to make as little noise as possible, he took the sheets from the newspaper, crumpled them one by one, and scattered them on the floor between the door and the bed. He put his pistol on the nightstand, undressed, and blew out the light.

The night darkened as he lay in bed, trying to sleep. No sounds came from the street or from other parts of the hotel. He was hungry and worn out and wound up tight. He needed to rest, to sleep. A thousand images came to him, including Ben Meredith riding away in the broad afternoon, the dark girl speaking to him in the night, and Art Meredith lying on the dirt floor in the light of the lantern.

He drifted in and out of sleep. In one scene, he was telling the girl about having to do what he did to Art Meredith. He returned to a waking state, in the dark.

He did not remember the words he used in telling her, but he had a clear sense of the common phrase she had used in response. *Así son las cosas.* That's the way things are.

———

DELAINE HAD DRESSED and was washing his face when a knocking came at his door, followed by the voice of Deputy Blackmur announcing himself.

Delaine located the key, unlocked the door, and opened it. "Come in," he said.

The deputy took off his hat as he walked inside. "I understand you wanted to talk to me, so I decided to come up before I started my day."

Delaine closed the door and left the key in the lock. He met the deputy's dark-brown eyes and said, "I have a possible crime to report. Would you like to sit down?"

The room had two chairs. The deputy took one, and Delaine took the other, setting it less than four feet away so he could keep his voice down.

The deputy had his face set in a firm expression and his eyes fixed on Delaine. "Tell me about it."

"I have found a woman who is being held against her own will, and she says she would like help to get out."

"Where is this?"

"About fifteen miles from town, in a line shack near the foot of the breaks."

"Out in that same country where men have been looking. Is she Mexican?"

"Yes, but her name is not Guillermina Martínez. She says it is Rosa Linda, which I take to be her first name. She did not give her last name. She says she's from Albuquerque."

"How old is she?"

"About eighteen."

"What's her story?"

"She seems to be part of an operation I mentioned to you, that I had heard of, with men transporting women for the purposes of using them as prostitutes in places like mining camps and logging camps. She says they've been holding her in this out-of-the-way place while they wait for some others to arrive, and when things are clear, they'll take her to meet the others and move on."

The deputy made an audible breath through his full mustache. "There's only so much we can do if they're all of age, but if we're sure they're being held against their will, we have more of a case."

"Here's the deal. I think the two men from Trinidad got off track looking for the runaway girl because they caught wind of this one being held there. And I think someone did away with them because they got too close to their operation. And I think Ed Hiller, following up on the same lead, met with the same end."

The deputy drew his eyebrows together. "How would any of them know to look there?"

"There's a man in town here named Mason Mardell. I imagine you've heard of him. From whatever sources he has, he knew of a dark girl being held in that line shack, and for a small price, he gave that information. I think he gave the same information to Stevens, the bird studier, who may have been some kind of a detective on the trail of a girl who had been kidnapped. A white girl, as he put it. Mardell, that is."

JOHN D. NESBITT

"This seems kind of elaborate," said the deputy. "They kill four men because they're hiding one girl."

"I think they're protecting the larger operation, and maybe as an additional motive, the two men who have been holding her have been using her."

The deputy let out a long puff of breath. "Do you have any idea of who these two birds are?"

"Yes. I saw them through the binoculars. One is Ben Meredith, and the other is his pal Crawford. I don't remember his first name."

"Lou, I believe."

"I think so. I haven't seen him since the first time they dropped by our camp, so I think he's been on guard when Meredith goes for supplies."

The deputy's chest went up and down. "The story becomes more credible when you mention those two. How did you talk to her with them around?"

"Meredith rode off in the afternoon, and the girl came out of the shack after nightfall, to use the outhouse. She said the other one was asleep. Drunk, or a word that means that."

"And you're sure she's not this Martínez girl?"

"I take her word for it, and her story is different."

"I don't suppose she witnessed them doing anything to any of these other men."

"No, she said she heard them make a brief comment about one man not causing any more trouble."

"How long did you talk to her?"

"Not very long. Maybe five minutes or a little more."

"She just spilled it all out."

"I think it helped that I spoke Spanish."

"Oh. And everything she said was in Spanish?"

"That's right."

"You're sure you didn't misunderstand anything?"

"Quite sure. She's got a clear way of speaking, like many of them do, and to the extent that she had an accent, it was one I'm familiar with. I spent quite a bit of time in New Mexico."

"Not Castilian Spanish, like they speak in Spain."

"Not everyone in Spain speaks the same Spanish, but that's a different matter."

The deputy looked past Delaine at the spot where the crumpled newspapers were piled up, and he came back. "Did you ride straight in here last night to tell me that?"

"Um, no. There's a separate story to tell, and a more serious one, which I was going to get to."

"Let's hear it."

"After I talked to the girl, I rode back to the ranch, thinking to spend the night and come in here in the morning. But when I was putting my horse away, someone came up behind me and stuck a gun in my back. He took my gun away from me, but I laid my hands on a field hoe and gave him a good one on the side of the head."

"A field hoe."

"The one I used for grubbing out cactus. You might have seen it."

"Oh, yes."

"It's got a good, heavy head on it. And a thick handle."

"I know the type. Who was the man?"

"Art Meredith."

The deputy sagged and let out a long "Whew."

"I don't know if he talked to his brother. I don't think his brother saw me out there, or they would have tried something. I don't know why Art would make this move against me at that time. Percy said he went to town, but I don't know that much for sure. I don't know if he knew about Ed Hiller."

"He did. I saw him here in town yesterday, and I asked him a few questions. Among other things, I asked him if he knew anything about the carriage that you and Ed Hiller saw. I didn't mention my source, but of course he had heard you brought Ed in, and so he could have figured I got that detail from you."

"I shouldn't be surprised. I knew he was pretty thick with his brother."

"Did you leave him there where you hit him?"

"Yes, I did. Percy may have found him by now."

The deputy bore down on Delaine. "I'm going to have to go out there. You seem to have a knack for being where your fellow ranch hands die."

Delaine had expected some kind of suspicion. He said, "I'm not trying to hide at all what happened to Art Meredith. I did what I had to do, right there in the barn. I'm guessing that he wanted to hand me over to his brother, but I didn't have any time to think about that. I acted, right then and there. Even if Percy moved him, he'll tell you where the body was. And as for Ed Hiller, I told you once before that if I had done that, I wouldn't have brought him right into town."

"I don't doubt that the circumstances are different. It's just one big thing after another, and if I go out there, I might as well look into this other thing as well, about this girl who's being held, and see if I can pull things together."

"I'll go with you if you want. Show you where the line shack is. Show you where I found Ed Hiller. It's on the way."

The deputy studied him. "If there's two of them, I'd like to have at least two on my side. Three is better. Sometimes just the appearance of numbers makes a jaybird think twice."

"I can check out of this room at any time. But I need to get something to eat. I haven't had anything since early yesterday morning."

"I don't think this is any time to be sitting around the dining room, talking to Miguel Cuenca. Let's see about buying something at the store to eat on the trail."

"All right."

"I'm going to the stable to have my horse gotten ready. Is yours there?"

"Yes."

"I'll meet you there, and we can pick up something to eat on the way out of town."

———

WHEN DELAINE ARRIVED at the stable, the sorrel ranch horse had been brought in. He brushed and saddled it while the stableman worked on the deputy's horse.

Deputy Blackmur showed up as Delaine was putting on the bridle. His manner was brisk. "I've asked around, and it looks as if the only one available to go with us is a kid. I don't want some kid along to get hurt, but he says he can at least hold the horses for us, and he's big enough that he looks like a man. He says he knows you."

"What's his name?"

"Hal."

"Hal Needham. He's all right. I wouldn't want him to get hurt, though."

"We'll keep him out of the way. He can do some good by being present and by holding the horses as necessary."

———

CLOUDS WERE PILING up in the northwest as the trio rode out of town. A cold wind blew, and it smelled like snow to Delaine. He had bought bread and cheese, and he had more bread than he needed, so he gave part of the loaf to Hal. The kid looked as if he was still trying to grow into his body, and he disposed of the bread in short order.

Near the turnoff to the Lazy T, they met Percy in the buckboard. The boss had a disturbed expression on his face, and he barked at Delaine.

"Where in the hell have you been? You didn't come in all day, and then this morning I see the horse you took out, but you're nowhere around. Then I find Art. Did you have anything to do with what happened to him?"

Hal gave a surprised look.

Delaine said, "He came up behind me and stuck a gun in my back. I didn't have a choice. He took my gun, so I got my hands on the hoe and gave him one with it. Right there in the barn where you found him."

"Well, he's done for." Percy motioned with his head toward the bed of the buckboard, in back of him, where a canvas covered a shape.

"I know. I went and reported it to the deputy."

Percy's light-blue eyes, which had a glaze to them, moved back and forth. "What are you doing here, Hal?"

"I'm going with them."

Deputy Blackmur said, "We were on our way to the ranch to check with you, and then we're going on to see about another matter. A related matter."

"I don't suppose you can tell me what."

The deputy remained circumspect. "I hope to be able to before long."

Percy turned his troubled eyes toward Delaine again. "I don't like any of this. You come and go as you please. Two of my men have died when you were around, and I'm not gettin' an explanation."

"I'm sorry, Percy. I'm sorry for what happened to Ed. I don't know who did it. I can only guess. As for Art, I can't be sorry for that. I had to look out for myself."

"What did he have against you?"

"I'm not sure. But I was uncovering some crooked things his brother was tied up in, including, I think, what happened to Ed. If you think Art was straight and honest, I might not be able to convince you otherwise, but he lied to me and Ed about where his brother worked, or at least he changed his story. Ben was up to no good. I can't tell you any more than that right now."

Percy's eyes went from Delaine to the deputy and back. "I don't like it. What do you expect me to do? Art was my right-hand man. Maybe he knew about some shady things his brother did, but he never took anything from me. So what am I supposed to do? Huh?"

Deputy Blackmur said, "I'm sorry for all the trouble this is causing you, Percy. We can't change what's happened so far, but we might be able to put a stop to some other things and bring someone to account."

"But what am I supposed to do?"

The deputy glanced at the buckboard. "It would be helpful if you took him the rest of the way into town. You know where to take him. Ed Hiller's already there."

"And where are you-all going?"

"Farther out. Depending on what happens, there may be more news before long."

"None of this news has been good so far."

"I know. And I see it much more often."

"I'll go," said Percy. His manner was still agitated as he fussed with the reins. "I don't know what else I can do."

The three on horseback went on. The grey clouds became thicker and darker, and by the time the group reached the work site, a few snowflakes were floating down.

Delaine pointed out where they had worked and camped, and the group moved on. When they came to the place where he had found Hiller's body, there was nothing to suggest that anything out of the ordinary had happened there. Most of the snowflakes melted as they hit the ground, but some clung to the thin blades of dry grass.

Delaine directed the group north and a little to the west. The snowfall was still light, and the breaks came into view when they were about two miles away. Closer and closer, he did not see the shack, although he was sure he was going in the right direction.

At last the shape appeared, a quarter of a mile away. The roof was turning white, and snow was sticking on the rough side of the building. Thin layers of snow had accumulated on the rails of the corral, which was empty.

The deputy called out at a distance of fifty yards, identifying himself. He called out again at twenty yards. The group rode up to the door, and after calling a third time, the deputy dismounted and handed his reins to Hal. Standing to one side at first, he opened the door and went in. He came out and said, "Empty."

He walked around in a fifteen-foot circle, stopped, and said, "Here."

Delaine followed his pointing hand and saw hoofprints pressed into what would have been the first snow, an hour or so earlier, and covered with the light snow that had fallen since. Once a person knew what to look for, the indentations were apparent.

"Looks like three horses," said the deputy.

Delaine, aware that no one had said in Hal's presence who it was they were after, said, "Might be that the party who left yesterday afternoon received some kind of orders and came back with another horse."

"Could be." The deputy was gazing to the southwest. "Looks like the trail goes that way."

"It does. I haven't been over there," said Delaine, though he had a sense of what might lie in that direction.

"I have, but not from here. The ranches are not close together out this way." The deputy seemed to be chewing on a particle like a grain of coffee. "If these tracks keep going in the same direction, I think they'll lead us to the Big Eight."

15

_____

DELAINE HAD NO DOUBT NOW THAT BEN MEREDITH and Lou Crawford had been working for the Big Eight all along. Delaine imagined looking down on this big country. The trail they were on at the moment led southwest toward the area where he had understood the Big Eight to be. The route of the carriage that he and Hiller had seen on that clear morning had been heading west-northwest toward that same general destination, so that the two routes made a broad "V." Whoever decided the movements must have decided that it was time for Rosa Linda to join the other three women.

Light, dry snow continued to fall. Delaine was able to shake it off his hat and coat, but it stuck on the sorrel horse's ears, mane, and neck. Deputy Blackmur, leading the way, seemed absorbed in his own thoughts, for he did not speak or give hand signals. Hal Needham rode behind, bouncing in the saddle at times. He did not have gloves, so he switched hands on the reins and kept one hand in a coat pocket.

They arrived at a layout of ranch buildings in the early afternoon. Snow covered the ground and was more than an inch thick on the roofs. The largest buildings, which sat back and faced east toward the trail coming in, were a tall red barn with a gambrel roof and a two-story white ranch house with brown trim. A hedge of lilac bushes between the two had gone out of leaf, and most of the yellow leaves had fallen from a broad cottonwood tree. On the north or right side as the riders slowed down was a large bunkhouse, followed by a separate building that appeared to be a cook shack and eating area. Across the yard, on the left, sat a couple of smaller buildings. One looked like an equipment shed, and the other might be a spring house or meat house, with canvas covering what would be screen windows.

Deputy Blackmur stopped in front of the bunkhouse and gathered the other two close by. "Let's try here first," he said. "Hal, you stay with the horses. No matter what you hear, don't come in. If something happens to us, you ride like hell. You know the way to town from here?"

"Yes, sir. How do I know if something happens?"

"I can't predict."

All three dismounted. Hal held the reins as Delaine and the deputy walked to the door.

The deputy rapped five times on the door and waited with his hand on his pistol. The door was opened by a man Delaine did not recognize.

"I'm Deputy Blackmur from the Laramie County Sheriff's Office, and I'd like to look inside."

The man opened the door wider, let them in, and retreated to a bunk. The bunkhouse had about twenty beds, in two rows. A couple of men lounged on bunks, three sat around a wood-burning stove at the left end, and two sat at a table nearby, playing cards. Delaine counted seven men, then an eighth who rose from a bunk in a dimmer area. Ben Meredith and Lou Crawford were not among them.

A man rose from a chair by the stove. He was not wearing a hat, but from his brown hair, blue eyes, flushed complexion, and stubbled face, Delaine recognized the lead rider for the Big Eight.

"I'm the foreman," said the man. "What do you need?"

"What's your name?"

"Ross Mitchell."

"I'm looking for Ben Meredith and Lou Crawford."

"They ain't here."

"I can see that. I have reason to think they came here, though, and I'm warning you and the rest of the men here to stay out of the way."

"What do you want them for?"

"I think you have a good idea. And they might not be the only ones. Where's your boss?"

"He's in the big house."

"We're going to talk to him. For right now, I'm telling all of you in here not to leave. I've got a man outside, and I'm going to give him orders to shoot anyone who comes out the door. I'll be back with more questions, and I'll want them answered."

"You can't come in here and treat us like a bunch of criminals," Mitchell said.

"Don't tell me what I can do."

None of the other men had come forward. Delaine recognized the other two men at the stove as the two who had been driving the carriage. Mitchell's fellow rider with the beard was one of the men playing cards.

"You're not going to find anything—"

"Stay put. We'll be back."

Mitchell glared at Delaine.

The deputy led the way outside into the grey afternoon and stopped next to Hal and the horses. He said, "I know they can go out the back door, so we have to stay on our toes and watch our backs. There's more men here than I counted on. Hal, hang onto the horses and follow us to the house. Again, if we don't come out, don't you go in. Ride for it."

The deputy led the way. He signaled for Hal to stay, then walked up onto the porch, knocked on the door with his pistol butt, and held the six-gun ready. Delaine stood by his side.

A man with blond hair and clean indoor clothes answered the door.

"I'm Deputy Blackmur of the Laramie County Sheriff's Office, and I want to talk to your boss."

"He's not available."

"I said I want to talk to him. I have reason to believe there are crimes being committed here, so don't interfere." The deputy pushed his way in, and Delaine followed. They stood in a front room with couches and padded chairs.

A voice from within called, "Who is it?"

"A sheriff," said the blond man.

Footsteps sounded, and a door at the other end of the room, which had been ajar, was pulled inward. Ben Meredith charged out, with Lou Crawford on his heels. The blond man dashed aside, and the two hired men opened up on the deputy. They did not seem to see Delaine at first.

The deputy fired back. Crawford dropped his gun, grabbed his mid-section with both hands, and fell. Meredith fired again. The deputy spun to one side and dropped, and another shot went past him and crashed through a window.

Meredith's gaze and pistol barrel turned toward Delaine. By now, Delaine had drawn his own pistol and held it with both hands. In that motion, he had thumbed back the hammer. He lowered the tip of the barrel until he lined the sights and squeezed the trigger.

The pistol bucked in his hands, and when it lowered, he did not see Meredith. Then he did. The man was lying on his back.

A third man appeared at the inner door, a tall man with a greying mustache and dark hair, pressed around the edges where a hat had been. He wore a dark herringbone wool coat, and a watch chain sparkled as he pointed his pistol at the crouched form of the deputy and eared back the hammer.

Delaine had cocked his own pistol again and brought it into position. He pulled the trigger, and the man stood up taller, opened his mouth, and fell to one side.

A faint commotion came from the deputy. He had come to a crouch and was facing the center of the room.

"How many?" he said.

"Three down," Delaine answered.

"Where's the other one?"

"I don't know." Delaine had lost track of the blond man. he crossed the room where he had seen him last, and he found him on all fours behind a couch. Delaine pointed his pistol and said, "Get up and come out."

The man rose and surveyed the damage.

By now, Delaine had placed the third man as the one he had seen on a few occasions in town. "What's your boss's name?" he asked.

The blond man said, "Albert Marcus."

The deputy had risen to his feet. His face was pale, and his right coat sleeve was soaked with red. "That's the owner," he said.

Delaine felt guilty that all three men had come out shooting at the deputy. The blond man had said there was a sheriff, and that was what they looked for. One or two of them might not have even seen Delaine. But this part was done.

The deputy spoke to the blond man. "Is there anyone else in this house?"

"No, sir."

"Then see if you can find me some cloth to wrap this arm."

"Yes, sir."

The deputy spoke to Delaine. "Go out and tell Hal we're all right."

With his arm wrapped up and his coat pulled on again, the deputy said, "Let's go to the bunkhouse."

Six of the eight men were still there. The two who had driven the carriage were missing.

"Where are the other two?" the deputy asked.

Mitchell said, "They left. I told them not to, but they did."

"Well, I'll send warrants after them." The deputy leveled his eyes on Mitchell. "Now, you can cooperate, or we can do this the hard way. I want to know if you've got any women hidden here."

"Nothing of the sort."

"Then let me tell you this. Those shots you heard

in the house? That was your boss and his two hard cases. They're all lying on the floor. I think I'm going to find something here, and if you hold out on me, the rest of you can consider yourselves under arrest for complicity."

Mitchell's face had gone queasy. "We're ranch hands. We can't help it if there's somethin' else goin' on. But I'll tell you, no one of us had anything to do with it." Mitchell turned and waved his arm. "You can ask any of them."

"I want to see what's here," said the deputy.

Mitchell and a man Delaine did not know put on hats and coats and led the way. Dusk was gathering as they crossed the yard and walked to the building with canvas tacked on the outside. Mitchell took a bolt out of a hasp and opened the door. A dull light was glowing inside.

"Go in ahead of me," said the deputy. "I don't want anyone locking me in." To Delaine, he said, "You come in and see if you can recognize any of them."

Delaine followed Mitchell and the deputy into the building, which was a room about twelve feet by sixteen. Burlap was covering the same areas that were covered by canvas outside. One lamp hanging from a rafter cast shadows on two rows of tiered bunks, four on each side, eight bunks in all.

Bags and clothing were piled on the top bunks, and in each lower one, a woman sat against the wall, covered with a blanket.

The deputy spoke. "I'm Deputy Blackmur of the Laramie County Sheriff's Office. I'm taking charge of things here. If you don't mind, I'd like you all to stand up under the light here so we can see what we've got. Don't worry. No one's going to touch you."

The women crawled out, and still draping the blankets around them, they stood together. Delaine thought he recognized the larger, dark-haired white woman with cloudy features. The two with brown hair could quite well be the other two, although one looked younger. The fourth was dark-haired and bronze-complexioned, the same height as the one he had spoken to in the dark.

"*¿Me conoces?*" he asked. Do you know me?

"*Sí,*" she said. Yes.

Delaine nodded to Deputy Blackmur.

The deputy said, "Ladies, there was a little trouble at the house, but it's all over. We're going to take you to town." He turned to Mitchell. "Is there a carriage here?"

"It's in the barn."

"Go get it ready." Deputy Blackmur turned to the youngest-looking woman. "What's your name?"

"Georgiana Fullmer."

"How old are you?"

"Seventeen."

"Do you think someone has been looking for you?"

"It could be. This turned out a lot different than I thought."

———

A FIRE WAS BLAZING in the fireplace of the lobby of the Dunfield Hotel. The four women had been provided with clean clothes and had had the opportunity for a bath and a meal. They sat on one side of the sitting area, while Miguel Cuenca, Francisco Gutiérrez, Percy Calvin, and Delaine sat on the other side. The deputy was standing with his back to the fire. He was wearing a clean, pressed shirt, with the right sleeve puffed up with the bandage underneath.

"Who's this?" he said, looking at the entrance.

A woman in a dark traveling coat and a black scarf was coming through the door. As she faced the group, Delaine saw that it was Rachel.

He rose to meet her. "Is there something wrong?"

"I heard there was trouble and more trouble. Men being killed at two ranches. I hired a man to drive me here. Thank God you're all right."

"Well, yes. It hasn't been easy, but I'm here. Come on over. The deputy is about to say something."

He ushered her toward the group. Miguel Cuenca gave her a nod of recognition, and he gave a mild frown in Delaine's direction. The others were waiting with attention.

Delaine said, "This is my friend, Rachel Valera. She came here from Overton to see if everything is all right. I hope she can join us."

"Go ahead," said the deputy.

Delaine and Rachel sat down.

Deputy Blackmur cleared his throat and said, "I hope I can go through this once and it'll be enough. I pieced my information together from several sources, including these four women and Mr. Delaine. So I'll begin." He cleared his throat again. "I'm sorry. I got a little bit of a chill last night." He drew himself up and said, "Here goes. There was trouble here before anyone knew it. Or at least anyone in town. A land-holder and businessman was engaged in an illicit trade, which I think we understand without my having to go into details. When a man from Trinidad, Colorado, came looking for his runaway daughter, he got off on the wrong track, thinking that a woman who was being held might be his daughter. He got too close, and the big businessman's henchmen took care of him. A nephew of his came, followed the same track, and ended up the same way." The deputy paused, nodded in the direction of Miguel Cuenca and his nephew, and went on. "Excuse me if I pass over this with what seems to be not much feeling, but I am trying to cover what seem to be the facts." The deputy seemed to catch a second wind. "And then a man who said he was a field scientist went around, asked a few questions, and was found dead in town here, or at the edge, at the railroad station. It turns out he was looking for one of the female persons we found at the Big Eight ranch yesterday evening. Then a fourth man, who worked at the Lazy T, who seemed to take interest in some reward money, was found dead in a manner similar to that of the two men from Trinidad, Colorado."

Deputy Blackmur paused. "I had reason to believe that one or more women were being held on or near the Big Eight. Assisted by Mr. Delaine and a young man from town, who is working today, I went from one place to another, and to make short a story that I think is already well known, the owner of the Big Eight and his two henchmen who had been holding one woman were killed. The two men who transported her here, and later three others, escaped. I am asking for warrants for them. I do not have enough evidence to arrest anyone else for unlawful sequestration."

Delaine thought, the Big Eight riders gave the others cover by bullying, but they didn't do enough to be brought to account.

The deputy continued. "I believe that the people responsible for the killings are no longer alive, so I do not expect to bring charges against anyone in that regard. Let me see. What else. The youngest woman is going to be returned to her family, and the other three are free to go."

Miguel Cuenca raised his hand, and in his loud voice, he said, "Ahem. I would like to clarify something if I could."

"Go ahead."

"So no one is going to be arrested or tried for the deaths of my two family members?"

"As I think I said, I do not have proof, but I have strong reason to believe that the men responsible are no longer alive."

"I just wanted to be clear on that," said Cuenca. "I have no objections to their being dead." He gave a jaunty toss of the head. "And my commendation to you. At this time, then, I think I can withdraw my offer for a reward, which was for information leading to arrest or conviction."

"That's up to you," said the deputy.

Delaine thought, so much for Mason Mardell and his expectations.

"Then I think our work is done here." Cuenca slapped his nephew on the knee and said, "*Vamos.*"

People stood up amid a scraping of chairs. Delaine waited to see if anyone wanted to speak to him. After a minute, Rosa Linda stepped away from her small group. It was the first time he had seen her up close and in clear light. She was of medium height with shoulder-length black hair and a bronze complexion, and she had a soft expression on her face.

"I want to thank you for helping me," she said to him in English.

"I was glad to be able to. This is my friend, Rachel

Valera. Rachel, this is Rosa Linda. She is from Albuquerque." Giving his attention to the younger woman, he said, "And what do you think you'll do now? Will you go back to your family?"

"I don't know. I think they have forgotten about me."

Rachel put her hand on Rosa Linda's arm. "Oh, no. Nobody has forgotten you. Your family is always your family. Your parents are always your parents, and you are always their daughter."

Rosa Linda's eyes were moist. "I know. It is very good of you to say that. I think you are right." She nodded. "I think I will go back. It is worth the trouble."

A LOOK AT: DARK PRAIRIE
A DUNBAR WESTERN MYSTERY

In a town where indifference and disbelief cloud the pursuit of justice, one cowboy vows to right their wrongs.

Taking up work at the Little Six Ranch in Winsome, Dunbar finds himself immersed in the dealings of Tut Whipple, a prominent water project developer. What begins as a simple inquiry into stolen beef soon spirals into something far darker with the disappearance of Annie Mora.

As Dunbar delves deeper into the young girl's disappearance, he becomes embroiled in the intricacies of Whipple's schemes and the mystery surrounding a recently constructed dam and reservoir. With each step closer to the truth, he faces off against increasing dangers.

But in a land where ruthless men hold sway, Dunbar welcomes a showdown on the dark prairie.

AVAILABLE NOW

ABOUT THE AUTHOR

John D. Nesbitt is the author of more than fifty books, including traditional Westerns, crossover Western mysteries, contemporary Western fiction, retro/noir fiction, nonfiction, and poetry. He has won the Western Writers of America Spur Award four times—twice for paperback novel, once for short story, and once for poem. He has won the Western Fictioneers Peacemaker Award twice—once for novel and once for short story. He has been a finalist for the Spur Award twice, the Peacemaker eight times, and the Will Rogers Medallion Award eight times. He has also received two creative writing fellowships with the Wyoming Arts Council—once for fiction, once for nonfiction—and he has won the fiction award four times with the Wyoming State Historical Society.

www.johndnesbitt.com